“Do you … ny women … ”

“Only ones I’m related to.” His grin turned devilish. “Unfortunately.”

The heat inside Amanda boiled, spread through her, weakening her knees. The mere presence of this man two feet away called to her, urged her to move closer, as if he somehow held a power over her she could not resist.

And didn’t want to resist.

“So, anyway,” Nick said, “I came to apologize for my state of dress just now.”

“The lack of it, you mean?”

He grinned again. “Yes. I hope you weren’t offended.”

“Traumatized beyond recovery,” Amanda declared. “I’ll probably have to spend the rest of the day in bed.”

His grin blossomed into a full smile and his gaze dipped to her toes, then rose to her face once more in a swift, hot sweep.

Amanda’s cheeks burned as his gaze caressed her....

Praise for Judith Stacy's recent titles

THE NANNY

"...one of the most entertaining and sweetly satisfying tales I've had the pleasure to encounter."

—The Romance Reader

THE BLUSHING BRIDE

"...lovable characters that grab your heartstrings... a fun read all the way."

—*Rendezvous*

THE DREAMMAKER

"...a delightful story of the triumph of love."

—*Rendezvous*

THE HEART OF A HERO

"Judith Stacy is a fine writer with both polished style and heartwarming sensitivity."

—Bestselling author Pamela Morsi

DON'T MISS THESE OTHER TITLES AVAILABLE NOW:

#619 BORDER BRIDE
Deborah Hale

#620 BADLANDS LAW
Ruth Langan

#621 A PERILOUS ATTRACTION
Patricia Frances Rowell

Judith Stacy

Married by Midnight

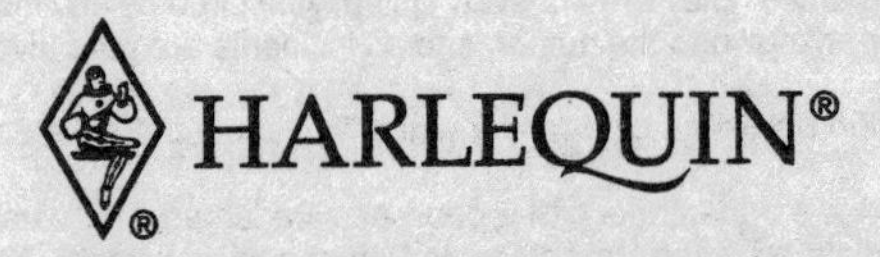

TORONTO • NEW YORK • LONDON
AMSTERDAM • PARIS • SYDNEY • HAMBURG
STOCKHOLM • ATHENS • TOKYO • MILAN • MADRID
PRAGUE • WARSAW • BUDAPEST • AUCKLAND

ISBN 0-373-29222-8

MARRIED BY MIDNIGHT

This edition published by arrangement with Harlequin Books S.A.

Visit us at www.eHarlequin.com

Printed in U.S.A.

Available from Harlequin Historicals and JUDITH STACY

Outlaw Love #360
The Marriage Mishap #382
The Heart of a Hero #444
The Dreammaker #486
Written in the Heart #500
The Blushing Bride #521
One Christmas Wish #531
"Christmas Wishes"
The Last Bride in Texas #541
The Nanny #561
Married by Midnight #622

To David—my Superman
To Judy and Stacy—my Kryptonite

Chapter One

Los Angeles, 1896

Another wedding. Her third in as many months. Could she really be expected to show excitement about yet another trip down the aisle?

At least none of the weddings had been her own.

Trying to look interested in the chatter of the three other young women in the bedchamber, Amanda Van Patton eased onto the foot of her friend's bed and gripped the carved post. *Trousseaus, invitations, china patterns.* Amanda feared she might scream if she heard those words one more time.

"Oh, and look at this." Cecilia Hastings, the bride-to-be, pulled another trousseau gown from her massive redwood closet and held it in front of her.

It was a promenade dress, pale teal with a matching parasol and hat that Amanda admitted would look wonderful on Cecilia, with her dark hair and green eyes. Another round of "oohs" and "aahs" rippled from the other women. Amanda managed an "oh, lovely."

Perhaps if she weren't so tired she might enjoy this impromptu fashion show, she decided, as Cecilia emerged from her closet with a lavender-and-ivory afternoon dress. Amanda had just arrived at the Hastings mansion in the West Adams district of Los Angeles, making the trip from her home in San Francisco in her uncle's private railroad car. She had already had a busy day before she'd set out on this journey.

"Oh, it's darling," she murmured as Cecilia presented another promenade dress. While the other two women in the room—friends of Cecilia's whose names Amanda had already forgotten—fawned over the pink creation and its wide-brimmed, white hat with matching flowers, Amanda kept her seat.

No, she wasn't tired, she admitted to herself. Only bored.

She glanced out the window at the moonlight illuminating the darkness and wondered how much longer she'd have to sit here before she could tactfully retire for the evening.

And why shouldn't she be bored? She'd just gone through this with her cousins—twice.

Since she was thirteen, Amanda had lived with her aunt and uncle and their four daughters in their Nob Hill mansion. Uncle Philip's wealth had given the family the best of everything—culminating in her cousins' weddings.

The twins, a few years younger than Amanda, had married within weeks of each other. Prior to that the Van Patton household had been in chaos for an entire year. Flower selection, dressmakers, menus, musicians and the endless stream of tedious details required to stage a wedding had been the topic of conversation morning, noon and night.

As a bridesmaid for both of her cousins, Amanda had been dragged through each facet of the planning. She'd managed to keep a smile on her face—in public, anyway—through the whole ordeal. She wasn't sure she could do it much longer.

She drew in a fortifying breath as Cecilia whirled around the bedchamber holding a pale yellow ball gown in front of her, and the other young women broke into applause.

"Radiant..." Amanda said, calling upon her considerable store of bridal compliments.

Luckily, Cecilia's wedding ceremony was only two days away. Amanda straightened her shoulders. Somehow, she'd get through it. She had to.

After all, she was the sole representative of the Van Patton family present at the Hastings-St. John wedding. Both of her cousins were still off on their own honeymoons, and Aunt Veronica had come down with a case of the hives at the last minute. Uncle Philip was too busy—or too smart—to attend weddings.

That left only Amanda to put in an appearance on behalf of the Van Pattons at what one Los Angeles newspaper's society column had already proclaimed "the wedding of the season." The prominence and wealth of the Hastings family allowed for no less.

Amanda pulled her lips upward, forcing a smile as Cecilia headed into the closet once more.

If it hadn't been a wedding that brought Amanda to Los Angeles she probably would have enjoyed the trip. The Hastings and Van Patton families had been friends for years. They visited back and forth, hosted each other on holidays and occasionally vacationed together. The time they spent together had diminished in the past few years, since Cecilia's father had died, and everyone had grown older and moved on with life.

But the families stayed in touch. They had, in fact, known each other for more years than Amanda had been part of the San Francisco branch of the Van Patton family. She'd only been sent to live with them eleven years ago when, at age thirteen, her father had passed away and her mother had fallen on hard times.

Amanda had been accepted into the family, even if she hadn't fit in very well.

"Breathtaking," she muttered now as Cecilia displayed her going-away dress, a cream-colored ensemble trimmed with green flowers and lace.

While the other women circled the gown, commenting on the fabric and cut, Amanda cast a furtive glance toward the clock on the marble mantel above the fireplace. After eleven already. Surely this would end soon—even Cecilia Hastings couldn't have that many more dresses to display.

As if her thoughts had somehow conjured up a tangible excuse for escape, the bedchamber door burst open and a stout woman with well-coiffed gray hair steamed in. She planted herself in the center of the room, silencing all the young women abruptly, and turned to Cecilia.

"What did you dream last night?" she demanded.

Cecilia paused, holding her black-and-white lace riding habit before her. "Aunt Winnie, where have you been all day?"

"Busy. Very busy," she declared, waving her hands. "Now, what did you dream last night?"

Cecilia gestured toward Amanda, who rose to her feet. This was a member of the Hastings family she'd never met.

"Aunt Winnie, this is Amanda Van Patton," Cecilia said. "My aunt, Winnifred Dubois from New York."

"Of course. The Van Pattons of San Francisco." Winnifred crossed the room to Amanda. "What did you dream last night?" she repeated.

"I beg your pardon?"

"I interpret dreams," Winnifred declared. She leaned closer and lowered her voice. "Not professionally, of course."

"No, of course not," Amanda said, and couldn't help smiling.

"Never mind." Winnifred turned back to Cecilia. "The bride-to-be should go first."

"Let me think." Cecilia pressed her lips together. "I don't believe I dreamed anything last night."

"Nonsense. Of course you dreamed something. Everyone dreams, every night," Winnifred said. "Your brother is an excellent example."

Cecilia exchanged a look with the other women. "I'm not sure Nick's dreams could be the best example of anything."

Giggles muted by hands pressed to lips rippled through the room as Winnifred took exception to Cecilia's comment.

But Amanda heard none of the conversation, only the thudding of her own heart as it suddenly beat double time in her chest. Her breathing quickened as it always did when Nick was mentioned.

Tall, handsome Nick. Black hair. Green eyes.

Was he in the house somewhere? Amanda wondered. Here, under the same room with her? Steps away? At this very moment?

She let her heart run wild, her mind fill with memories of Nick.

The first time she'd laid eyes on him.

Their moonlit encounter in the snow-covered forest. The night he'd ruined her for all other men.

Amanda drew in a breath and stilled her runaway thoughts. If Nick was, in fact, here in the house tonight, it wouldn't matter. He may as well be miles away.

Really, Nick had always been miles away.

Amanda sank onto the bed and pressed her lips together. She couldn't wait to get this wedding over with and go back home.

Nick Hastings sank lower in his leather chair and stretched his long legs up, propping his heels on the corner of his desk. At the end of this tiring day the house was finally quiet—and it hadn't been quiet for weeks. Thanks to the wedding.

A short time ago he'd heard the doorbell chime and feminine voices drift down the hallway to the study, where he'd closed himself in after supper. More of Cecilia's friends stopping by, or yet another guest arriving for the big day.

Across the desk from Nick sat his two oldest friends, Ethan Carmichael and Aaron St. John. Both were dark-haired, neither quite as tall as Nick; all of them had just passed their thirtieth birthday. Between them sat the bottle of Scotch they'd been working on for the past hour or so.

Occasions such as this were a rarity for the three of them. With large companies to run, they seldom had time for an evening of cigars, open collars and conversation.

Which was probably a good thing, Nick decided as he took another sip of Scotch. His head had started to buzz three drinks ago.

"Thank God this wedding nonsense is almost over with," Ethan declared, puffing his cigar. He elbowed Aaron, who was sitting next to him. "Now you can get on with the honeymoon."

Ethan fell into a fit of laughter, and Aaron grinned stupidly. Nick dropped his feet to the floor and thumped his fist on the desk.

"That's my sister you're talking about."

Ethan gulped down his laughter with a swig of Scotch.

"Yes, your sister. A woman for whom I have the utmost respect, and whom I love more than life itself," Aaron said. "But after so long a time, you can understand how I'm...anxious to have this whole thing over with."

"A hard-fought battle," Ethan agreed, saluting him with his glass. "How long have you and Cecilia been engaged now?"

"Fourteen months, two weeks and five days," Aaron said.

Ethan shook his head. "This wedding business...damn lot of nonsense, if you ask me."

"How many parties and the like?" Nick asked.

Aaron rolled his eyes. "Dinners, receptions, engagement parties and celebrations—hell, I've lost count. Not to mention the hours spent with the florist, the clergy, looking at china patterns, talking about honeymoon plans."

Ethan grinned and sipped his drink. "But well worth it after you walk down the aisle."

Nick rapped his knuckles against the desk and pointed at Ethan. "None of that kind of talk."

A light knock sounded and the door opened. Cecilia stepped inside the study, smiling at the three of them.

"I see you boys are behaving yourselves," she said.

They clattered to their feet. Aaron, the first to rise, crossed the room to stand beside her.

Cecilia glowed. Nick had seen that happiness on her face for months, growing more luminous as the weeks passed. Now, with the wedding two days away, she was positively radiant.

She smiled up at Aaron and he down at her. They moved close, as if drawn to each other instinctively, but were careful not to touch.

They were in love. Any fool could see it. Nick wasn't sure why it made his chest ache a little.

Must be the Scotch, he decided, and took another gulp.

"Can I steal you away for a few minutes?" Cecilia asked, gazing up at her intended.

Aaron followed her out the door without a backward look.

Nick watched the two of them disappear and the

door close. He and Ethan dropped into their chairs again.

"Seems it's worth it," Ethan said. "The wedding hoopla, I mean. Worth it to be married, from the looks of those two. Lately, I've found myself thinking that I wouldn't mind being married."

Nick's gaze came up quickly. "You're joking."

His friend shrugged. "No, not at all. I guess I've come to the point in my life where having a wife, looking toward the future, producing children, seems, well...it seems—"

"Appropriate." Nick sat back in his chair. "Actually, I've been thinking the same."

"Really?"

He nodded. "Really."

The idea had come as a surprise to Nick, too. He'd had no time or energy for such thoughts until lately.

Since his father's death six years ago, Nick had focused his efforts first on maintaining, then increasing the wealth his father had left him to manage. Nick had the welfare of his mother, his sister and a parade of relatives on his shoulders. The house, still under construction at the time, had had to be to finished—and paid for, of course. So that they could feed their own families, the workers in his father's businesses had depended on him to keep those businesses going, keep them profitable. All of them had depended on Nick.

It had consumed him, driven him, nearly beaten him at times. He'd been but twenty-five years old when his father had died, out of college only a short time and not quite ready to take life so seriously.

But he'd persevered. He couldn't—wouldn't—fail

the many people who relied on him. He wouldn't fail the memory of his father. Or fail himself.

With mentoring from some of his father's friends, and an uncanny instinct for business he hadn't known he possessed, Nick had doubled the family fortune. Now, on his own, he was about to triple it.

He sat back in his chair again. "I have everything else in life. A successful business, a good home, financial security. What the hell am I going to do with it?"

Ethan raised an eyebrow. "Think you'll hold on to all that money? Even with that Whitney project you've started?"

Nick shifted in his chair. "It will make me a fortune."

"If it doesn't bankrupt you first," Ethan said. He nodded. "Gutsy move on your part, I'll give you that. Going it alone on such a huge undertaking is risky."

This wasn't the first time someone had expressed concern about his latest business venture. It was a massive project, already months in development, with thousands spent, and they'd not even broken ground yet.

But he'd investigated it thoroughly, looked at it from every angle, consulted with experts in the field. Nick was confident he could pull it off without additional partners or financial backers. In fact, that was the *only* way he wanted to complete this project.

Somewhere in the middle of a sleepless night a few months ago, the thought had come to Nick that he had no one to leave his fortune to. The notion had been floating in the back of his mind ever since.

"I suppose," Ethan said, "having a wife, then a family, is the next logical step."

Nick sipped his Scotch and nodded. "It makes sense."

Ethan snorted a laugh. "Just who the hell do you think is going to marry *you?*"

"I could ask you the same," Nick said. "You've got a list of faults a mile long."

"Me?" Ethan rocked forward in his chair. "I can't even think where to start naming all your shortcomings. You'd never find a woman willing to marry you."

"Like hell."

"I could find a wife quicker than you," Ethan told him.

Nick grunted. "In your dreams, maybe."

"Want to bet?"

Nick gazed across the desk at his friend. Over the years the two of them had wagered on most everything imaginable. Neither man liked to lose.

"You're not serious," Nick said.

"Why not? We both want to get married. Why not make the whole process a little more interesting?"

Nick stroked his chin. "What did you have in mind?"

Ethan thought for a moment. "We'll both go wife hunting, and whichever of us is married first will be the winner."

Nick frowned. "I don't know that I've got time to court a woman right now, with this Whitney project going."

"Then we'll set a time limit," Ethan said. "We'll give it, say, thirty days."

"A month?" Nick shook his head. "Aaron's engagement lasted over a year."

"But he made a slow study of it," Ethan said. "You and I will handle it differently. We'll select the woman we want and make an all-out marital assault. Sweep her off her feet. Then insist on an elopement."

Nick shook his head. "I don't know..."

"Look at the benefits. No long courtship. No long engagement. None of the parties, receptions or wedding preparations Aaron had to suffer through. Thirty days of concerted effort to land a wife, then it's back to business as usual."

Nick considered the notion for a moment and found himself warming to the idea. "It makes sense. But..."

"What's the matter? Don't think you can charm a woman into marriage in thirty days?"

Nick sat up straighter. "I've got plenty of charm."

"Can't maintain it for a month?"

"I can maintain."

Ethan laced his fingers together and placed them behind his head, sinking deeper into the chair. "I'm not seeing a problem, myself. I'm quite certain I can find a wife in that time. If *you* don't think you can handle it—"

"I can handle it," Nick insisted.

"Well then?"

Nick considered his friend for a moment. "So what does the winner get?"

"Besides a wife in his bed, at his beck and call, every single night?" Ethan nodded toward the whiskey bottle on the desk. "How about a case of the finest Scotch in the city?"

Nick contemplated the bottle, then his friend and

the idea he'd suggested. He'd thought about his future for a while now, and having a wife was certainly a part of that. Nick hadn't envied Aaron and all the wedding rituals he'd gone through, so the quicker the whole thing was over and done with, the better.

And a case of Scotch was always good.

"All right, you're on," Nick said, and came to his feet.

Ethan rose from his chair. "So here's the wager. The first one of us to be married—"

"Legally married," Nick interrupted.

"—to a woman—"

"A living, breathing woman."

"—shall be declared the winner." Ethan glanced at the clock on the mantel. "We'll give ourselves until midnight, thirty days from today. Deal?"

Excitement stirred in Nick's belly as he shook his friend's hand. "You've got yourself a deal."

After all, what could go wrong?

Chapter Two

She'd dreamed about Nick.

Amanda came awake as the first golden rays of sunlight streamed into her room. She rolled over and studied the ceiling. If Cecilia's Aunt Winnie asked her what she'd dreamed about last night, she wouldn't know what she'd say. She certainly couldn't tell the woman the truth.

Settling onto the thick feather pillows, Amanda glanced at the window and the slice of sky visible between the drapes. From all appearances the day was dawning clear and bright. If this weather held, Cecilia would have a perfect June wedding tomorrow. Nothing else was acceptable for a Hastings.

Today would be filled with last-minute wedding preparations. Cecilia and her mother, Constance—and Amanda, simply because she was present—would probably spend hours going over them.

"Damn..." Amanda cursed and pounded her pillow. Wedding thoughts were only slightly more undesirable than recollections of Nick and the dream she'd had last night.

A light rap sounded on her door, and the maid she'd brought with her from San Francisco slipped inside. Dolly was a slight woman, no older than herself, with curly brown hair that frequently sprang from under her white dust cap.

"My Lord, Miss Amanda, you should see what all's going on downstairs, even at this hour of the morning. Everybody's hopping like grease on a hot griddle—just like home, when the twins were getting married," Dolly said, pushing back the heavy, green floral drapes. "And when I walked by Miss Cecilia's room just now, I couldn't help but glance inside. Her mother, Miz Constance, was with her. I can't say for sure, but I think she was crying."

Amanda pushed herself upright in the bed, her first thought to go to Cecilia and see what was wrong. But tears the day before a wedding weren't uncommon, and Cecilia's mother was there to comfort her.

"Are you sorry I brought you down here with me?" Amanda asked.

"Shoot, no," Dolly declared, grinning broadly. "I wouldn't miss this for nothing."

While Dolly selected clothing from the closet, Amanda slid out of bed. Even though the house was filled to capacity with out of town guests and relatives, Constance had given Amanda a comfortable room on the second floor.

Amanda walked to the window, her bare feet silent on the carpet. Outside stretched the mansion's rear lawn—thick grass, shrubs, flower gardens, a gazebo and towering palm trees.

"My, it's pretty here," Dolly said, joining her at the window. "One of the cooks told me it don't hardly ever rain down here. Wouldn't mind living in a place like this."

Amanda smiled. "What else did the cook tell you?"

"Oh, you know, just talk," she answered. "Mostly about Mr. Nick."

"Nick?" Amanda's breath caught. She forced herself to look unconcerned, hoping Dolly hadn't noticed. "What about Nick?"

The young woman grinned dreamily. "How handsome he is. Lordy, he's a looker, according to all the maids. And just as nice as the day is long. Good to his mama, generous with the staff."

Amanda's heart lurched. She wasn't surprised to hear any of those things about him.

"I'm plum crazy about him already, and I haven't even laid eyes on him yet." Dolly grinned. "'Course, that's nothing you don't already know, I'm sure, seeing as how you've been friends with him for so long."

"Actually, I haven't seen Nick in years," Amanda said.

Ten years. Since that night in the snow...

"Oh, really? Well, how come?" the maid asked. "I thought your families had been friends since way back."

Dolly had come to work for the Van Pattons only a year ago, so she didn't know all the family history. Surprising, given how the servants liked to talk.

"That's just the way things worked out," Amanda said, and turned away.

"Now, if you don't mind me saying so, Miz

Amanda, there's a story here you're not telling,'' Dolly said.

Amanda smiled. Dolly was so intuitive she seldom got away with anything around her. She could have simply said that she didn't want to talk about it, and the maid would have respected her privacy—and remembered her place. But since Dolly had come to the Van Patton household, Amanda found she was more comfortable talking to her than her cousins, aunt or friends.

So telling her now what had happened ten years ago might be just what she needed to put it in perspective, Amanda decided. She'd have to face Nick over the next few days. Perhaps this would help her prepare—and keep her from making a fool of herself.

''It was the autumn I turned fourteen,'' Amanda said. ''Only six months before that I'd been shipped off to the Van Patton home by my mother, who could no longer care for me after my father's death.''

She didn't need to tell Dolly that she'd been born into a distant, poorly regarded branch of the Van Patton family, or that Uncle Philip and Aunt Veronica had agreed to take her in. Amanda was quite certain the servants had already told that part of the story.

''It was a difficult adjustment for me,'' Amanda said, but that didn't begin to describe the problems she'd struggled with.

Etiquette, table manners, conducting herself with proper decorum. Living up to her aunt and uncle's expectations. Living down her past.

Everything had been uncomfortable. The opulence of their home, the servants, the family meals.

''On top of that,'' Amanda said, ''I'd suffered

through a growing spurt and shot up five inches. I changed, matured. I had long, ungainly arms and legs I didn't know quite what to do with. Nothing I wore seemed to fit right."

"Lordy-me, Miz Amanda, do I remember those days!" Dolly commiserated, shaking her head. "Bosoms and hipbones suddenly poking out. The monthly misery. Being angry and sad and happy all at the same time. And *nobody* understanding."

Amanda laughed softly. "I suffered no more than any other young girl blossoming into a young woman. But it seemed worse back then, on top of everything else."

"So what happened between you and Mr. Nick?"

"We vacationed near Tahoe with the Hastingses. They were strangers to me. The twins were quite young then, but my cousin Rachel was sixteen, Daphne seventeen, both beautiful young women at ease with everything and everybody around them."

Dolly raised a brow. "Including Mr. Nick?"

She nodded. "Including Nick."

He'd been nineteen that autumn. The most handsome young man Amanda had laid eyes on in her life. She'd spent the whole holiday too addle-brained to think of anything to say to him, and too tongue-tied to speak even if she could have thought of something to say.

Until that night...

Amanda still remembered how warm it had been, despite the snow that blanketed the ground. A full moon illuminated the forest around the magnificent mountain home the Van Pattons referred to as a cabin.

"It was late. Daphne and Rachel slipped outside

and I went with them. We met Nick and two other young men from the neighborhood. It was all quite innocent. A playful snowball fight broke out.''

Amid squeals and laughter, the six of them had scattered into the woods, scooping up the cold snow, hurling it at each other as they darted among the trees. One of the young men had picked up Daphne and tossed her into a snowbank. Another had chased Rachel, threatening the same.

''Then, somehow, I found myself alone with Nick. I threw a snowball at him. He dodged it easily and charged right at me.''

Quick as a wink, he'd swept her feet from under her and sent her crashing toward the ground. But at the last instant he'd caught her, kept her from falling. He'd pulled her upright and held her by both arms as she gripped his sleeves.

Moonlight had shimmered through the pines, casting beams across his face as they stood staring at each other. Breathless, Amanda had marveled at his strength—the strength of a man. Had marveled at his quickness. His agility. His masculinity.

He'd knocked her to the ground, but he'd saved her from the fall just as effortlessly. In that instant Nick Hastings had taught her how a man should treat a woman. With tempered strength, compassion, gentleness.

At once, her arms and legs had seemed to fit her body, and she knew why she'd been saddled with the womanly curves she'd found so uncomfortable. Suddenly, Amanda had been at home in her body, glad for the first time that she was a young woman. Understanding, too, that Nick was a young man.

"The next thing I knew, I was in his arms," Amanda said, looking out the window at the yard, but seeing that snowy forest instead.

They'd stayed that way for a long moment, gazing into each other's eyes. Nick's beautiful green eyes, looking only at her. His fingers clutching her arms possessively...

He'd eased closer. She'd smelled his masculine scent, seen the shadow of dark whiskers on his chin. Only the two of them had existed in the snow-covered world.

"Then he kissed me," Amanda said.

It wasn't anything more than a pressing of lips, a brush of bodies. But it had taken Amanda's breath away, left her shivering and shaking.

"So, what happened then?" Dolly asked, leaning forward.

"The others came crashing through the trees and Nick ran off with them."

Amanda had stood there alone, knowing she'd never be the same again. She'd fallen in love with him. And he'd ruined her for every other man she met afterward.

"And that was that?" Dolly asked.

Amanda drew in a breath, remembering the aftermath of the moment that had changed her life.

"The next morning when Nick walked into the dining room for breakfast, he took one look at me and walked out again."

Dolly uttered a disgusted grunt. "You are kiddin' me."

"No, I wish I were. After that, if we happened

upon each other, he never so much as made eye contact, just turned and left at the sight of me.''

''Humph,'' Dolly said, and her expression soured. ''I don't like that Mr. Nick at all, anymore.''

''Rachel mentioned that Nick had asked about me later that night, the night we kissed. Afterward, he wouldn't even look at me,'' Amanda said.

''Why do you reckon he did that?''

''I'm not certain.''

She didn't know for sure. But she was left with the crushing assumption that he'd learned who, exactly, she was. Not a real Van Patton, only a distant, destitute relative they'd taken in out of the goodness of their hearts.

''And you never saw him again?''

Amanda shook her head. ''He never came with the Hastings family when they visited San Francisco. He was in college, traveling in Europe, then working at the family business.''

''What about when you all came down here to visit?''

''I always found an excuse not to come. Aunt Veronica never seemed to realize the situation. She had four daughters to contend with and probably appreciated that I wasn't one of her problems.''

Dolly shook her head. ''A young woman never forgets her first kiss. Especially if it's from a good-looking older boy like Mr. Nick.''

That was certain. Amanda had never forgotten that night. Never stopped measuring every man she met by her one encounter with Nick. She'd often wondered if he even remembered that night. And if he did, had it meant anything to him?

Surely not what it had meant to her.

"So," Amanda said briskly, shaking off the memories, "that was that."

Dolly grunted again. "Still, I don't like the man. I don't like what he did. Kissing you, then treating you like you were dirt, or something."

"It was a long time ago. He's probably changed."

"I still don't like him," Dolly declared.

Amanda was glad Dolly hadn't asked any more about Nick. She didn't want to admit that, after all this time, thoughts of him left her as breathless as they had that moonlit night so many years ago.

"I'd better take a bath," Amanda said, leading the way across the bedchamber to the bathroom down the hall. She was better off pushing the whole matter out of her mind. She'd grown up, filled her life with things that mattered to her.

Somehow over the next few days, she would get through this wedding and return home. Amanda was confident she could pull it off.

All she had to do was keep her distance from Nick.

Chapter Three

"Damnation..."

Nick slumped against the sink, braced his arm on the cold porcelain and squinted into the mirror.

He looked like hell.

He felt like hell.

But what did he expect after consuming his share of a bottle of Scotch last night?

Pushing away from the sink, he saw that Jackson, his valet, had already filled the claw-footed tub for him, as he did every morning. Nick stripped off his flannel drawers and eased into the water. He dunked his head and threaded his fingers through his dark hair, slicking it off his face.

During his morning bath Nick usually reviewed his day ahead—people he planned to meet, appointments scheduled at his office downtown, things that required his attention. But this morning all he could think about was Ethan and that damn bottle of Scotch. Nick seldom drank to excess. Now he remembered why.

A discreet knock sounded on the bathroom door, and Jackson, a slight man with graying hair, slipped into the room bearing a tray with a cup of coffee, then disappeared just as silently. Nick wasn't sure how the man always knew his needs so instinctively, but he appreciated it.

Sipping the coffee, Nick washed, dried and dressed in fresh underdrawers and the white sleeveless undershirt Jackson had left for him. When he moved to the mirror once more, he thought he looked a little better. He felt a little better, too.

Yet something nagged at him. Something from last night. What was it?

Dragging the razor across his lathered jaw, he thought back to yesterday. The Whitney project came to mind, but he could recall nothing out of the ordinary with it. Just the usual worry that he stood to lose a large fortune if the deal fell apart.

No, it wasn't the Whitney project. Nick rinsed the razor under the tap, mentally reviewing the previous day. Finally, he recalled last night in the study. Cecilia had come in. Ethan and he had been left with the bottle of Scotch to finish off. Then Ethan suggested—

"Hellfire." Nick's head came up quickly.

He'd made a wager to find a wife in thirty days.

"Damn...!" Nick eyed his reflection sharply. What had he been thinking? He'd bet Ethan a case of Scotch that he would be married by midnight in thirty days—twenty-nine days, now. What the hell was wrong with him?

Grumbling, Nick finished shaving and went into his adjoining bedchamber. Jackson had disappeared, but he'd laid out Nick's suit for the day. Nick yanked on his white shirt, mentally berating himself for drinking so much, for agreeing to that ridiculous bet.

He stopped in the middle of his room as another thought occurred to him.

Even before last night he'd considered getting married. Having a wife wasn't such a bad idea. In fact, it would ease his burden in life considerably.

No more young eligible women being pushed in front of him at social events. No more mothers, grandmothers and aunts looking him over, sizing him up as husband material.

Maybe Ethan's idea had some merit. Nick fastened the button on his left sleeve. Getting the whole wedding thing over and done with quickly had its advantages.

He exhaled heavily. No, it wasn't right—not for his future wife, anyway. Women lived for that sort of thing. Parties, receptions. Certainly her wedding. He couldn't rob her of that once-in-a-lifetime event.

He fiddled with the button on his right sleeve. Of course, finding a wife in a month's time would be a challenge to any man, but who was more up to it than he? He could sweep a woman off her feet as well as anyone.

Finding the right sort of woman would be imperative. Nick had no intention of falling desperately in love. He'd known that for some time now. He'd known, too, that what he wanted was a wife who was compatible.

He'd learned the hard way what "love" could do to a man.

Nick paused. Compatible. Yes, that's what he

wanted. It was what he would look for. Compatibility. If he found that, everything else would fall into place.

The door to his bedchamber burst open. Nick swung around as Cecilia swept into his room, her dressing gown billowing behind her, her hair a mass of tangles.

While never in a thousand years would Nick consider walking into his sister's or mother's room unannounced, the women in the house thought nothing of bursting in on him when it suited them. Such as now, when he wore only his drawers and shirt, with one cuff buttoned.

Cecilia stopped, flung out both hands and cried, "It's over! The wedding is off!" She burst into tears.

"What?" Nick went to her.

Constance dashed into his room, hot on her daughter's heels. She, too, wore her dressing gown. Her graying hair, woven into a braid, hung down her back.

"Cecilia," Constance said, "please, calm down."

"What happened?" Nick asked.

"It's off! The wedding! Aaron—Aaron never really loved me at all!" Cecilia collapsed into racking sobs against Nick.

He gathered her into his arms and turned to their mother. "What the hell happened?"

"I have no idea. I found her this way in her room a few minutes ago," Constance said, her eyes wide. She touched her daughter's shoulder. "Cecilia, dear, you must tell us what happened. Why do you think Aaron doesn't love you?"

"Because he *doesn't,*" Cecilia wailed, lifting her head from Nick's shoulder. "Cancel the wedding. The flowers, the food, the reception—cancel it all!"

Nick saw his mother sway as over a year's worth of planning and preparing evaporated before their eyes. He reached out and steadied her. She clamped her hand onto his arm.

"Let's just all calm down," Nick said. "First—"

"No, there's nothing to discuss!" Cecilia said.

"Cecilia, you don't mean that," Constance insisted.

"Yes, I do!"

"Nick, do something!"

"Look, both of you—"

"Stop!" Aunt Winnie blasted into the room wearing a ruby-red dressing gown, her hair so neatly styled it looked as if she'd sat up in a chair all night. "I could have predicted this would happen! Cecilia, what did you dream last night?"

Cecilia wailed anew and buried her face in Nick's shoulder. Constance clutched him tighter.

Winnifred marched over to them. "Someone's dream predicted this. Nick, what did you dream last night?"

"I—I dreamed I was flying," he said.

Winnifred's eyes squinted together. "Were you flying over broken objects?"

"No." He peered down at his sister, trying to see her face. "Cecilia, you have to tell us what happened."

"Were you flying with black wings?" Winnifred persisted.

"No."

"White wings?"

"No. Listen, Cecilia, Aaron loves you. Just last night—"

"He doesn't!" she insisted.

"Were you shot at while flying?" Winnifred asked.

"No."

"Were you flying naked?"

"Aunt Winnie!" Nick eased Cecilia away from him and tilted her face up. "Tell me what happened."

"Yes, dear, tell us everything," Constance said, finally pulling herself together.

Cecilia sniffed and dragged her hand across her cheeks, wiping away her tears. "Last night when Aaron was here he—he said something. I thought nothing of it at the time, but when I woke this morning I realized what it really meant."

"Did it come to you in a dream?" Aunt Winnie demanded.

"No," Cecilia said.

"What did he say?" Nick asked.

"He said he—he wanted to cut our *honeymoon short.*" She collapsed into tears again. "Because of *business.*"

"Aha!" Constance declared, as if everything were clear to her now.

Nick stared at the two of them. "What the hell's wrong with that?"

"Oh, Nick, *really.*" Constance shot him a look and gathered her daughter into her arms.

Cecilia gave Nick a whack on the chest. "Oh, I should have known you wouldn't understand!"

He plowed his fingers through his hair. "I could understand it if you could explain it."

"He wants to come back early because of business," Cecilia said, swiping at her tears again. "That means he cares more about his business than he cares about me. If he really loved me he would want to be with me as much as possible. But he doesn't."

"That's not what it means," Nick insisted.

"Yes, it is! I won't marry a man who cares more about his business than he cares about me!" Cecilia clenched her hands into fists. "You don't understand! Nobody understands!"

"Cecilia—"

"Dear—"

"What did Aaron dream last night?"

"I understand."

Nick looked up as yet another woman wearing a dressing gown walked into his bedchamber. This one he didn't know. But Cecilia obviously did because she rushed to her.

And, Lord, this woman was pretty. Tall, with thick brown hair that curled to her waist. She looked vaguely familiar, but Nick was certain he would have remembered her if they'd met.

"I couldn't help but overhearing as I was going down the hall," she said, gesturing toward the door and casting an apologetic look at Constance.

"That's fine," Constance replied, seeming relieved to have her here. "Go ahead, Amanda."

"Amanda?" Nick stared harder at her.

She ignored him and took both of Cecilia's hands. "I just went through this same thing with both my cousins, only weeks ago when they married."

"Amanda Van Patton?" Nick asked, as a foggy memory crept into his mind.

"It's last-minute jitters, that's all," Amanda said. "Things seem worse than they really are."

"Amanda Van Patton? From San Francisco?"

"Hush, Nick," Constance hissed.

"No," Cecilia protested. "That's not the case here. It's not just jitters."

"Yes, it is," Amanda told her. "Now, listen to me, Cecilia, and listen well. Aaron loves you. You know that. His asking if he could cut the honeymoon short means *just that.* Nothing more. It doesn't mean he doesn't love you, or that he thinks more about his business than he does you. And he did ask you, didn't he? He didn't tell you."

"Well, yes," Cecilia said, and sniffed.

"You'll be his wife," Amanda said. "His business responsibilities will be your responsibilities, too. Aaron is a smart man. If he really thinks he needs to come home sooner, then you should consider that he has a valid reason."

A heavy silence fell over the room while the wedding of the season hung in the balance. Cecilia chewed her bottom lip. Nick was certain his mother held her breath. He was having a little trouble breathing himself, but for an entirely different reason. This woman was Amanda Van Patton? Recollections surfaced in his memory, vaguely matching the beautiful woman who stood in front of him now.

Finally, Cecilia sniffed and said, "Yes, I suppose you're right. I hadn't thought of it that way."

"Talk to Aaron. Listen to what he says. Tell him how you feel," Amanda said. "You two need to do what's best for the both of you."

"All right," Cecilia promised, sniffing again and drawing in a breath. "I will."

"So the wedding is on?" Constance asked, almost

in a whisper, as if afraid of what the answer might be.

Cecilia pushed her chin up. "It's on."

"Thank goodness," her mother declared, pressing her hand to her throat. Then she dashed for the door. "I have a hundred things to do today."

"I must talk to Aaron right away," Cecilia declared, hurrying after her.

"What about your dreams?" Aunt Winnie called, following the other two women. "I must know what you dreamed."

Nick hardly noticed the three women leaving the room as he stared at Amanda, standing in profile before him.

She'd been little more than a child when he'd last seen her. But now she was a woman. All woman.

Beautiful, yes. But more than that. She'd handled the situation with Cecilia with an intelligence and a command seldom found in women. And that made her even more attractive.

"Amanda?"

She turned and gazed up at him with the biggest, bluest eyes he'd ever seen. Nick's belly clenched.

"I didn't recognize you," he said. "You don't look as I remember...but I don't see how I could have forgotten."

Amanda gave him a half smile and wiggled her finger at him. "Actually, what you've forgotten is your trousers."

She turned briskly and walked out of the room.

Nick looked down at himself, then slapped his palm against his forehead. "Oh, my God..."

Chapter Four

Amanda pushed her bedroom door shut and fell back against it. Heat swept through her, flushing her cheeks and threatening to burn her from the inside out.

Then she giggled. A silly, schoolgirl giggle.

Since agreeing to come to the Hastings home she'd worried and wondered what would happen when she saw Nick again. Would she be so overwhelmed by the sight of him that she'd stutter and stammer? Trip over something? Faint dead away? Would she make a fool of herself by his mere presence?

None of that had happened. Instead, the first time she saw him he'd been in his underwear.

"What happened?" Dolly asked, turning away from the closet. "Why was Miss Cecilia crying?"

They'd heard her sobs on their way to the bathroom down the hall. Dolly had returned to Amanda's room, leaving her to see what the problem was.

"Everything's fine with Cecilia. Just last-minute nerves," Amanda said.

Dolly's eyes narrowed. "Then what's so all-fired

funny? I can see that smile on your face, plain as day.''

''Nothing,'' Amanda insisted, trying again to swallow her grin. ''It's nothing.''

A knock sounded on the door. Amanda's heart lurched. Was it Nick?

She admonished herself for having the thought. More than likely it was Constance, coming to thank her for helping. Or Cecilia wanting to talk.

She opened the door and her heart thundered in her chest. Heat flooded her cheeks again.

It *was* Nick.

In the ten years that had passed since she'd last seen him his features had hardened, become more angular. A straight nose, square jaw, dark full brows...the face of a man looked down at her.

He'd grown larger, too. His shoulders were wide and straight, his chest full and muscular. Her nose barely reached his chin.

His dark hair was damp, hanging over his forehead. The white shirt she'd seen him in moments ago was buttoned now, but the tail hung loose and the collar stood open. She glimpsed the fabric of his white cotton undershirt and his coarse, black chest hair curling over the top.

He also wore trousers.

He must have hopped into them and hurried after her, because even now he was pulling up his suspenders.

A moment passed while he just looked at her, as if he'd forgotten what he wanted to say, or perhaps couldn't bring himself to say it. Amanda didn't know which. All she knew for certain was that her mouth had grown so dry she couldn't have answered had he asked her anything.

Then he smiled. It pulled at the corners of his mouth, lifting them ever so slightly.

Amanda fought back her own answering grin and wagged her finger at his legs. "I see you found your trousers."

Behind her, she heard Dolly approach, and sensed her craning her neck for a better view.

Nick's smile widened and he glanced down at himself. "Sorry about that. I didn't realize..."

Amanda crossed her arms in front of her. "You didn't realize? Is that because you routinely have so many women in your bedchamber?"

"Only ones I'm related to." His grin turned devilish. "Unfortunately."

The heat inside Amanda increased, spread through her, weakening her knees. The mere presence of this man two feet away called to her, urged her to move closer, as if he somehow held a power over her she could not resist.

And didn't want to resist.

She took a step backward. She could have sworn he leaned forward, but maybe it was her imagination.

"So, anyway," Nick said, "I came to apologize for my state of dress just now."

"The lack of it, you mean?"

He grinned again. "Yes. I hope you weren't offended."

"Traumatized beyond recovery," Amanda declared, hoping the sarcasm in her voice could somehow take the edge off her churning emotions. "I'll probably have to spend the rest of the day in bed."

His grin blossomed devilishly and his gaze dipped to her toes, then rose to her face once more in a swift, hot sweep. Amanda's cheeks burned as his eyes caressed her.

"Well, if there's any way I can assist you in that, please let me know." Nick gave her a nod and headed back down the hall.

Amanda just stood there for a moment, watching him walk away. Long legs, straight back, muscular—

"Oh, gracious." What was she doing? She slammed the door, fanning her face with her hand.

"That was him, wasn't it?" Dolly asked, her eyes bulging. "That was Mr. Nick?"

All Amanda could manage was a nod.

"Did you see that man's *feet?*" Dolly asked, more an announcement than a question. "Land sakes, he has the biggest feet I've ever laid eyes on. And you know what *that* means."

Amanda's face flushed anew.

"Help me, Lord," Dolly beseeched, turning her face upward and clutching her hands to her chest. "I am in love."

"Only twenty minutes ago you said you didn't like Nick."

Dolly turned to her as if she'd lost her mind. "Did you *see* that man?"

Amanda reined in her own runaway thoughts, forcing herself to regain her composure. "He was pleasant looking."

"Pleasant looking? Lordy, Miz Amanda, that ain't the half of it." Dolly nodded her head wisely. "He was giving you the look."

"The look?"

"You know what I mean," Dolly said. "He got an eyeful of you, and he liked what he saw. Believe me, I know."

Yes, Dolly did know. She had an uncanny ability to read people's expressions. Her intuition ran far deeper than Amanda's ever had.

But Amanda didn't want to think about the possibility that she might be right.

"I came here with the intention of avoiding Nick," Amanda declared. "That's what I intend to do. Now, I'd better get on with the day. Maybe I can hurry this wedding along, get it over with sooner, somehow. The quicker I get back home the happier I'll be."

"You're gonna avoid Mr. Nick?" Dolly gave her a knowing look. "We'll just see about that...."

Nothing like making a good impression.

Nick gave his necktie a tweak as he trotted downstairs, cringing inwardly at what had happened in his room. A beautiful woman in front of him and he'd had no trousers on.

He paused at the bottom of the steps. The situation could have turned out much more embarrassing. In fact, it almost had.

The warmth that had simmered in him since Amanda had sashayed out of his bedchamber increased a little more. She'd had on a dressing gown, buttoned up to her throat and cinched at her waist. But those curves of hers, hips and breasts clearly defined by the flow of fabric, with none of the armor of underwear most women insisted upon wearing to disguise their shape and keep him from seeing their figure...

When he'd gone to Amanda's bedchamber to apologize, he'd gotten close enough to smell her. He'd almost made a complete fool of himself all over again.

Nick ground his teeth together and hurried toward the breakfast room. Enough of those thoughts. He had a lot to do today, and remembering a beautiful woman like Amanda in her dressing gown would only keep him from thinking straight.

The comfortable, sunny yellow breakfast room was situated at the back of the house. Windows offered views of the grounds. Since it was early, none of the other houseguests were up yet, which suited Nick fine.

A servant in a gray uniform and crisp white apron came in as Nick sat down at the head of the table. She filled his cup from the silver service on the buffet and presented him with the morning newspaper. He told her what he wanted for breakfast and she left again.

Unfurling the paper, he reached for his cup. A fragrance tickled his nose. It wasn't the coffee.

Amanda stood in the doorway.

In contrast to earlier, her hair was done up atop her head, with little tendrils curling at her ears. She wore a pale blue gown. The skirt was drawn across her front, then lifted high to a bustle in the back. The toes of her high buttoned shoes peeked from beneath the skirt. Leg-o'-mutton sleeves on her jacket tapered to her wrists.

"Good morning." Nick lurched to his feet, catching the newspaper before it slipped to the floor.

A few seconds passed while Amanda just stood

there, as if reluctant to enter the room. Finally, she did.

"I see you've dressed for breakfast," she said.

Nick stepped away from the table, looked down and tapped his toes on the floor. "Shoes and socks this time."

She glanced down and he could have sworn her cheeks colored. Odd reaction to his feet, he thought.

Nick held the chair to his immediate right, and Amanda lowered herself into it. He lingered for a moment, looking down at her, held captive by the long line of her neck, the loose curls of her fine hair, her slim shoulders and the scent that wafted up.

"Is something wrong?" Amanda asked, turning her head to look back at him.

"No, nothing," Nick said, fearing that he'd moaned aloud or something. He gave her a quick smile.

She smiled, too—a lovely, shy little smile. Nick dropped into his chair and picked up his napkin. It seemed a good idea to have something over his lap at the moment.

The servant came in again and poured juice at Amanda's request. She declined a hot breakfast, preferring pastries and fruit from the platter already on the table.

"Don't let me disturb you," she said to Nick, nodding toward the newspaper beside his plate.

He was quite certain nothing the *Times* reported today could be as interesting as the woman seated at his elbow.

"No, it's all right. I can read later—"

But before he could finish his sentence, Amanda

pulled a tiny tablet and the nub of a pencil from her skirt pocket and turned her attention to them.

For some reason, that didn't quite suit him. "I'm sorry I didn't recognize you earlier," he said.

"It's all right."

"It's been a long time."

"Yes, it has." She glanced up at him, then turned back to her tablet once more.

"Yes, it has," he echoed, and couldn't help but think he was usually better at talking to women than this.

"How's your family?" Nick asked.

"Quite well, thank you."

A few more minutes dragged by.

"Are you planning to be in town long?" he asked.

"No," Amanda said. "I'll be going home immediately after the wedding."

Nick wasn't certain what he was doing wrong. He'd never had to work this hard at conversation in his life.

Generally, women fell all over him, hanging on his every word, giggling at his jokes. This one, however, didn't seem to care if he sat here with her or not. Somehow, that made him try harder.

"I guess you'll help out with all the last-minute wedding preparations today?" he asked.

That got a bigger response from Amanda than he'd elicited so far, but it wasn't favorable. She cringed, held up her hand as if to ward off the possibility, and gave herself a little shake.

"I fear that will be my doom—destiny," she said, and turned back to her tablet.

Nick was about to run out of small talk. Maybe if

he knew what his competition was, he'd be better able to hold her attention, he decided.

He tilted his head to get a look at the tablet she was writing on, and saw that she'd made a list of some sort.

Probably some litany of the inane things women spent their time on. Nick leaned closer, unable not to. Lord, she smelled delightful. Lavender or something.

Just then Amanda sat back and frowned. She gave a breathy little sigh.

''Is something wrong?'' he asked, glancing from her tablet to her face again.

Surely something was amiss. The fact was obvious from the look on her face—the lines of concentration, the frown. How endearing she looked, probably worried over some shopping problem she faced today. Nick wondered at the workings of the feminine mind. The smallest things threw them.

Amanda tapped her pencil against her bottom lip. Nick shifted in his chair.

''I might be able to help,'' he offered, dragging his gaze away from her mouth.

She laid her pencil aside. ''Do you know anything about concrete?''

He stilled, then leaned back. ''Concrete?''

''Yes, concrete. It's used in construction to form—''

''I know what concrete is.'' He looked down at her tablet. ''Why do you want to know?''

''I'm going to erect a building.''

His frowned. ''You're going to do what?''

''Erect a building.''

Nick just stared at her, not sure he'd understood her correctly.

"I'm going to erect a building," Amanda said again. "Erect. A. Building. *Erect.* Are you understanding this?"

"I assure you, I have firsthand knowledge of erec—never mind." Nick drew in a breath. "Why are you...putting up a building?"

"It's a long story," Amanda said, picking up her pencil again, "and not a very interesting one, really."

The servant came into the room and served Nick his breakfast. He picked up his fork and bit into the eggs.

"Go ahead. Tell me. I'd like to hear all about it," Nick said. "Are you building a flower shop? A dress shop, maybe? Or one of those hat places where women like to wile away the afternoon?"

"I'm building a refuge for women with children who've been abandoned by their husbands."

Nick froze, staring at her. He knew he should say something, but couldn't think of a darned thing. Anyway, it was almost impossible to speak with his foot buried so deeply in his mouth.

"All is well. All is going as planned," Constance announced as she breezed into the breakfast room. "Today I'm going to—"

"I have to go, Mother," Nick said, rising from his chair, glad to be interrupted before he made an even bigger fool of himself in front of Amanda—though he didn't know how that would be possible.

"But don't you want to hear about the wedding plans?" Constance asked, as if she couldn't imagine why he wouldn't. ''The florist is coming over today—''

''I'll hear about it later,'' Nick promised, tossing his napkin onto his plate.

''Oh, well, all right.'' Constance turned to Amanda. ''We'll have such fun today. After the florist leaves, the dressmaker will be by for a final fitting.''

''Oh, yes...'' Amanda smiled bravely. ''Won't that be fun?''

''Has Cecilia showed you her trousseau yet?''

''Actually, she has. Last night,'' Amanda said.

''Well, you'll want to see it again,'' Constance declared. ''We'll do that this afternoon.''

''Lovely...''

The change in Amanda that Constance seemed not to notice didn't escape Nick. Right before his eyes Amanda appeared to wilt. Her shoulders slumped. Beneath her brave facade he caught a fleeting grimace of distaste.

Was it possible that she was as tired of hearing about Cecilia's wedding as he was?

He decided to take a chance.

''Actually, Mother,'' Nick said, ''I've already offered to show Amanda around the city this morning.''

Amanda's gaze came up quickly and landed on him with such gratitude that he thought she might launch herself into his arms.

''Really?'' Constance said, clearly disappointed.

Nick looked down at Amanda. ''Unless you want to change your mind and stay here today?''

Now she looked as if she might throttle him.

''No!'' She jumped from her chair, then forced a

smile. "I mean, no. I couldn't go back on my word after you so generously offered your time."

"Well, perhaps if you hurry back?" Constance suggested.

"Can't promise," Nick said. He cupped Amanda's elbow and the two of them hurried out of the room.

"Remember there's the rehearsal tonight," Constance called. "And supper."

"Don't worry, Mother, I'll be there." Nick led Amanda through the house to the foyer, stopping at the foot of the grand staircase. "Get your things."

"You're serious?" she asked, a little breathless. "You'll really get me out of this house today?"

"Sure."

Amanda gave him a saucy little grin. "You, Nick Hastings, are my new best friend." She turned, hiked up her dress and sprinted up the stairs.

Nick watched her, trying to remember why he'd avoided going to San Francisco for so many years.

He wondered, too, how he was going to keep Amanda Van Patton from going back.

Chapter Five

Amanda dashed into her bedchamber. ''I need a hat!''

''What's got you all fired up?'' Dolly asked.

''I'm going out,'' Amanda said, crossing to the closet. ''With Nick.''

''Oh, my word. I knew it,'' Dolly declared, pushing ahead of her and opening the closet door.

Amanda stilled. ''It's nothing like that. He's simply taking me out to see the city. That's all.''

Dolly nodded wisely as she pulled down a hatbox from the shelf. ''That's all? Uh-huh. Sure it is.''

Amanda pried off the top and lifted out the wide-brimmed hat, decorated with flowers and bows. She hurried to the mirror over the dresser and pinned it in place.

''Is this the same Mr. Nick that you intended to keep your distance from not an hour ago?'' Dolly asked.

Amanda glanced at the maid's reflection in the mirror. ''He's just being a kind host, that's all.''

Dolly studied her for a minute, then nodded slowly.

"All right. I reckon you know what you're doing. Besides, can't say that I blame you, good-looking as he is."

Amanda checked herself in the mirror one last time, then scooped up her handbag and headed for the door.

"You just watch yourself," Dolly called.

The sobering words rang in Amanda's head as she stepped into the hallway. Dolly was right. Nick had hurt her once before. Hurt her deeply, so deeply that some of the pain still lived with her today, all these years later.

"You sure you want to do this?" Dolly asked, walking to the doorway.

Amanda considered the question. Perhaps she should tell Nick that she'd changed her mind and didn't want to go with him today.

Somehow, she couldn't bring herself to say the words.

"I'll be fine," she declared.

Still, the idea caused her stomach to knot as she walked down the hallway. But the alternative meant spending the day with Cecilia and Constance, discussing the wedding. Amanda couldn't bear that.

Nor could she bear standing at the window watching Nick drive away without her.

"Be cautious," Amanda mumbled aloud as she reached the top of the staircase. She could do this, she told herself. She could spend the day with Nick without letting her feelings run away with her. She'd keep herself in check.

Somehow.

Amanda heard footsteps behind her in the hallway and, fearing it was Cecilia or Constance with a dire wedding crisis, hurried down the steps. At the bottom, she stopped. Nick wasn't there.

Had he already gone? What if he'd changed his mind and left without her?

A cold shiver passed through her. Old memories popped into her mind. Feelings of being young, newly arrived at her aunt and uncle's mansion. Not fitting in. Not being as worthy as everyone around her. Not being good enough...for Nick.

Amanda gave herself a shake, pushed her chin up and crossed the foyer. Of course she was good enough. Now. She hadn't been back then, when she was little more than a child, uncomfortable in her new life. But she'd learned how to conduct herself, and she did, in fact, fit in quite nicely.

She opened the front door and stepped out into the bright morning sunlight. The Hastingses' carriage waited at the foot of the steps and Nick stood beside it. Amanda felt her heart lurch, seeing him there waiting for her.

And because he looked so tall and handsome, Amanda's own words of warning sped through her mind again. *Be cautious.*

"All set?" Nick asked.

She stopped beside him. "Thank you for masterminding my escape today."

He smiled. "What are best friends for?"

Warmth rushed up Amanda's arm as she lay her fingers in his palm and accepted his assistance into the carriage. He climbed in after her and took the opposite seat.

When the carriage swung out of the driveway and onto West Adams Boulevard, Amanda sat back and tried to relax. It wasn't easy with Nick so close and her heart beating faster than normal.

"It's quite lovely here," Amanda said, peering at the passing neighborhood from beneath her wide-brimmed hat.

The West Adams district had become as famous as New York's Fifth Avenue, and Nob Hill, where Amanda's uncle made their home. Wide, tree-lined boulevards, wrought-iron and stone fences fronted the magnificent homes of some of the finest families in the city. Here, standards were set by people of affluence and wealth.

"My parents selected the site and designed the house," Nick said. "Father died shortly after construction began."

"He never got to live here?"

"No." Nick smiled gently. "But the house makes us all think of him."

Amanda turned back for a last glance at the Hastingses' home. A three-story structure with scrollwork and gingerbread, a witch's cap and onion dome, the house was painted ivory with deep blue and maroon trim. It was a grand home, and a fine legacy left by Nick's father.

"Don't you want to know where we're going?" Nick asked.

"Not really," Amanda said, and smiled. "I trust you."

"Now you've really put me on the spot," Nick replied, and gave her the same devilish smile she'd seen earlier.

That smile wound its way through Amanda and settled around her heart. If Nick got much more handsome, or smiled at her again, she didn't know how she'd bear it.

Maybe she shouldn't have come with him today, she thought again. Regardless of how dreadful another day of wedding preparations sounded, perhaps she should have stayed at the house and endured it, somehow. She'd come to Los Angeles with the intention of keeping her distance from Nick, knowing it was best for her. Dolly had been right to remind her of that. Now here she sat, facing a day alone with him.

Once more, Amanda cautioned herself to stay on guard, lest she lose herself completely in Nick's green eyes.

They rode in silence for a while, and that seemed to suit Amanda, Nick noted. He studied her face, turned toward the window so she could watch the passing scenery. Unlike so many other women, she didn't chatter about this or that, or feel the necessity to fill every moment with conversation.

Usually, that would have pleased Nick. Having lived with females his whole life, he thought that, in general, they talked too much. But now, with Amanda, it made him wonder what she was thinking.

Certainly, it wasn't anything remotely related to what *he* was thinking.

"Amanda, you're really very—"

Pretty, he'd intended to say. But when she turned to him and he saw that look of tired expectation on her face, it occurred to him that people probably told her she was pretty all the time—because she was. Nick didn't want to be like everyone else.

"Smart," Nick said. "You're really very smart."

She smiled then, a genuine, heartfelt smile that Nick was sure she seldom shared with anyone. He was inordinately pleased that he'd elicited it from her.

"The way you took care of that problem with Cecilia this morning," he continued. "You were the only one who seemed to have a handle on the situation."

She shrugged her shoulders. "All my wedding experience came in handy for something."

"What do you do with your time when you're not being dragged into everyone else's weddings?" Nick asked.

"Volunteer work, mostly."

Any other woman would have rattled off a list of clubs she belonged to and decorating projects she'd completed. But Amanda wasn't just any woman, Nick was fast learning.

"What sort of volunteer work?"

She seemed surprised that he'd asked. "Three days a week I work at churches, preparing meals and serving indigents. Twice a week I visit the orphanage."

"You enjoy doing that?" he asked.

"It breaks my heart, seeing the children." Amanda looked at him, tears instantly welling in her eyes.

Nick nearly bolted across the carriage to hold her, comfort her. He'd never felt a desire so strong in his entire life.

Amanda blinked her tears away. "But I can't stay away."

"Has this got something to do with that women's refuge you mentioned earlier?"

"Yes, it does," Amanda said. "So often women don't have the skill or knowledge to support themselves and their children when their husband leaves them or passes away. I want to provide a place where they can live while they get on their feet and learn how to provide for their children.''

Nick just stared at her. Good Lord, who was this woman—this Amanda Van Patton? Where had she been all his life?

''That's an incredible idea,'' he finally managed to say.

''Thank you.'' She smiled softly, and Nick's heart melted a little.

For the first time, he wondered what would have happened to his own family if things had been different when his father died. What if he'd been a boy, unable to take over the family business? Would his mother have known what to do? Where would she have gotten the help and guidance she needed to provide for their family?

''So, when are you starting this project?'' Nick asked.

''As soon as I raise the money.''

''What about your uncle Philip? He'd support your cause.''

''I don't want to ask him,'' Amanda said. ''It's a losing proposition, never intended to show a dime of profit. I can't expect him to spend his own money on it. Besides, I'd like the community to get involved, to realize what's happening and take part in solving the problem.''

''That's a tall order.''

She sat a little straighter on the seat and gave him a brisk nod. ''I have a plan.''

He grinned. ''Really?''

"I plan to stage a number of events for San Francisco's wealthy families to raise awareness of the situation and drum up support. Once I've secured the funds, I'll start on the refuge," Amanda said. "I need a building large enough to accommodate women and their children. It will require a kitchen, sitting rooms, a playroom for the children, and a place where they can receive medical care. I'll also require space so the women can receive training for the jobs they'll need to eventually become self-reliant. I want a safe location near schools, parks and churches."

She paused and blushed slightly. "Well, that's my plan."

"It sounds more like your passion," Nick said.

She considered his words. "You could be right."

"Any other passions?" Nick inquired, not sure why he'd asked such a leading question, yet anxious to hear her answer.

"Of course," she said simply. "But you'll have to figure those out for yourself."

"I warn you, I do love a challenge."

Amanda smiled and gestured out the window. "So, Mr. Tour Guide, what's that building over there?"

Nick had instructed the driver to take them through Los Angeles and give Amanda a look at the city. He pointed out the building where he had an office, then the shops along Wilshire Boulevard, which were bustling with people, delivery wagons, trolley cars and carriages. Gradually, the driver headed east, also on Nick's instructions, until the city faded into farmland.

Amanda leaned closer to the window, gazing at the open fields dotted with an occasional farmhouse.

"Perhaps now is a good time to ask where you're taking me."

"I want to show you *my* passion. My latest project," he explained, waving his hand toward the window. "The Whitney project, I'm calling it, named after the man who owned the majority of the land."

The carriage drew to a stop. Nick exited first, then helped Amanda to the ground.

Miles of farmland spread out around them, rimmed by a range of rugged mountains. Nearby was a dilapidated farmhouse—its roof blown off, windows smashed—shaded by a towering oak.

The driver handed a wicker hamper and blanket to Nick, then flicked the reins.

"Where is he going?" Amanda asked, watching the carriage drive away.

"Taking the team down to the creek for water."

Amanda glanced around at the vast openness, the isolation. "So we're out here alone?"

Nick nodded. "Just the two of us…and our passions."

Chapter Six

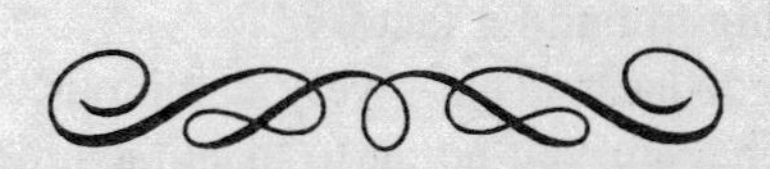

"Come here, let me show you." Nick dropped the wicker hamper and blanket under the tree, and took Amanda's elbow.

"This is the Whitney farm?" Amanda asked, walking alongside him.

"Most of it. Ezra Whitney owned the acreage to the north, and his son owned that to the south. It belongs to me now." Nick gestured to the old farmhouse. "This portion here in the middle will be mine shortly."

"It's not part of the Whitney farm?"

"No, it belongs to another farmer," Nick said. "It's been abandoned for years, as you can see by the condition of the place. We're tracking down the owner now, arranging for the purchase of the land."

Amanda looked up at Nick. "What if he won't sell?"

"Oh, he'll sell, all right," Nick told her. "He'll jump at the chance to unload this land."

"It seems like you're taking quite a chance," she said.

Nick shook his head. ''This tract of land is *perfect.* I'll have it, one way or another.''

Amanda gazed around. ''There must be a hundred acres.''

''Just about.''

''What do you plan to do with it?''

Nick stopped for a moment and surveyed the area. ''I'm going to build a factory.''

''My goodness. That's very ambitious,'' Amanda said. ''What are you going to manufacture?''

''Electrical parts,'' Nick said, and started walking again. ''Light switches and fixtures, sockets, wiring, bulbs. Everything needed to provide electricity to the public.''

''That's a very progressive idea.''

''It's the future.'' Nick pointed across the field. ''The main building will go right here. Come on, I'll show you.''

They crossed the field as Nick explained the layout of the factory complex, pointing and gesturing. Amanda asked questions—intelligent questions—that pleased him no end.

As he explained the reason for the placement of the warehouses, he realized he couldn't think of another woman he'd bring out here to look at his factory site—not even his mother or sister. But having Amanda here with him seemed the most natural thing in the world. He couldn't imagine not having her here, not telling her about his project.

''Has the architect finished the plans?'' Amanda asked as they walked toward the old farmhouse again.

''Almost.'' Nick grinned. ''I keep thinking of new things I'd like to add.''

"When will the factory open?"

"Early next year," Nick said. "I'm projecting it will turn a profit within two years."

"Two years?" she asked, her eyes wide.

He grinned. "I like to think long-term."

"I guess you do."

"Hungry?" Nick asked as they reached the shade of the oak tree. He gestured to the hamper. "I had the cooks prepare something for us. No easy task, with all the wedding preparations under way."

Amanda spread the blanket on the soft grass and sat down. Nick joined her, the hamper separating them.

A light breeze stirred the wisps of hair at Amanda's temples and her cheeks glowed a pale pink as she looked off across the field. Nick couldn't keep his gaze away. It was the first time he'd been to the old Whitney farm and found anything more interesting than the land itself.

Amanda turned back to him and saw that he'd been watching her. She flushed slightly and dropped her gaze. Nick thought her the most lovely woman he'd ever seen.

"Let's see what we have here," he said, briskly opening the hamper.

Inside was cheese and bread, some cold meat, fruit and a bottle of wine. Amanda set out the plates and cutlery while Nick filled their glasses.

"Do you intend to employ women in your factory?" Amanda asked.

Nick bit off a chunk of bread. "Men and women working alongside each other? I'm not sure that's a good idea."

"That sounds a bit old-fashioned for a man building a factory meant to take us into the next century," Amanda said, sipping the wine.

He shrugged. "Yes, I suppose it does."

"Well?"

Nick shook his head. "I don't know..."

"At least say you'll think about it."

"I'll think about it," he promised. "For you."

Amanda smiled, and Nick couldn't help smiling back.

"So," he said, helping himself to the fruit, "what made you decide to build this women's refuge?"

"I saw a need and wanted to fill it." She gestured toward the open field. "Sort of like your factory."

He sensed her evasiveness and again found himself desperate to know what thoughts lay in Amanda's mind.

He sipped his wine. "I think there's more to it than that."

Amanda paused. "Do you?"

"Yes. And I'd like to know the whole story." Nick grinned. "Besides, you trust me, remember? And I'm your new best friend."

Amanda set her plate aside and studied him. At first, it irked Nick a bit that she wouldn't simply tell him what he wanted to know. Did she not trust him? Could she believe he wasn't genuinely interested?

"All right, I'll tell you," Amanda finally said, leaving him feeling that he'd accomplished something with her. "You arranged my escape from the house today. I suppose I owe you."

Nick pushed the hamper aside and scooted a little closer to her on the blanket. But she gazed off across the field again, and for a moment he wondered if she really would tell him.

Finally, she looked back at him. ''My father died when I was eleven years old. Mother was quite devastated, of course. She was also quite unprepared to make a life for us. She'd never worked. She had no skills, no training. Nothing that would allow her to get any sort of decent job.''

Nick shifted on the blanket. What Amanda was telling him was something highly personal and surely painful. Maybe he'd have been better off letting it alone, not insisting she tell him. Then, just as quickly, he disregarded the notion. He wanted to know everything there was to know about Amanda.

''It didn't take long before the little money my father left us was gone,'' Amanda said. ''We lost our home. Mother didn't want to accept charity.''

''But what about your uncle? The man's worth a fortune.''

''Yes, but Uncle Philip was a distant relative of my father's, and Mother didn't know him,'' Amanda said. ''Finally, though, when things got really bad, she sent me to live there.''

''Why didn't she come herself?''

''As I said, Mother wouldn't take charity,'' Amanda told him. ''For me, yes. But not for herself.''

''But still...''

Amanda thought for a moment. ''I think Mother was intimidated by them. Their money, their lifestyle. She knew she wouldn't fit in.''

''But she sent you?''

''She never intended for me to stay with them. She

simply wanted them to take care of me until she could get on her feet and make a home for the two of us."

"But that never happened?"

Amanda glanced away. "No. She died."

"I'm so sorry," Nick whispered, and had never meant anything more in his life. Instinctively, he covered her hand with his. She felt fragile and small, her fingers warm against his skin. Amanda gave him a wan smile, then withdrew her hand, seemingly not comfortable with too much sympathy directed at her.

Nick wondered why he'd never heard about Amanda's background when she'd first come to live with the Van Pattons. Their families had been close. Why had he not known these things about her?

Amanda drew in a deep breath, as if pushing the old memories to the recesses of her mind, where they belonged. "So, if Mother could have found decent work and a place to live, things would have turned out very differently for us."

"And you think you can right that wrong by building your refuge?"

"Yes."

Nick studied her for a long moment, absorbing the determined spark in her eyes, the set of her jaw. He nodded. "I think you can, too."

"You do?" she asked, and seemed a little surprised. "You hardly know me."

"I know you well enough to see that once you put your mind to something, Amanda, you'll see it through. Which," Nick said, "is a quality I very much admire."

Another shy smile tugged at her lips, pulling him even closer to her. Something about this woman called to him, intrigued him, lured him. He leaned forward, his gaze locked with hers, and kissed her.

Nick's heart thundered in his chest as he pressed his mouth against Amanda's. He hadn't known he was going to kiss her, hadn't meant to do it. Yet it seemed the most natural thing in the world.

Sweet. Oh, she tasted sweet. Slowly, Nick blended his lips with hers, savoring the feel of her, then pulled away.

It was a chaste kiss. Nothing hot or sweaty or passionate. But heat pumped through Nick with an intensity he hadn't expected.

He looked at her face, inches from his. He felt her hot breath on his skin, and knew he wanted to kiss her again. More than that, he wanted to devour her. Smother her with the passion suddenly boiling inside him.

Nick drew back from her. Her pink lips were wet, her cheeks flushed and her blue eyes wide. Everything about Amanda summoned him, beckoned him to lean forward again, kiss her once more.

Should he? He sure as hell wanted to.

"We should get back to town," he said, surprised at how low and raspy his own voice sounded.

Amanda nodded, seeming to understand his dilemma and their situation clearly. "Yes, we should."

They tossed the remains of their picnic into the hamper. Nick got to his feet and gazed across the open field, annoyed to realize that the old Whitney farm would never be the same again.

Not after kissing Amanda.

"What did you dream last night?"

Amanda glanced to her left and saw Nick's Aunt Winnifred take the seat beside her in the music room of the Hastings home. While the wedding party was at the rehearsal, Constance had named Winnifred hostess for the evening. Amanda and the other ten houseguests had just finished supper and were now gathering in the music room for the evening's entertainment Constance had arranged.

"Well?" Winnifred asked, leaning a little closer.

Around them, voices blended pleasantly and skirts rustled as everyone settled into chairs.

"Let me think," Amanda said, stalling. Last night she'd dreamed of Nick, but she didn't intend to tell Winnifred.

It wasn't the first time she had experienced a dream in which Nick played a starring role. Over the years, the vision of him often crept into her slumbers. And much to Amanda's distress, the dream was always the same.

Her, in a crowded room, when Nick walked in. He crossed the room, speaking to everyone—but her. She reached out to him as he drew near. Yet he always stayed an arm's length away. She could never quite touch him. Never get him to look at her. Never get him to speak to her.

Amanda had often wondered what the dream meant, wondered why it continued to periodically invade her sleep. But she certainly couldn't ask Winnifred to interpret it for her.

"How did you become interested in dreams?" she asked instead.

"It's quite fascinating," Winnifred declared, snapping her fan open. "Dreaming is universal. It's common among people of all lands, all cultures. Dreams are a sign of prophecy, a prediction of the future or a message of some sort. The Bible shows the significance of dreams. Some of the greatest thinkers believed in the power of dreams. One merely has to understand the signs and interpret them correctly to unravel their secrets.''

''And you've studied this extensively?'' Amanda asked.

''Oh, no, of course not,'' Winnifred said. ''I interpret by instinct. Though my natural, logical thought process. It's a gift. Now, tell me what you dreamed last night.''

Amanda decided to indulge the woman. It seemed harmless enough. She thought quickly, recalling a past dream that she hoped would satisfy Winnifred. ''All right,'' she said, ''here's what I dreamed.''

Winnifred's features pulled together in tight concentration as she settled back in her chair, listening.

''I dreamed I was standing at the train station,'' Amanda said, ''waiting for a train.''

Winnifred's lips pressed together. ''Was it raining?''

''No.''

''Were small animals with you?''

''No.''

''Were you wearing purple?''

Amanda drew back slightly, eyeing her. ''No.''

''Hmm…'' Winnifred's eyes narrowed and her lips pressed together so tightly they nearly disappeared. A moment dragged by while she stared straight ahead, tapping her fan against her palm. ''Aha!'' she cried.

Amanda jumped.

"I know what your dream means," Winnifred announced. "It indicates your dislike for certain kinds of food."

Amanda frowned. "It does?"

"Certainly."

"Doesn't it mean that I'm anxious to go somewhere? Or, perhaps, looking forward to the arrival of someone or something new in my life?"

"Oh, no, no," Winnifred said, waving away the idea.

"But the train, and the train station...?"

"Foods," Winnifred assured her.

"Well, all right...if you're sure."

"Of course I'm sure. I told you, I've been blessed with a gift." Winnifred gave a brisk nod, then levered herself out of the chair and walked away.

She circulated through the room, chatting with the other guests, then gave a brief introduction as a pianist popular in the city made her entrance. Winnifred resumed her seat beside Amanda, and the performance began.

Amanda clasped her hands in her lap, determined to focus her thoughts on the young woman seated at the piano. A full minute passed before she realized her mind had drifted.

To Nick.

To their kiss.

So much for her vow to keep her distance from him. Not only had she jumped at the chance to spend the day with him, she'd allowed him to kiss her.

Not that she could have stopped him.

Not that she wanted to stop him.

Determinedly, Amanda recalled ten years ago,

when Nick had treated her so shabbily. When he'd broken her heart. Why hadn't that incident made her hate him?

Through the years, whenever the Hastings and Van Patton families had gotten together, the conversation always included news of Nick. His mother talked about how well he ran the family business, what a good man he'd become.

And from all Amanda had seen since her arrival in Los Angeles, his mother had been right. Nick was a good, decent man. Maybe if he weren't, Amanda could find an excuse to dislike him. If he had a major fault, she could point to it and tell herself that no, she shouldn't involve herself with him, and here was the reason why. But so far she'd found nothing. No reason not to still care about him.

What did it mean? That she herself suffered from some horrific personality flaw that wouldn't allow her to forget him?

The song ended and polite applause rippled through the room. Amanda forced her attention to the pianist and clapped her hands, smiling her appreciation, nodding in agreement when Winnifred cast a glance her way. The pianist took her seat again and resumed playing. Amanda slipped into her own thoughts once more.

Today. Alone with Nick. Just the two of them rambling through town, then into the countryside. She'd told him things she seldom shared with anyone. He'd explained his Whitney project, as if he couldn't wait to tell her about it.

And then he'd kissed her.

Amanda sighed deeply, remembering the taste, the

feel of his lips. In the decade since he'd last kissed her, Nick Hastings had gotten better at it. Though their exchange this afternoon was little more than a brushing of lips, Amanda sensed a command, a passion that had caused her stomach to tingle—still, hours later.

Applause again interrupted Amanda's thoughts, and she realized the song had ended. Quickly she joined in, glancing around, hoping no one had noticed her lack of attentiveness.

Voices drifted in as the applause died. Amanda turned to see the wedding party enter the room.

Nick. Tall, sturdy, handsome Nick Hastings.

Amanda's heart thumped into her throat and hung there. Her stomach fluttered. She didn't need Winnifred to interpret these signs. Amanda already knew what they meant.

The dream she'd had so often in the past that she wouldn't allow herself to share with Winnifred popped into her mind. Now, at this moment, the dream became a reality.

Amanda in a crowded room. Nick entering. Would he ignore her, hold himself aloof, just out of her reach, as he always had in her dream?

"Winnifred," Amanda whispered, "do you believe that dreams can come true?"

"Oh, of course," she told her.

Amanda's pounding heart seemed to skip a beat as she watched Nick standing in the doorway. Ten years ago he'd kissed her, then ignored her. This afternoon after he'd kissed her, he'd announced they were leaving.

Would he now treat her the way he had all those

years ago? Once more, would he ignore her? As he always had in her recurring dream?

Amanda drew in a fortifying breath.

Nick's gaze swept the room, landed on Amanda and stayed there. He smiled. Someone spoke to him, but he ignored the man and walked straight toward her.

Her heart raced as he drew near, stopped in front of her and took her hand. Amanda rose, her gaze locked with his, neither of them aware of anyone else in the room.

Her awful dream hadn't come true.

At least, not tonight.

Chapter Seven

"I love weddings," Ethan said.

"Is that so?" Nick grumbled as he stepped out of the house onto the rear lawn, where the wedding reception was under way.

Late-afternoon sun shone brightly on the lawn, where a white, gauzy tent had been set up, crowded with tables covered with white linen and bouquets of fresh flowers. Fine china and crystal gleamed. Musicians played as elegantly attired couples swirled on the dance floor.

"Absolutely," Ethan declared, as he fell into step beside Nick.

"Since when?" Nick asked, though he wasn't much interested in the answer. Not with the problem that was on his mind, delivered to him just now from his office downtown.

"What's not to like?" Ethan helped himself to a glass of champagne from a passing waiter as they stopped in a shady spot near one of the refreshment tables. He took a second look at Nick. "What's wrong with you? No, wait. Let me guess. Another problem with your Whitney project?''

Nick fumed for a moment, annoyed now with Ethan as well as the problem he had to deal with. Yet he didn't intend to discuss it with his friend. ''It's nothing,'' he said. ''Routine business.''

''Humph.'' Ethan grunted in disbelief, then shook his head. ''That project is going to bankrupt you. I've said it before and I'll say it again—you'd better pull out before you sink every cent you have into it, and lose it all.''

''This project will work,'' Nick insisted, keeping his voice down with considerable effort.

Ethan glanced at him. ''Who are you trying to convince? Me or yourself?''

Nick glared at him. ''I don't need to convince anyone.''

''Relax, will you? This is supposed to be a party—your sister's wedding reception.'' Ethan gestured with his glass toward the guests, then sighed contentedly. ''Look at all these lovely young women, dressed in their finest, all so beautiful, just waiting to be...well, now, who have we here? Who is that gorgeous creature talking with old man Ramsey?''

Nick's gaze followed Ethan's to the edge of the crowded dance floor. His simmering annoyance edged closer to anger as he realized it was Amanda whom Ethan had noticed.

''How did I miss her earlier?'' Ethan set his glass aside. ''Seems I need to rectify this situation immediately.''

While Nick couldn't blame Ethan for his attraction to Amanda, he wasn't about to let him get near her.

He planted his palm on Ethan's chest, stopping him in his tracks. "Stay away from her."

Surprised, Ethan backed up a step. "What's this?"

"Leave her alone," Nick told him, none too kindly.

A knowing smile crept over Ethan's face. He glanced at Amanda, then back to Nick, nodding wisely. "I see. You've staked a claim yourself?"

Nick just glared at him.

"Don't I at least get to know the fetching young woman's name?" Ethan asked.

"Amanda Van Patton, from San Francisco."

Ethan studied Amanda for a few moments, then nodded in approval. "So, you've selected your prey."

Nick's eyes narrowed. "My prey?"

"Yes, for our wager. Don't pretend you've forgotten."

Nick rubbed his forehead. Actually, he had forgotten, and was annoyed now at being reminded of it. "That bet was a stupid idea," he said.

Ethan shrugged. "You certainly haven't wasted any time. Seems you're off to a quick start. And Miss Van Patton is quite lovely. Why are you wasting your energy with that Whitney project when, in twenty-eight days, you could be rolling around under the covers with her?"

"Shut up."

"Sorry." Ethan held up his palms and backed up a step, smiling. "Seems I'd better get going if I'm to have any chance at winning that case of Scotch."

"Look," Nick said, "I want no part of that bet."

"Oh, no, no. Not on your life." Ethan glanced toward Amanda again. "We're not quitting now. Things are just getting interesting."

Ethan tugged at his vest and swaggered toward the dance floor.

Nick watched him go, his annoyance growing. That damn bet, bad news from his office, then Ethan eyeing Amanda. How much worse could this day get?

He kept watch until he saw Ethan approach a group of young women seated at one of the tables—across the lawn from the dance floor. Satisfied, he turned back to Amanda. She glanced up and their gazes met.

Nick's problems simply floated away. He felt lighter than the air itself as he was drawn on some unseen current across the lawn to her. He butted in front of Olin Ramsey and took Amanda's hand. "May I have this dance?"

She cast an apologetic look at Mr. Ramsey, and Nick led her away.

Once Nick had her in his arms and they were whirling among the other dancers, a deeper sense of calm washed over him. Which seemed odd, since Amanda also caused an excitement to simmer inside him. Yet they danced the whole song through without speaking. Nick couldn't think of one damn thing to say, and luckily, that seemed to be all right with Amanda. She, too, seemed content with them simply gazing at each other.

When the song ended, Nick laced his fingers through Amanda's, keeping her at his side. The music began and he swept her into his arms once more.

"The wedding was lovely," Amanda said, gazing up at him.

"I thought you didn't like weddings."

"I don't," she said, then smiled. "But all the work, the planning and the headaches seem worth it the moment the bride walks down the aisle."

Nick glanced at Cecilia and Aaron, seated together at a table. "They do seem happy."

"So does your mother," Amanda said.

He followed her gaze to the table where Constance sat. "Who's that man?" Nick asked.

"Your aunt Winnifred introduced us," Amanda said. "He's Charles Osborne. Don't you know him?"

"No," Nick said. But he didn't know every one of his mother's friends, nor had he paid much attention to the guest list. He certainly didn't know this Charles Osborne, a man about his mother's age, with a full head of snowy hair, sharp eyes and a military bearing.

"He and your mother seem to be having a wonderful time," Amanda said. "Which is more than I can say for you."

His attention snapped back to her and the knowing look on her face. "You noticed?"

"I noticed," Amanda said. "What's wrong?"

While he'd been adamant about not revealing to Ethan what was bothering him, it seemed quite natural to tell Amanda. "I just received an update on the search for Danton Moore."

"The man who owns the center tract of farmland you want for your project?"

"Yes," Nick grumbled. "I don't know what's so damn difficult about tracking down one old farmer."

"Is this going to hold up the project?"

"No," Nick insisted. "I won't let it."

Amanda gave him an encouraging nod. "You'll find your Mr. Moore."

"Damn right I will," Nick said.

The song ended and he turned, taking another look at his mother and Charles Osborne.

"Why don't you go over and meet the man?" Amanda suggested.

Nick nodded. "Yes, I will. Come with me?"

Amanda gestured toward Olin Ramsey, still standing nearby. "I owe Mr. Ramsey a dance."

Nick escorted her over, satisfied to leave her safely in the care of the elderly gentleman, and headed toward his mother's table.

Amanda watched him walk away, thinking not for the first time that day how handsome he looked in his tuxedo. Certainly the most redeeming quality about the wedding, she decided.

Winnifred approached, and for once didn't ask what she'd dreamed the night before.

"Lovely wedding," the woman declared. "Just lovely."

Olin Ramsey, balding and slightly stooped, nodded. "A fine-looking young couple, certainly."

"Where are Cecilia and Aaron honeymooning?" Amanda asked.

"Europe, of course," Winnifred said. She nodded to the table where Constance sat. "Mr. Osborne has recently returned from there."

"Does he live here in Los Angeles?" Amanda asked.

"Visiting. He's related to the Davenports, I understand," Winnifred told her.

"It's the Wades," Mr. Ramsey said. "He's here visiting the Wades."

''Oh, well, yes,'' Winnifred said, dismissing the contradiction with a wave of her fan.

With considerable effort, Mr. Ramsey drew himself up straighter. ''Mrs. Dubois, may I have this dance?''

''Of course.'' Winnifred laid her hand in his and allowed him to escort her to the dance floor.

Amanda smiled as they moved into each other's arms, then jumped when a wisp of breath warmed her cheek.

''Good afternoon, Miss Van Patton.''

A tall, dark-haired man about Nick's age stood beside her.

''Allow me to present myself,'' he said, and bowed slightly. ''Ethan Carmichael. I'm a close friend of Nick's. His oldest and dearest friend, actually. He asked me to keep you company while he's occupied.''

''He did?'' Amanda's gaze leaped to Nick, who was standing at his mother's table talking with Charles Osborne.

Ethan nodded and offered his arm. ''Would you care to dance?''

She stole another quick look at Nick, then assessed Ethan for a moment and decided he appeared harmless.

''Very well,'' she said.

They moved onto the dance floor and fell in step with the other couples.

''I understand you're visiting from San Francisco,'' Ethan said.

''Yes, I plan to return first thing tomorrow morning.''

''So soon? Why the rush?''

"I have a number of things there that require my attention."

Ethan favored her with what Amanda was sure he considered to be his most charming smile. "Your departure will surely be our loss."

Their dance continued for a few more moments before Ethan frowned down at Amanda and his expression grew serious. "Amanda—may I call you Amanda?"

"You may."

"Amanda, I realize this is hardly the time or place for such a conversation, but I feel it's my duty to pass along a word of warning to you about Nick."

"A warning?" she echoed, not sure to what Ethan could possibly be referring. "What sort of warning?"

"The man's riddled with faults."

"Is that so?"

"Oh, yes," Ethan said. "Drinks to excess. Gambles. Carouses at all hours, with all manner of people."

"You don't say."

"And his business deals." Ethan made a little tsking sound. "They tend to run a bit, shall we say, on the shady side? Good breeding prevents me from going into too much detail, you understand."

"Yes, Mr. Carmichael, I believe I understand exactly," Amanda said, realizing now that she'd become caught in some sort of rivalry between Ethan and Nick.

Ethan sighed heavily and shook his head sadly. "Nick puts up a good front, but deep down, he's not the sort of man any decent woman would want to get mixed up with. A woman like yourself, for instance."

Amanda raised an eyebrow. ''And you're a good friend of Nick's?''

''A very good friend,'' Ethan insisted. ''But that doesn't mean I don't see him for what he is. Or would want a woman—such as yourself—to be hurt because of him.''

''How very noble of you, Mr. Carmichael.''

He smiled. ''Please, call me Ethan. And may I say, Amanda, that you—''

''Move.''

Nick appeared at Ethan's side and gave him a shove hard enough to push him two steps away.

''Amanda, could I speak with you a moment?'' Nick asked pleasantly, ignoring the guests who'd turned to stare.

Amanda glanced back at Ethan as Nick escorted her away from the dance floor. ''He said he was a friend of yours. Is that true?''

Nick stopped abruptly, his brows pulled together. ''Did he say something to offend you?''

''No, not at all,'' Amanda said. ''But he did make some...odd comments. About you.''

''Pay him no mind.'' Nick's waved away her words with his big hand, dismissing them and Ethan. ''Would you come with me? There're some people I'd like you to meet.''

Amanda spent the evening with Nick and the friends he introduced her to. Business acquaintances, mostly, men who ran successful firms in Los Angeles and throughout California. Some were married, others were accompanied by young women. Amanda felt at ease among them, and at ease with Nick seated beside her.

Shortly, Ethan joined their table, escorting an attractive young woman. Amanda had met her earlier. Julia Prescott, tall and blond, was here visiting her aunt, having recently arrived from Europe, where she'd lived the last year, recovering from the sudden death of her husband.

Nick never let Amanda stray too far from his side. They danced, ate and visited with friends as the evening wore on and the reception drew to a close.

After the honeymoon couple departed and the last guests headed homeward, a wave of emptiness descended upon Amanda as she stood near the deserted dance floor. She was tired and felt a bit like her surroundings—the burned-down candles, the wilting floral arrangements. But the wedding had been lovely. It was the only one she'd attended that she'd actually enjoyed.

Amanda glanced up at Nick as she stood at his side, bidding goodbye to some friends. The evening breeze blew slightly, bringing with it the scent of flowers and blooming shrubs. Faint light shone from the house, illuminating his face. Despite the long, draining day, Nick looked strong, absolutely tireless—and handsome, of course. Amanda was sure he was the real reason she'd enjoyed this particular wedding so much.

They walked with the final departing couple to the rear porch and said their goodbyes. Behind them, Constance supervised as the servants began the long process of clearing away all remnants of the reception, as the musicians packed up their instruments.

"Well, I guess that about wraps it up," Nick said.

He seemed reluctant to leave the porch. Amanda

wondered if he, like herself, wanted these final few minutes together to last as long as possible.

Eventually, when there was no reasonable excuse to stay any longer, they walked inside and headed toward the staircase.

An unnatural quiet hung over the house in the wake of the day's festive atmosphere. Guests staying at the Hastings home had already gone up to their bedchambers.

Nick rested his palm against Amanda's elbow as they climbed the steps together, and held on to her as they stopped in front of her room. There he glanced up and down the hallway, then eased closer, lowering his head.

Amanda's back pressed against the door to her room. Was he going to kiss her? Her heart speeded up considerably as the possibility occurred to her. She felt his warm breath on her cheek and smelled his heady, masculine scent.

If he tried to kiss her, should she let him? Amanda gazed up at him, caught in the spell of his deep green eyes. Yes, oh yes. She'd let him kiss her.

"Would you like to do something together tomorrow after church?" Nick asked, his voice low.

Amanda reined in her runaway thoughts, admonishing herself for thinking that he'd kiss her—that he'd want to.

"I can't," she said, surprised to hear how tight her own voice sounded. "I'm leaving in the morning."

He frowned and eased back a little. "Leaving?"

"Yes, I'd always intended to return home immediately after the wedding. Dolly is packing my things now," she said. "We'll leave right after breakfast."

"But—why?"

Because when she'd planned the trip, she'd wanted to leave as quickly as possible, to avoid any undue contact with Nick. She hadn't trusted herself in his presence, had been afraid of what she might do.

But she couldn't tell him any of that. Not now. Not when her heart still pounded wildly in her chest at his closeness, and despite his obvious intentions otherwise, she still wished he'd kiss her.

She pulled in a breath, trying to calm herself. "My aunt and uncle are expecting me home tomorrow afternoon."

"You won't consider staying longer?" he asked softly.

Amanda gazed up at him. More than anything, she wanted to stay. Here. With Nick. But she didn't dare.

She glanced away. "No. I should go home."

Nick touched his finger to her chin and turned her to face him. "You're sure?"

"I'm sure," Amanda whispered.

"Well, then..." Nick backed up a step. "If you're sure."

They stood like that for a moment, just looking at each other. Finally, Nick nodded.

"Good night," he said, and walked away.

Chapter Eight

"Did you ever see a prettier bride in your life?" Dolly exclaimed as she breezed into Amanda's bedchamber.

Amanda stood in front of the dresser, her emotions churning in the wake of her encounter with Nick in the hallway moments ago. He'd seemed surprised that she was leaving, and not altogether pleased about it. Standing next to him, she'd found her heart soaring at the possibility of not returning to San Francisco. She's wanted to blurt aloud that she'd stay—stay forever.

But Nick hadn't asked her to.

He hadn't even kissed her goodbye.

Amanda drew in a ragged breath. Yes, leaving was the right thing to do.

No matter how much it hurt.

Dolly seemed not to notice Amanda's distress. "Me and some of the other girls stood at the windows and snuck us a peek today at all the goings-on out back. Lordy-me, what a to-do."

"Yes," Amanda murmured, "the wedding was lovely."

Dolly stopped abruptly. "What's wrong?"

Amanda walked to the dresser, hoping to avoid her maid's gaze. But Dolly knew her too well.

"I'm just tired," she said. "That's all."

Dolly planted a fist on her hip. "Now, Miz Amanda, you may as well go on and tell me, 'cause I can see plain as day that something's bothering you. Did somebody say something that upset you?"

"No, of course not." Amanda glanced at her momentarily, then looked away again.

A moment passed before Dolly said, "It's that Mr. Nick, isn't it."

Amanda's gaze came up to meet Dolly's. She could deny it, but didn't have the strength. Besides, Dolly would see right through her lie.

"Yes," she admitted. She drew in a fortifying breath and straightened her shoulders. "But we're leaving in the morning, just as we'd planned."

"You love him, don't you," Dolly said softly.

"No," Amanda insisted, and looked into her eyes. But after a few seconds she had to turn away.

Dolly took a step closer. "Maybe you should stay. See what happens with Mr. Nick."

"No," she said. "I can't stay. I simply can't."

"Because of your feelings for him?"

"I don't have any feelings for him," Amanda insisted.

"Well, if'n you don't, then why don't you just stay here a couple more days?" Dolly asked, almost in a challenge. She nodded wisely. "It's because you love that man."

"It's not love. Nick doesn't feel that way about me, and—"

"And you don't want to be hurt again, like when you were younger."

Amanda drew in a deep breath and let it out slowly. "Exactly."

"You don't think he cares about you?"

"No, not really."

"I think you're wrong," Dolly said. "I think you owe it to yourself to stay here and—"

"Get hurt again?" Amanda demanded, her heart aching.

Dolly shrugged. "Maybe you should give the man a chance."

Amanda shook her head. She couldn't bear it. She couldn't bear it if she woke in the morning, saw Nick, and he simply ignored her. Better to leave things as they were. Better to leave now.

"No," Amanda said. "We're leaving in the morning and—"

A knock sounded on the door, with so much force it caused Amanda and Dolly both to jump. They looked at each other.

"That ain't no gentle rap from one of the dignified ladies in this house," Dolly said.

Amanda gulped. She'd thought the same.

Dolly crossed the room toward the door, but Amanda caught her elbow. "That's all right. I'll get it."

Dolly's eyebrows rose. "Your cheeks are all flushed and you're breathing fast—just because you *think* that *might* be Mr. Nick at the door. Don't try to tell *me* you don't love that man."

The pounding sounded again. Amanda opened the door and, as Dolly had predicted, there stood Nick. His tie was pulled down and his collar stood open. He looked agitated.

"Could I speak with you?" he asked, obviously struggling to sound pleasant.

Amanda stepped into the hallway and closed the door behind her.

"Why are you so hell-bent on leaving tomorrow?" he asked.

"I told you already, I'd always planned to leave. My aunt and uncle are expecting me," Amanda said.

"That's it? That's the only reason you're going?"

"My charity work is there. The orphans. The indigents. They depend on me," Amanda said. "And I want to start on my women's refuge. You know how important that is to me and—"

"I want you to stay."

Amanda gasped softly. She gazed up at him, unsure if she should trust her own ears. "What?"

"I want you to stay," he said again, doing his best to contain his simmering agitation. "I'll get my mother up here to issue a formal invitation, if you like. Hell, I'll parade every person in the house before you if it will change your mind."

Her heart thundered in her chest. He wanted her to stay? Everything inside Amanda cried out to accept his invitation.

But nagging doubts intruded on her thoughts, memories of when she was young. Certainly, she was all grown-up now. She wasn't the same lost young girl—far from it. Nothing created self-doubt in her now, and hadn't for years. Nothing, that is, except Nick. Why was that?

Amanda wasn't sure. In fact, she didn't even want to think too hard on the subject.

All she knew for certain was that she couldn't bear being hurt again. Not by Nick.

Amanda shook her head. "I'm sorry, Nick, but I have to go home tomorrow."

He frowned at her, his unhappiness over her decision etched in the taut lines of his face. "There must be something I can say to convince you to stay."

Amanda gulped, fearful that the knot of emotion in her throat would dissolve into tears. "It's better this way."

"The hell it is."

"I—I really have to leave."

Nick glared at her. "There's nothing I can say? Nothing I can do?"

She gulped again, forcing the words through her tight, dry throat. "I can't think of anything."

Nick's face softened and a little grin pulled at his lips. "Wait, I just had an idea." He leaned closer and braced his arm on the wall beside her head. "I believe a great man once said that a kiss is worth a thousand words."

Amanda's heart pounded harder, robbing her of breath as she gazed up at him. "I've never heard such a thing."

"Then let me demonstrate." Nick brushed his fingers along her cheek and lowered his head. "But I have to warn you, this kiss will be a more memorable kiss than the last two."

"The last two?" Amanda asked.

"Yes. Out at the Whitney farm, and at Tahoe." He eased back a little and raised an eyebrow. "Have you kissed so many men that you've forgotten?"

"No, of course not," she said, and felt her cheeks flush. "But I didn't think you'd remembered. About the Tahoe kiss, I mean. It was so long ago, and—"

"I'd prefer to forget that first one myself," Nick said, shaking his head. "Not my finest moment. I suppose I owe you an apology for kissing you like that. I had no idea. It wasn't until I spoke with your cousin that I realized."

"Realized what?"

"That you were only fourteen." Nick uttered a gruff laugh. "There I was thinking myself all grown-up, all wise and worldly, and I mistook you for being much older."

Amanda gasped. "I had no idea."

"I was…embarrassed, and thought it best if the whole thing were forgotten."

"Oh, Nick…" Amanda splayed her palms against his chest and gazed up into his handsome face, as relief ten years in coming washed over her. "That's why you never spoke to me again? That's the reason? Because of my age?"

He straightened at the feel of her hands, and drew in a quick breath. "Of course. What else?"

A little giggle slipped through Amanda's lips. "All these years I—I thought… Oh, never mind. It's not…"

Amanda's words trailed of as Nick slid his hand to the back of her neck and lowered his mouth to capture hers.

She moaned softly as his lips covered her own,

warm and moist, in a deep kiss that was nothing like the quick brush he'd given her at Tahoe or at the Whitney farm. Gently, he worked their mouths together, finally parting her lips and slipping his tongue inside.

Another moan rattled in Amanda's throat at the sheer delight of their kiss. Nick slid both arms around her and drew her close, pulling her fully against him. Amanda latched on to his arms and held on tight.

He lifted his head and gazed down at her, his eyes as hazy as she felt. "My God..." he whispered, looking at her, seeming to see her in a wholly different light.

"Ask me again," Amanda said softly.

He looked confused, a little dazed. "Ask you what?"

She grinned. "Ask me to stay."

Nick smiled broadly, suddenly understanding. "Stay. Please?"

A giddy giggle escaped her throat. "Yes, I'll stay."

"Westlake Park," Nick announced, gesturing to the expanse of green grass and trees on the outskirts of the city.

Amanda smiled as he assisted her from his carriage. Sunday-afternoon visitors strolled the paths that crisscrossed the park, as others picnicked on bright colored blankets. Children fed the ducks at the edge of the lake. Vendors hawked lemonade, popcorn and caramel apples.

"It's lovely here," Amanda said, taking Nick's arm as they walked.

"This area along Wilshire Boulevard was a weed-choked ravine for years. It's just been developed into this park,'' Nick said. He motioned toward the red-roofed boathouse. ''Feel like a boat ride?''

''Certainly,'' Amanda said.

He squinted one eye at her. ''I warn you, matie, I'm a black-heart pirate on the water.''

She giggled. ''I'll take my chances.''

While Nick secured a rowboat for them, Amanda waited in the shade. The afternoon sun was tempered by a layer of clouds, the heat relieved by a breeze. She wore an apricot-colored skirt, striped blouse and a wide-brimmed hat, and carried a parasol—one of her many outfits her aunt had sent down this week.

Nick helped Amanda into the small rowboat and took up the oars. As he propelled them across the lake amid the other boaters, Amanda thought once again how dashing he looked, dressed in white trousers, a blue jacket and necktie, sporting a white boater hat.

She'd been in Los Angeles a little over a week now, and somehow, Nick continued to grow more handsome. And more attentive.

In the first few days following the wedding, all the houseguests had left, save for Amanda and Winnifred, and Constance had taken to her bed for a much-needed rest. Nick had made certain Amanda stayed busy. He'd escorted her to supper at some of the city's finest restaurants, and they'd attended the theater Saturday night.

''Any word on finding your Mr. Moore?'' Amanda asked, adjusting her parasol and making herself comfortable in the little boat.

''What's this? A woman who'll discuss business

on Sunday?'' Nick grinned. ''I certainly can't throw you overboard now.''

Amanda smiled. ''I knew you were a kind-hearted pirate.''

''As it happens,'' Nick said, pulling on the oars, ''the elusive Danton Moore has been located in Oregon. My attorney, the investigator who located Moore and an assistant to help with the negotiations and legal paperwork will go up there by the end of this week and conclude my business with him.''

Amanda couldn't help but admire Nick's confidence. In the week she'd spent with him, she'd seen a fearlessness about him. Certainly, he couldn't run so successful a company, or make his Whitney project a reality, without it.

''I saw your friend Ethan Carmichael yesterday,'' Amanda said. ''Your mother and I were having lunch at the tearoom and Ethan came in. Julia Prescott was with him. You remember Julia? We met her at Cecilia's reception. The widow in town visiting her aunt. Anyway, Ethan seemed quite taken with her.''

Nick raised an eyebrow at her. ''Ethan?''

''They sat together in a quiet corner near the back. I got the impression that he cared deeply for her.''

''Ethan?'' Nick asked again. ''Ethan Carmichael?''

''Why is that so hard to believe?''

Nick opened his mouth as if to say something, then apparently changed his mind. ''Don't put too much stock into anything Ethan does.''

''But I saw the signs.''

''Signs?''

''The signs of being in love.''

Nick paused in his rowing, stowed the oars and

looked at her skeptically. "How do you know so much about being in love?"

"From my cousins," Amanda said. "I watched all four of them being courted and then marrying."

"So you're something of an expert on the subject? This, from a woman who doesn't like weddings?"

"Just because I don't want to suffer through any more wedding preparations doesn't mean I don't understand love," Amanda said. "There's a difference."

Nick took up the oars again. "All right, then, tell me what these signs of love are."

"Well, there're a number of things, according to my cousins," Amanda said. "Racing of the heart. Dampened palms. Difficulty concentrating. The wearing of big, silly grins. Oh, and a squishy stomach."

"Squishy?" Nick asked.

Amanda touched her fingers to her stomach. "Yes, squishy. The belly feels mushy, tingly—squishy."

"Sounds very scientific."

Amanda giggled softly. "Well, those are the symptoms—as reported by my cousins."

"The whole thing sounds rather embarrassing," Nick insisted. "It's different for men."

"I wouldn't be so sure," Amanda said. "Not after what I saw yesterday. Not only with Ethan, but with Charles Osborne. Your mother and I ran into him, too. He seems quite taken with her."

"I don't know about that man," Nick grumbled.

"What's wrong with him?"

He just shook his head. "Something. Can't put my finger on what, exactly."

"Does it trouble you that your mother may be romantically interested in him?" Amanda asked gently.

"No, of course not," Nick insisted. He paused, then said, "I just don't want her to be hurt, that's all."

Amanda smiled. "That seems a normal reaction."

"My parents' marriage was...well, it suited them, I suppose." Nick gazed off across the water, then turned to Amanda again. "Maybe I should have Osborne checked out."

Amanda's eyes widened. "Do you mean through an investigative service? Nick, you're not serious."

"Dead serious."

He gave her a look so hard, so intense, it caused Amanda to shiver, despite the warm sun.

"You—you know such people?" she asked.

"Certainly."

"I think you're making too much of this," Amanda said. "Mr. Osborne and your mother simply enjoy talking with each other."

Nick mulled over her comments for a moment. "Maybe you're right. I guess Osborne is a decent enough man, since he's a friend of the Malloys."

"The Malloys?" Amanda paused. Hadn't Mr. Ramsey mentioned that Mr. Osborne was staying with the Wades?

She shook her head, dismissing her concern. Mr. Ramsey was elderly and probably confused. Anyway, it was likely that Mr. Osborne knew the Malloys and the Wades both.

"If it will make you feel better," she said, "should I see your mother and Mr. Osborne together again, I'll keep watch for any further signs of love."

Nick grinned. ‘‘Oh, yes. What was that stomach ailment again?’’

‘‘Squishy,’’ she said.

‘‘Squishy.’’ He grunted. ‘‘Sounds like a lot of nonsense to me.’’

Amanda didn’t say anything. She didn’t have to. She already knew the ailment existed. Because that’s the way her own stomach felt every time she thought of Nick.

Did he feel even an inkling of the same for her? She couldn’t know—could hardly bring herself to speculate.

But after spending this week with Nick, dare she hope?

Amanda gazed across the little rowboat at him. Yes, she could hope.

Chapter Nine

"Your cheeks are looking a little flushed," Dolly said, taking Amanda's hat from her as she entered her bedchamber. "And I don't think it's from being outside."

"What do you think it's from?" Amanda asked, trying to sound innocent.

She already knew what Dolly's response would be. After nearly three weeks at the Hastings house—three weeks with Nick—Amanda knew she was losing her struggle to remain distant from him.

Dolly looked pointedly at her. "Are you ready to admit your feelings for that man?"

"We're just friends," Amanda insisted.

"Humph." Dolly snorted in disbelief and headed for the closet. "Did you and Miz Constance have a good time at your meeting this afternoon?"

"Yes, very nice," Amanda said, drifting to the window.

Over the last three weeks, Constance had taken Amanda to the many ladies' clubs, social and civic groups she belonged to in the city. She'd introduced

Amanda to her friends. They, along with Winnifred, had attended luncheons and teas with the socially prominent people in the city.

"Constance has certainly gone out of her way to make me feel at home here," Amanda said, pulling back the drape and gazing at the afternoon shadows slanting across the grounds.

"And why do you suppose that is?" Dolly asked pointedly.

"Because she's nice," Amanda told her.

"Yeah…sure."

Amanda pressed her head against the windowpane, angling for a glimpse of the carriage house at the rear corner of the property.

"He's already come home."

Amanda swung back from the window, the familiar jolt warming her stomach. "Nick's home?"

"I saw his carriage go down the lane just before you walked through the door," Dolly said, waving toward the window. She shook her head. "This whole family is liable to end up penniless the way that man's taken to coming home early these last few weeks."

Amanda dashed to the mirror, turning her head left, then right, checking her hair. "Maybe I should change my dress? Wear the pink one?"

Dolly shook her head slowly. "If you don't mind me saying so, Miz Amanda, it ain't the color of your dresses that's bringing that man home from work early."

Amanda gave her a hopeful smile. "You don't think so?"

"I'm dang near positive."

Warmth pooled in Amanda's heart. In the past few

weeks she'd spent most of her time with Nick. They were both growing quite comfortable in each other's company, she knew. Yet seeing him, being close to him, still brought a tingle to her stomach. Just as it always had.

Dolly crossed to the writing desk in the corner of the room and picked up a small envelope. "Before you go downstairs, read this. You got a letter from your uncle this morning."

Amanda took it. "Nick might be interested in hearing how the family is doing." She ripped it open and read it over quickly. The smile disappeared from her face. "Oh, dear..."

"Good afternoon, sir."

Nick looked up from behind his desk in the study as the Hastingses' butler, Vincent, stepped into the room. Gray-haired and slightly shrunken with age, the man had been with the family for as long as Nick could remember.

"Might I bring you something?" Vincent asked in that way he had of looking but never seeming to focus on anything.

"No, I'm fine," Nick said. "Is—"

"She arrived moments ago," Vincent said. "Along with your mother and your aunt."

"Thanks. That's all," Nick murmured, and placed his leather satchel on his desk.

"Yes, sir." Vincent moved silently out of the room.

Nick opened his satchel, a little uncomfortable that his thoughts were so apparent—even to the butler. Of course, his intentions toward Amanda had hardly been secretive these last few weeks. The two of them had become somewhat of an item in the city. He'd taken her out for supper, to the theater, to the park. He'd sat through two music recitals and a dramatic reading. Once he'd even joined Amanda and his mother and aunt at that silly tearoom the ladies liked so much, and had endured a lunch of cold soup and miniscule sandwiches. Oddly enough, he'd enjoyed every moment of it, though he had sent the company errand boy out to fetch him something decent to eat as soon as he returned to his office.

Nick unloaded the ledgers he'd brought from the office and dropped them on the desktop. For the past week he'd taken to coming home early in the afternoon. To work, of course. At first he'd told himself that he could concentrate better here. No street noise, no interruptions.

With a sigh, Nick sank into the leather chair behind his desk. Truth was, here at home he could hardly concentrate at all. Because of Amanda.

The first day he'd come here to work she'd seen him from the hallway and stepped in to greet him. A lovely sight she was, too, her dark hair all done up atop her head, dressed in attire that hugged her curves and swayed when she walked, begging to be taken off one delicious layer at a time.

Nick squirmed in his chair as his desire for her made itself known yet again. Even when he was at his office this pleasurable ache wouldn't leave. Everything reminded him of Amanda, somehow. Everything made him think of her. Everything made him want her. Nick could hardly get any work done—not even on his Whitney project.

To make matters worse, Amanda lived under his own roof. She slept just down the hall from him, only steps away. At night, his body tense and aching, Nick lay in bed thinking of her, hardly getting any sleep at all.

He'd kissed her twice more, since that night he'd gotten her to agree to postpone her return to San Francisco. Nick sank farther into his chair, remembering the feel of her in his arms. Her warm lips. Her breathy little sighs. It had taken all the willpower he could muster to do no more than kiss her. Still, he couldn't stop imagining her bare breasts cradled in his palms, her silky legs—

"Damn it..." Nick pushed himself out of the chair and stalked to the window. If he didn't get himself under control he wouldn't be fit to be seen in the presence of a lady ever again.

For Amanda was a lady. Raised and educated to be just that. Damn lot of trouble dealing with such a woman, Nick thought, gazing out at the rear lawn. Proper care had to be taken when dealing with a lady. No breach of decorum was allowed. No hint of impropriety.

Even though the two of them lived under the same roof, Amanda insisted upon bidding him good-night at the foot of the stairs and going up to her room alone every evening. And every evening Nick stood at the foot of the stairs watching her bustle sway as she climbed the stairs, imagining her sweet little bottom beneath it. Fighting the urge to run up the stairs after her.

Amanda was, indeed, a lady, and he wanted no less

in a woman. Which, to his way of thinking, explained why she always held back.

Nick leaned his shoulder against the window casing, remembering the times he'd kissed Amanda. He sensed passion in her—great passion smoldering just beneath the surface. He wanted her to give in to it—urged her to do so with his kisses—but she wouldn't.

He grunted and turned away from the window. He sure as hell could use some of that self-control.

Yet for all her reluctance, Amanda was just the sort of woman he wanted. He'd made a careful study of his requirements, as any man in his position would do, and Amanda filled them all to the letter.

Pretty, charming, educated, articulate, well dressed, well informed. Amanda was all those things. Yet she was more. She was smart. She asked intelligent questions, made intelligent remarks. Her compassion seemed limitless. Nick couldn't imagine any woman he knew—including his own mother or sister—volunteering time at an orphanage, or feeding indigents. Absolutely no woman he knew would even consider the thought of building a refuge for women and children.

He enjoyed her company. She made him laugh. He looked forward to seeing her at breakfast each morning, and was infinitely pleased that she was the last person he saw at night. She listened to his problems, listened and genuinely understood.

In short, Amanda was compatible with his lifestyle. A matter of no small significance, to Nick's way of thinking. It was imperative that two people be compatible. What good were silly grins and squishy stomachs if a husband and wife couldn't talk to each other? How far would damp palms and racing hearts take a couple when things got difficult?

In short, Amanda was perfect for him.

The only real surprise was that she could stir such strong feelings of passion in him.

Those feelings presented themselves with another surge of urgency. Nick muttered a curse and flopped down in his chair once more. Determinedly, he set his satchel aside and opened one of the ledgers. Surely columns of figures would get his mind off Amanda.

He'd gotten only halfway down the first page when a rustle of skirts and petticoats and a welcome, familiar fragrance intruded upon his thoughts. Amanda.

She stepped into the doorway dressed in a lovely green gown. Nick's chest tightened at the sight of her. The feeling arrowed downward, worsening his already uncomfortable condition. He resisted the urge to get to his feet and go to her as he usually did when she walked into a room.

Amanda stopped short, her cheeks pale, her lips drawn together. "Nick..."

Her greeting, more a plea, drew him out of his chair. His heart lurched and he hurried to her side, overwhelmed with the need to learn whatever was wrong and fix it immediately. The notion swelled in his chest.

"What is it?" he demanded, the words coming out more harshly than he'd intended.

She didn't seem fazed by his tone, just held up the small envelope in her hand. "I received a letter from Uncle Philip. He says I must return home. Immediately."

* * *

''Someone's dream predicted this,'' Winnifred announced. ''Nick, what did you dream last night?''

Nick settled his mother into her chair at the foot of the dining room table, then took his own seat at the opposite end. The servants began serving supper, though no one at the table appeared anxious to eat. Certainly not Nick.

''Aunt Winnie, I don't think my dream last night had anything to do with Amanda receiving that letter from her uncle this afternoon,'' he said.

''Nonsense,'' Winnifred declared. ''What did you dream?''

''Let's see...'' He paused, remembering. ''I dreamed I was in the forest on some sort of wild-game hunt.''

''Hmm...'' Winnifred mumbled thoughtfully. ''Was it day or night?''

''Day.''

''Was there a water source nearby?''

''No.''

''Had you recently eaten pork?''

''No, Aunt Winnie.''

''Hmm...''

''Well, at any rate,'' Constance said, glancing at Amanda, ''we certainly don't want you to leave.''

Amanda smiled weakly at Nick's mother. ''Thank you.''

''Perhaps if I wrote to Philip and Veronica on your behalf?'' she asked, casting a hopeful look at Nick.

''I would certainly appreciate your assistance,'' Amanda said. ''But I don't think it would make any difference. According to Uncle Philip, Aunt Veronica is quite lonely now, with the twins married and gone.

She misses me. Besides, Uncle Philip doesn't want me to wear out my welcome here."

"Nonsense," Constance said. "We're thrilled at having you here. Aren't we, Nick?"

His gaze met Amanda's and he nodded earnestly. "Yes."

"Uncle Philip is concerned that it's unseemly," Amanda said, "my being here alone for this long, without Aunt Veronica to chaperon."

Nick had never felt so helpless in his life. The last thing he wanted was for Amanda to leave. When she'd read her uncle's letter to him in the study earlier, he'd wanted to charge to San Francisco and set the man straight. Yet he had no right to do so. No right to insist Amanda stay.

The thing that made her so desirable—one of the things, anyway—was that she was a proper, dignified woman from a proper, dignified family. The Van Pattons were quite right to insist Amanda return home. She'd been here much too long already. Young, single women didn't just travel where and when they chose. Coming to Cecilia's wedding had been grounds for an exception. But staying longer—especially this long—simply wasn't done.

"Still," Constance said, "there must be something we can do. Perhaps if—"

"Aha!" Winnifred cried.

Startled, they all turned toward her.

"I know what your dream means," she declared.

Nick rubbed his forehead. "What does it mean, Aunt Winnie?"

"Your trek through a forest on a big-game hunt indicates you're unhappy with your footwear."

He looked at his mother and Amanda, then at his aunt once more. "My footwear?"

"Certainly," she declared.

"The hunt through a forest doesn't, perhaps, suggest a search for something? Something that's missing in one's life?" Amanda asked.

"Oh, no, dear. Walking on all that rough terrain. Footwear, of course."

"Thank you, Aunt Winnie," Nick said. "I'll check into buying some new shoes...tomorrow."

Amanda turned to look at him just then, sending a stab of dread through his belly. Tomorrow. Tomorrow, Amanda would be on her way back to San Francisco.

She pulled her gaze from his and rose from her chair. "I really must go see to the packing. I should be ready to leave first thing in the morning."

Nick lurched out of his chair, watching her.

"Thank you for having me in your home," Amanda said to Constance. "I appreciate the kindness you've shown me. I'll miss you all."

"We'll miss you, too, dear," Constance said.

"Write to me about your dreams," Winnifred said.

"I will." Amanda dared one brief glance at Nick, then hurried from the room.

He watched her go, felt something inside himself go with her. Nick tossed his napkin onto the table and went after her. He caught up with her at the top of the stairs.

"Amanda?"

She turned and came toward him without so much as a second thought. He took her hands, pleased that she would come to him so easily.

"Stay," he said.

She managed a small smile. "I wish that I could."

"Then do it. Stay."

"I'm needed there."

"You're needed here."

"I have responsibilities. Uncle Philip was right to remind me of them," Amanda said. "The orphans—"

"We have orphans in Los Angeles."

"And the hungry indigents at the churches?"

"I'll ship them some food. As much as you want."

Amanda smiled, then tears welled in her eyes. "I can't defy my uncle."

And that issue was the one Nick knew he couldn't overcome.

"Good night, Nick," Amanda whispered, and hurried into her bedroom.

"Damn it," he swore, and stomped back downstairs.

Amanda closed her bedchamber door and fell against it. She squeezed her eyes closed, forcing back tears.

"I guess this means we're leaving in the morning."

She opened her eyes to see Dolly across the room, folding down the bedcovers.

"Yes," Amanda said, pushing away from the door. "We're leaving in the morning."

"If you don't want to go—"

"I can't refuse my uncle. You know that."

Dolly nodded sadly. "Yeah, I reckon I do."

"Besides," Amanda said, "I've been given no reason to stay."

"Mr. Nick cares for you," Dolly said. "I see it in

his eyes every time he looks at you. I hear it in his voice when he speaks.''

Amanda sniffed and swiped at the single tear that rolled down her cheek. ''What does it matter if he does? I'm leaving in the morning.''

''You need some time to think on this. I'll get up extra early and do the packing,'' Dolly said quietly, and slipped out the door.

It was early for bed, but Amanda changed into her nightclothes, anyway. She couldn't face going downstairs again, seeing anyone, discussing her situation once more. She didn't want to dissolve into tears, and her emotions were strung so tightly she knew that could easily happen.

Nothing remained but to resign herself to her fate. Her uncle had issued a decree and she had to obey.

Though she didn't have to like it.

Fastening the top button of her nightgown, Amanda stood by the window, gazing outside. Evening shadows darkened the lawn. In the distance, lights twinkled in windows. She plucked the pins from her hair, allowing it to fall down her back.

Was Dolly right? she wondered. Did the maid see something in Nick that showed he cared?

''Just my luck...'' Amanda muttered, turning away from the window. She fetched the chair from the writing desk and placed it in front of the open window. Sitting down, she drew her bare feet up and hugged her knees.

Just her luck that Nick would care for her when she had to leave.

Maybe this was meant to be. Perhaps it was fate. Was she intended to fall in love with someone different? Was there a better, more suitable beau out there somewhere?

Amanda searched the heavens out the window, the tiny stars twinkling in the blackness. No, she couldn't imagine such a thing.

Regardless of the way he'd treated her ten years ago, she'd lost her heart to Nick and never recovered it. She'd loved him since she was fourteen years old. She loved him still.

And she was sure she always would.

An odd peace came over Amanda at the realization. For weeks—years, really—she'd tried to convince herself that what she felt for Nick was a schoolgirl crush. Now, sitting here in the dark, facing her own feelings, she knew that wasn't true. She loved him. And there was nothing she could do but accept those feelings, accept them—and go on with her life, somehow.

Amanda sat in the chair, thinking and stargazing, until her feet began to tingle. She rose and lay on the bed, sinking into the down coverlet and feather pillows, and stared at the ceiling, thinking, wondering, imagining....

Faintly, from somewhere in the house, she heard a clock chime. It was late. She couldn't sleep.

Rising, Amanda put on her robe and slippers and opened the door to her room. Every door down the hallway was closed tight. The house was silent.

While it wasn't proper for a young woman to set foot from the upper floor in her nightclothes, Amanda didn't hesitate to slip along the hallway and down the staircase. What difference could it make now? She was leaving in the morning, anyway.

A lamp had been left burning here and there, offering enough light to guide her. The rear lawn and recollections of Cecilia's wedding reception drew Amanda through the house. How handsome Nick had looked that day. How heady it had felt to be in his arms on the dance floor, and at his side, chatting with friends. She wanted one last look to seal it in her memory.

But as she neared the rear of the house, she heard a sound from along the hallway. Amanda stopped and looked down at herself. Nightgown, robe, slippers, hair loose about her shoulders. Somehow, coming down here had seemed less frightening up in her room.

She was about to turn and dash upstairs again when she heard a cough.

Nick.

Amanda moved down the hallway and around the corner to the doorway of his study. Light spilled out.

Chapter Ten

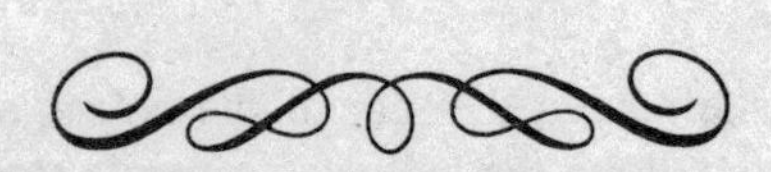

From the doorway, Amanda saw him seated behind his desk. Slumped deep in his chair, Nick had stretched his long legs up to the corner of the desk. Dark suspenders cut vertical lines on his white, open-collared shirt. A ledger lay on his lap and he held a stack of papers in his hand, but he stared across the room, seeing none of it.

Amanda's heart ached anew. She should go. She knew it. She should turn and leave immediately. It was the proper thing to do. But silently Nick called to her. An irresistible force bade her to stay…to go to him.

She stepped inside the doorway. "Nick?"

His gaze came up sharply and swung to her. He squinted into the darkness, then jumped to his feet, sending the ledger and the stack of papers flying.

"Amanda…" he whispered, as the flurry of white pages floated to the floor around him.

"Sorry," she said. "I didn't mean to startle you."

"No, no, it's all right," he assured her, coming around his desk. "Come in. Please, come in."

Amanda glanced down at herself and smoothed her hand along the front of her dressing gown. "I shouldn't be here...like this."

He stopped in the center of the room, as if he feared he might scare her away. "No, it's fine," he said, and his gaze scanned the length of her. Then, determinedly, he focused on her face. "Really, it's fine."

"No—"

"Please don't go."

The sincerity, the depth of his voice stopped Amanda and drew her into the room.

"Couldn't sleep?" he asked.

She shook her head.

"Me, neither," he said.

"You're working?" Amanda gestured toward his desk.

He shook his head. "Thinking, mostly. About you. About how I don't want you to leave in the morning."

"I have to go. You know that," Amanda said.

"No. I don't accept it."

"You have to."

"Well, I don't."

Even in the faint light Amanda saw the intensity in Nick's face. She read his thoughts—because she'd had them herself. Defy her uncle. Stay here, at all costs.

But Amanda couldn't do that.

She stepped around him and dropped to her knees beside his desk, picking up the papers littering the floor. "You're only making this more difficult."

Nick knelt beside her, his arm brushing hers. Through the fabric of her gown and robe, she felt the heat that radiated from him. Determinedly, she scooped up the papers.

His hands covered hers, stilling them. She gazed up at him, unable not to. For a long moment they remained that way, both on their knees, simply looking at one another.

Then Nick kissed her. He caught her shoulders and sealed their mouths together with a searing kiss. Amanda gasped, and tossed the papers into the air once more.

He deepened their kiss and locked her in his arms, pulling her tight against him. Her breasts tingled as they met the wall of his chest. Their thighs brushed. Heat swept Amanda, binding her to him.

Nick kissed her cheek, her jaw, then dropped his head to trail his lips along her throat. Amanda looped her arms around his neck and sank her fingers into his soft hair.

Claiming her lips again, Nick eased her backward onto the carpeted floor. He stretched out beside her and slid his hand upward to capture her breast.

Amanda gasped again. Dizzying thoughts sped through her head, too quickly to name. Instinctively, she leaned into him.

Nick groaned, then spread another trail of kisses down her throat to the top of her nightgown, savoring the taste, the feel of her flesh.

He lifted his head, his breath hot against her face. ''You're staying. I can't let you leave.''

''But, Nick—''

''I want you to stay, Amanda,'' he said, his voice raspy. ''I want you to stay forever.''

"What?" Amanda pulled away from him, out of his embrace, and sat up. "Forever?"

"Forever."

"You're saying you...what?"

Nick took her hand. "I'm asking you to marry me, Amanda."

"Oh, Nick..."

"You care about me, don't you?" he asked, almost as an afterthought.

"Of course I do," Amanda said, her heart full and racing. "I love you, Nick. I've loved you since that night in Tahoe."

He raised his brows. "You have?"

"Yes." Amanda dropped her gaze.

A big, wide smile broke over his face. "Amanda, you are the most amazing woman I've ever known. You're perfect for me—perfect. I can't imagine not having you in my life. I want you with me. Always."

He caught her hand and pulled it to his lips, kissing it softly. "Will you marry me?"

"Oh, yes, Nick." She wrapped both arms around him and threw herself against him.

He caught her and buried his nose into the thick hair brushing her neck, drinking in its scent, its softness. "You'll have the finest wedding this city has ever seen. The most elegant gown, the—"

Amanda pulled away, distancing herself from him. She shook her head. "A big wedding? No..."

Nick scooted closer to her on the floor and captured her hand once again. "Fine, then. No big wedding. Whatever you want."

She smiled. "Just the two of us. That's all I need."

Nick smiled, too. "Then how about tomorrow? There's no reason to wait, is there?"

"Tomorrow?" Amanda could hardly believe what she was hearing. "Tomorrow...tomorrow is—perfect."

He took her into his arms again and eased her onto the floor, cushioning her head with his arm. Gently, he kissed her lips. "You've made me a very happy man."

The clock on the mantel chimed twelve times.

"Midnight," Nick whispered, tracing her cheek with the tip of his finger. "By this time tomorrow we'll be man and wife. You'll like being my wife."

"I will?"

"I guarantee it," he said, and gave her a devilish smile.

Nick covered her lips with a deep kiss, then slid his leg atop hers. His hand captured the mound of her breast. But this time, Amanda caught his wrist, stopping him.

Nick lifted his head and smiled gently at her. "We'll be married in a few hours. We don't have to wait."

"Now?" Amanda's gaze bounced around the room, then to him again, her eyes wide. *"Here?"*

"Well..." He looked at her. A long moment dragged by. Then he gave her a quick smile. "No, not if you don't want to."

Nick got to his feet and pulled her up with him. They walked hand in hand out of the study and up to her room.

"I'd like to buy you a ring," he said in a low voice,

"if that's not too much wedding preparation for your taste."

Amanda shook his head. "No. A ring would be fine."

"We'll go in the morning."

"We should tell your mother."

They stood there together, then Nick leaned down and kissed her quickly on the lips. "Good night."

"Good night," she said, then went into her room.

"You're doing no such thing!"

"Mother, it's what we want," Nick explained. He rounded the breakfast table, Amanda at his side. Never had he thought his mother would become so enraged when he announced their wedding plans.

"No!" Constance declared. "No son of mine—and no daughter of my dearest friend—are getting married in a civil ceremony in some judge's office. I absolutely forbid it."

"It's my fault," Amanda said. "I don't want a big wedding."

"We're perfectly happy with it," Nick said.

"No," Constance said, brushing past the two of them.

"Look, Mother, this isn't your decision—"

"Nick, please," Amanda said, laying a hand on his arm. "What would you suggest, Constance?"

She paused, drawing a breath. "A service here. At home. In the garden. I'll have the minister come over this afternoon."

"Nothing fancy. And no guests," Nick told her. "We don't want a big fuss made."

Constance nodded. "Fine."

Nick looked at Amanda. ''Is that all right with you?''

''Perfect,'' she said. ''And thank you, Constance.''

Nick's mother didn't seem to hear as she headed for the door. ''I've got a dozen things to do.''

Nick offered Amanda his arm. ''May I take you to buy that ring?''

She looped her arm through his. ''I'd like that.''

''I now pronounce you man and wife.'' Reverend Hammond closed his Bible. ''You may kiss your bride.''

A lump rose in Amanda's throat as Nick turned to her. They stood together in the gazebo Constance had decorated with candles and vases of fresh flowers. She, along with Winnifred and the silver-haired reverend, looked on.

Twilight settled over the lawn as Nick laid his hands on Amanda's shoulders and gazed deep into her eyes. The sight of his handsome face intently studying her, the gentle smile on his lips, seared into her. Her heart raced as the love she felt for this man filled it to overflowing.

He smiled sweetly, almost secretively, then kissed her tenderly on her lips. Amanda blinked, afraid she'd cry from sheer happiness.

''Congratulations,'' the minister said, interrupting them.

''Thank you,'' Nick replied, shaking his hand.

Constance stepped forward, sniffing, opening her arms. ''Oh, Nicky...''

He wrapped his mother in a hug and she kissed his

cheek. She turned to Amanda, gathered her in her arms and gave her a motherly kiss, too.

"Thank you for everything. It's lovely," Amanda said, gesturing to the flickering candles and the fragrant flowers.

"And you are a beautiful bride," Constance said, standing back, looking at her.

She'd had no time to buy an appropriate dress, so she'd worn an ivory gown with pale blue trim that her aunt had sent down with her other belongings the first week of her stay in Los Angeles. It made a fine wedding gown.

"You two will have a long and happy life together," Winnifred predicted, giving Nick, then Amanda, a hug. She paused. "But just to be certain, you each must tell me what you dream tonight."

"Mrs. Hastings?" Vincent stood a discreet distance from the gazebo. "Your carriage is ready."

"Yes, of course. Thank you, Vincent," Constance said.

"I must be on my way," Reverend Hammond said. He presented the paperwork for them to sign, making their marriage legal. Nick scrawled his name quickly across the bottom. Amanda took the pen, warm from Nick's hand, and signed her name.

"Good luck to you both," Reverend Hammond said. He nodded and left.

"Winnifred, are you ready?" Constance asked.

"Ready, as always," she replied. "A perfect evening for traveling. I know. Last night I dreamed a giant bird was circling the house—a good sign."

Nick caught Amanda's hand and looped it through

his arm, patting it gently. When his mother and aunt left the gazebo, he planted a quick kiss on her cheek.

They followed the women through the house to the front portico, where the servants were busy loading trunks and bags into the carriage. Constance had arranged an impromptu vacation for herself and Winnifred, leaving the newlyweds alone in the house.

"I've handled everything with the staff," Constance said to Nick, standing beside the carriage. "We're staying at the Hotel Del Coronado. We'll be back in a few weeks. If any—"

"San Diego isn't that far, Mother. If anything comes up, I'll notify you."

"Yes, all right." She looked back and forth between the two of them. "Well, goodbye."

After another round of hugs and kisses, Nick assisted his mother and aunt into the carriage, then slid his arm around Amanda's shoulder and waved as they drove away.

When they were out of sight, he turned her in his arms. "I'll take you on a honeymoon soon," he promised.

"I understand," Amanda said. Their wedding ceremony had been so sudden. She knew Nick couldn't walk out on his business for weeks, with only a day's notice.

"As soon as I can get things settled at the office, we'll go anywhere you like," he said.

They returned to the rear lawn, where Constance had arranged for their wedding supper to be served. A small table laid with a white linen cloth, sparkling china and crystal and a glowing candelabra awaited them in the gazebo.

Amanda managed to eat a little, but hardly tasted the food, while Nick ate as if it were his last meal. He offered a toast to the two of them. By the time dessert was served, Amanda's stomach was in such a knot she couldn't eat another bite. All she could think of was what awaited her tonight. With Nick. In his bed.

Together they walked upstairs. Nick held her elbow firmly. He stopped outside the door to her bedchamber.

Amanda's heart pounded as she managed to raise her gaze to look at him.

"I'll come for you in a while," he said softly. He lifted her hand and kissed it. "Take your time. No rush."

Amanda nodded and slipped into her room.

Except that it wasn't her room. Not the one she'd used since arriving here for Cecilia's wedding.

Constance, in the midst of planning today's ceremony and arranging for her and Winnifred's trip to San Diego, had also moved Amanda's belongings into the master suite. Nick occupied it now, as well, his bedchamber separated from hers by a sitting room.

With the death of Nick's father prior to the completion of the house, the master suite had never been used. During the move this afternoon, Constance had told Amanda that she couldn't bear to occupy the suite without her husband. It would have made his loss seem all the greater.

Now it belonged to Amanda and Nick.

And a beautiful suite it was. Her bedroom was large, airy, filled with gracefully carved furniture and decorated in rich shades of blue. Amanda wondered what Nick's room looked like.

Then she gulped, realizing that she would find out shortly.

Across the room, Dolly paused from arranging clothing in one of the drawers. "If you don't mind me saying so, Miz Amanda, you look like you're scared to death."

"No, of course not," Amanda said, then realized that she'd been wringing her hands. "Well, maybe a little. I understand the...procedure, but..."

"It ain't so bad," Dolly said, waving her hand, "once you get the hang of it."

Amanda's eyes widened. "You've—?"

"Oh!" Dolly's cheeks flushed. "Well, now, Miz Amanda, you know I ain't never been married."

"Then how do you know?"

"Well, now, uh, it's, uh—it's because of my older sister. Yeah, that's what it is," Dolly said. "I heard my mama giving her advice just before she got married."

"Oh." Amanda leaned closer. "Well, what did she say?"

"My mama said that enthusiasm will make up for any number of shortcomings," Dolly said. She frowned. "'Course now, my sister's got seven children already, so I 'spect her enthusiasm's waning some. But she's kept her husband happy. He ain't strayed once."

"Enthusiasm?"

"I don't think you've got nothing to worry about," Dolly said, "what with Mr. Nick being a gentleman and all. Just remember it's all right to speak up."

Amanda gulped. "Speak up?"

"Sure," Dolly said. "Don't feel like you've got to put up with something you don't like. You're supposed to enjoy it as much as your man is. And if he's doing something good, tell him so. They like that—at least, that's what I've been told. You want help with your dress?"

Amanda shook her head. "I think I'd rather be alone."

"Well, all right, then. I won't come in the morning till you send for me. So good night," Dolly said, and left the room.

The quiet closed in around Amanda. Her heart thumped in her chest. Thoughts of Nick filled her mind. But it wasn't her love for him that she was thinking of at the moment.

She drew in a breath and straightened her shoulders. This was her wedding night. Thousands of women had been through this and had gone on to lead happy lives. Everything would be fine. Surely.

In the adjoining bathroom, Amanda bathed and slipped into the pale green nightgown and matching dressing gown Dolly had laid out for her. She sat on the bench in front of the vanity and pulled the pins from her hair. It curled down her back.

Amanda stopped abruptly, studying herself in the mirror. Should she have taken her hair down? Perhaps she should put it up again. Did this make her seem presumptuous? Easy? Experienced?

"Oh, goodness..." Amanda rose from the vanity bench and paced the room. She glanced at the door to the adjoining sitting room. Nick's room lay just beyond. What was taking him so long?

She looked down at herself. Was this the right gown to wear? What if Nick didn't like it? What if he hated the color green? What would he think of her when he saw his bride for the very first time?

A knock sounded, faint and distant. Amanda's breath caught. Who would be knocking? The house was empty, save for her, Nick and the servants.

She ventured to the door to the sitting room and opened it a crack. The knocking sounded again, louder this time. It came from the door that led to the hallway, Amanda realized.

Carefully, she crossed the room and opened it. Vincent stood in the hallway.

"Mrs. Hastings?"

Amanda gave a start, expecting for an instant that Nick's mother would answer the call.

"Yes, Vincent?"

"Begging your pardon, ma'am," he said, ducking his head, looking both embarrassed and apologetic. "But a wedding gift has arrived for you."

"A gift?" Amanda echoed, surprised that anyone outside the family knew the wedding had even taken place.

"Yes, ma'am," Vincent said. "Just arrived. He insisted—*insisted*—that it be delivered this very moment."

"Well, all right. Bring it in," Amanda said. As Vincent struggled inside with a heavy wooden crate of bottles, she stood back from the door, feeling a little odd that the first man to see her on her wedding night was the butler rather than her new husband.

"What is it?" Amanda asked.

"Scotch," Vincent said, placing the heavy load on the table. "A whole case of it."

"Who sent it?"

"Here's the note that arrived with it, ma'am."

Amanda took the folded paper from Vincent and opened it. "It's from Ethan Carmichael."

Chapter Eleven

Nick tossed the towel aside and studied himself in the mirror above the sink. He'd bathed and shaved extra close in the bathroom that adjoined his new bedchamber. Excitement hummed in his veins.

Next door, his new wife awaited him. The few times he'd kissed her, he'd sensed her passion. But also her reluctance. Understandable, given her inexperience, her innocence.

He'd have to go slowly with her, Nick reminded himself. It would be to his advantage in the long run. He wanted the night to be pleasurable for her. He'd do anything to make her happy.

Including wear the silk pajamas someone had given him last Christmas—which he'd never worn.

Nick eyed the soft, gray garments hanging near the door. He never wore pajamas. But he'd wear them for Amanda.

He pulled them on and glanced in the mirror again. Not wanting to seem anxious, he'd dragged out his preparations as long as he could. He didn't want to appear in Amanda's room too soon, before she was ready.

Still, he didn't want to leave her standing around waiting. Either way, he knew he was in for a long evening. Calming her fears, getting her to relax, gently coaxing her into his room...into his bed.

Another surge of wanting pulsed through him. That's where he wanted her tonight. In his bed. Not hers.

Nick drew in a breath, tamping down his desire. Rushing her would not do either of them any good.

He left the bathroom with the image of Amanda in his mind. When he eased into her room, what would she be wearing? Would she smile shyly? He prepared himself for the very real possibility that she'd seem frightened. She might even—

Nick stopped abruptly halfway across his bedchamber. Amanda was already waiting. The door to the sitting room was open and she stood just inside his room.

His heart thundered in his chest. What a vision she was! Covered from ankle to throat to wrist in a lacy, pale green dressing gown. Her dark hair curling about her shoulders. A pink blush on her cheeks.

Had he misjudged her? Here Amanda stood, in his room, waiting for him—*him.*

He walked forward slowly, struggling to keep his grin from blooming into a smile. "Amanda, I—"

"You received a wedding gift."

Nick stopped, the ice in her voice freezing his footsteps on the thick carpet.

She pulled her arm from behind her, revealing a large bottle. "Scotch."

Nick's stomach lurched.

Amanda raised her other arm, displaying a letter clutched in her hand. "From Ethan Carmichael."

"Oh, my God..." Nick felt the color drain from his face and his stomach twist into a knot. The bet. That infernal bet. "Amanda—"

"Let me read his note," she said, her voice hard and cold. "'Nick, you win. Enjoy both your prizes—your wife and the Scotch. I should have known better than to wager against you, especially where finding a wife is concerned. Congratulations, Ethan.'"

A wave of nausea roiled through Nick. "Amanda, I can explain—"

She pulled in a quick breath and her eyes widened. "It's *true?*"

"Listen to me, Amanda. It was just a silly bet," Nick insisted. "I'd forgotten all about it."

Horror tightened the lines of her face as reality sank in. "You made a bet with Ethan about finding a wife? About marrying me?"

"Let me explain," Nick said. He wanted to rush to her, take her in his arms and make her listen. But the look on her face, her rigid stance, held him in place.

"Is it true or not?" she demanded.

"Yes, but—"

"Oh, my God..." Amanda gasped. For a long moment, she just stared at him. Then a single tear slipped down her cheek. "You don't love me."

"Amanda, listen—"

"You don't love me at all!" A wave of tears washed down her face. "I'm just some prize in a wager!"

Nick's stomach twisted in a tighter knot. "If you'll just let me explain—"

"Do you love me?" she demanded, tears flowing unchecked. "Do you, Nick? Do you?"

"Amanda, please, listen. You mean the world to me. I care deeply for you. I want you—"

"Do you *love* me?" she demanded.

"You're the perfect wife for me," Nick told her. "What more could you want?"

She gasped. Her tears stopped. Color drained from her face. "You really don't…" she whispered.

"Damn it, Amanda, listen to me!" Nick stepped toward her.

"Get away from me! You never loved me! I never meant anything to you!" Tears gushed from her eyes again and she backed toward the sitting room.

"For chrissake, Amanda, I told you—"

"Leave me alone!"

"Amanda—"

She drew back the bottle of Scotch and hurled it at him. Nick jumped aside as it whizzed past his head. The bottle struck the mirror. Both exploded. Shards of glass and waves of amber liquid cascaded onto the carpet.

"I hate you!" Amanda screamed. She bolted across the sitting room into her bedchamber and slammed the door.

Nick went after her, but stopped at her door. "Damn it!" He drove his fist into the wall.

Nick cursed as a beam of morning sunlight streamed through the window of the sitting room and struck his face, waking him. He pushed himself upright and groaned. Every muscle ached from sleeping on the tiny settee all night.

He stood and stretched and pulled on the back of his neck, then looked at the door to Amanda's bedchamber. Still closed tight.

He'd slept on the settee in the sitting room all night, hoping she'd come out and talk to him, give him a chance to explain. Instead, he'd sat there alone, listening to her muffled sobs until late into the night.

All was quiet in her room now. For a moment, Nick considered going in, making her listen to him. He glanced down at himself. Showing up in her room at dawn, dressed in these idiotic pajamas, would do his cause no good. God only knew what she'd think of him then.

Careful to skirt the bits of broken glass in his bedchamber, he went into his bathroom, where he stripped off his pajamas, washed and dressed in a dark, pinstriped suit.

His wedding night had hardly turned out as he'd imagined—which he intended to make Ethan Carmichael pay dearly for in the very near future—but it wasn't anything that couldn't be fixed. Nick was sure of it. All he had to do was explain things to Amanda. She'd been too upset to listen last night, and really, he couldn't blame her. But Amanda was an intelligent, reasonable woman. That was one of the things that had attracted him to her. She would understand, once he explained it properly.

As soon as he got her out of her room, that is.

Nick gave his necktie a final tug. No sense in letting this thing go any further. It would only get worse. He needed to fix this situation with Amanda immediately. And he intended to start right now, even if he had to walk into her room unannounced.

Which might not be such a bad idea, he decided.

But when he reached the sitting room, he stopped, stunned to see Amanda. Nick's heart squeezed nearly to a stop.

There she stood, his new wife, dressed in a dark-blue gown, hair properly done up, waiting. But there was no hint of a smile on her lips. Instead, her cheeks were pale, her eyes swollen from the tears she'd shed.

Nick wanted to take her in his arms, apologize, explain, make her feel better—make things right between them. But when she lifted her gaze to him, he didn't dare go any closer.

"Good morning," she said, her voice soft and frail, as if it hurt her to speak.

"Amanda, please, let me explain. I never meant to hurt you. I never meant for any of this to happen."

"It's my fault, really." With some effort, she straightened her shoulders and drew herself up. "Before I agreed to marry you I should have made sure you loved me. I'll remember that...next time."

His heart lurched. "Next time?"

"Yes. I'm leaving today."

"Leaving—?"

"My uncle's lawyers will arrange for a divorce...or annulment...whatever is appropriate."

"No," Nick said, panic taking root in him. "I don't want you to go."

"You don't love me."

She said it quite simply, with no emotion or hurt in her voice. Just a statement of fact, one she accepted and knew was true. It made Nick's blood run cold.

"Amanda—"

"Goodbye, Nick." She lifted her gaze to meet his for only a fraction of a second, then turned toward her own bedchamber again.

"I don't want you to go," Nick said to her back. "You have to stay here so we can work this out."

She kept walking.

Nick gulped. He couldn't let her go. Not now. Not like this.

"Won't you at least give me a chance?" he asked. "A chance to make it up to you?"

Amanda didn't answer, didn't pause, didn't stop.

"A divorce will cause a scandal," he called. "Your uncle and aunt won't be happy."

She glanced back. "They'll understand."

"What about my mother? Can't you see what this will do to her?"

"She'll get over it," Amanda said, and turned away again.

"There'll be gossip from here to San Francisco and back. Is that what you want?"

She didn't respond.

Nick went after her, desperation clawing at him. "Don't go, Amanda. We can work this out. I'll do anything...."

She reached the door to her room and opened it.

"I'll build you your women's refuge."

Amanda stopped.

Thrilled with this small victory, Nick felt his spirits soar. "I'll build it for you here in Los Angeles. I'll start on it today. If you'll stay."

Slowly, she turned. But her expression held no warmth, no gratitude. She looked at him with new-found contempt. "You'd use my dream, the thing that I told you meant so much to me, to get me to stay? To get your own way?"

Nick cringed inwardly. He knew it made him look bad, but really, how much worse could he appear in her eyes? He didn't care. As long as she agreed to stay.

Nick simply nodded. "Yes."

She straightened, drawing on some inner strength she hadn't displayed yet this morning. Anger caused her breath to come a little faster. Nick was heartened that he'd gotten this much response from her.

"I'll think about it," she said, then turned sharply, went into her room and slammed the door in his face.

God knows what the servants are thinking, Nick mused, as he sat behind his desk in his study. Vincent had been in three times in the last hour asking if he needed anything. Surely the old butler and the entire staff wondered why Nick was working the day after his wedding, while his young bride was holed up in her room.

But at least she was in her room and not on her way back to San Francisco. Nick turned the page of the ledger he was trying to study, satisfied that he'd gotten her to stay.

The women's refuge she wanted was a small price to pay to keep her here. Even if she thought little of him for tempting her with it.

But once he explained everything, smoothed it all over, she'd understand, and their marriage would be on track again. After all, they were perfect for each other. Hell, by this evening he'd have her rolling around in bed with him, sealing their marriage.

Nick glanced at the clock on the mantel. Nearly noon. He'd sat here for hours trying to work, giving Amanda the time she needed to think things over. But he didn't intend to wait too long. No sense in her letting her think too much. Where Amanda was concerned, it wouldn't do his cause any good.

Nick left the study and sprinted up the stairs to the sitting room that adjoined their bedchambers. He eyed the door to Amanda's room. Beyond it, he heard soft voices and the rustle of skirts. Nick drew in a fortifying breath and knocked.

Amanda opened the door, her familiar scent washing over him. God, she was pretty. But more than that, her cheeks were pink again. She didn't look washed out, trodden down, overwhelmed and beaten by what had happened. Nick's stomach twisted into a knot. Was that a good sign?

She stepped into the sitting room and faced him squarely, giving him a very businesslike look.

"I've decided to accept your offer," she said.

Relief swamped him. A big smile bloomed on his face. He wanted to hold her, kiss her, bind her to him. More than anything, he wanted to make everything all right for her.

But she held up her palm, stopping him. "On one condition."

Nick's enthusiasm cooled. "Such as?" he asked, almost afraid to hear her answer.

"I will allow you to buy the land and build the refuge," Amanda said, "but then you will deed it to me, personally. I won't have you threatening to sell my refuge out from under me as a way to control my behavior.''

''You think I'd do that?'' he demanded. Irritation knotted in his chest.

''Yes,'' she said simply. ''I do.''

He didn't like this. Not at all. Yet her demand wasn't so outrageous that he could disagree with it. Besides, all that really mattered was that she was staying.

''All right, fine.'' Nick drew in a breath. ''So, you'll stay?''

Amanda glanced down, then up at him again. ''There's one more condition.''

Nick steeled himself.

''I'll remain here as you wish,'' Amanda said. ''But we will not live as man and wife. There will be no intimacy between us.''

Nick's jaw dropped. ''You mean we can't—you don't want us to...''

Everything in him rebelled. No, he wouldn't agree to that condition. How could they ever have a marriage—a real marriage—that way?

''You're not serious,'' he said.

Amanda raised an eyebrow and gave him a look so cold it caused him to shiver.

''Wanna *bet?*'' she asked, flinging the words at him like an openhanded slap.

Nick backed off a step. She meant it. With every bone in her body, she meant it.

His own determination hardened inside him. No, he wouldn't agree to this. Never in a million years.

''Amanda,'' he said, careful to keep his voice low, ''I care deeply about you.''

"No, you don't."

"Yes, I do."

"I don't believe you."

Nick pressed his lips together, struggling to control his rising temper. He couldn't agree to her condition. He couldn't *think* the words, let alone speak them.

But what was the alternative? She'd leave. Plain and simple. And Nick would not allow that to happen.

He blew out a big breath. "Fine. I agree to your conditions. All of them."

He expected she'd looked pleased, thrilled even, that she'd gotten her way. But she didn't.

Deliberately, she walked to the case of Scotch still sitting on the table where Vincent had left it last night. She picked up one of the bottles.

"I'm keeping this in my room with me," Amanda said. "So I don't...forget."

Nick moved in front of her, blocking her path. He eased closer and leaned down. "You keep that bottle. But mark my words, Amanda, you'll use it to toast the day you welcome me into your bed."

She gazed up at him for a long moment, then cut around him, went into her room and slammed the door.

Nick stood there, replaying in his mind the vision of her swaying bustle as she disappeared into her room. Determination hardened in his belly. He'd have her. Somehow. He wasn't about to let the perfect woman get away from him.

But where to start?

Nick mulled over the situation. Amanda didn't want to be his wife. Well, he'd just show her how wonderful it could be.

Chapter Twelve

Nick shoved his hands in his trouser pockets and stared at the dining table set for one.

"Where is Amanda?" he asked the servant bustling about the room, serving supper.

She paused and gave him a look that Nick judged to be on the edge of contemptuous. "Your missus is having supper in her room," she said, and disappeared out the door.

Nick grumbled under his breath. So, the servants knew what had happened between him and Amanda last night. Wonderful.

He dropped into his chair at the head of the table and tried to eat. The food was tasteless, and the ticking of the clock—the only sound in the room—pounded in his head.

Fine thing. Married less than twenty-four hours and here he sat, eating alone. Never mind the fact that he should be upstairs, rolling around in bed with his wife.

Annoyed, Nick pushed his plate away. Enough of this nonsense. He'd left Amanda to herself all day, ever since she'd delivered her conditions for remaining married to him this morning. He'd thought giving her time would help.

Nick looked down the long, empty table. Obviously, he was wrong. He needed to put an end to this at once.

He found Vincent, asked him to send Amanda downstairs immediately, and went to his study.

Dolly closed the bedchamber door and turned to Amanda. ''It's that Vincent fella. He says Mr. Nick wants you to come downstairs. Right now.''

Amanda heart seemed to skip a beat at the mention of Nick's name. After all that had happened, he still had that effect on her. Much to her dismay.

She laid down her pen and pushed her chair back from the writing desk. All day she'd been trying to compose a letter to her aunt and uncle, giving them the news of her marriage to Nick. The evidence of her repeated failures lay in crumbled balls in the trash container.

Amanda got to her feet and walked to the window overlooking the rear lawn. Only yesterday she'd stood in the gazebo at Nick's side, pledging her life, her love to him.

And all along, he hadn't loved her. She'd been but the prize in a wager with his friend.

Last night, when she'd first read the note that accompanied the Scotch, she couldn't believe it was true. She'd thought it was some sort of joke. After all, Ethan had said those awful things about Nick at Cecilia's reception. Nick had told her not to believe anything his friend said.

But when she'd confronted Nick with the note and the Scotch, he'd admitted it was true.

Emotion rose in Amanda's throat, but no tears formed. She'd cried herself out already.

Yet she couldn't help but think once again how close she'd come to having everything she wanted. As a child, she'd dreamed of living in a home where she was truly wanted, where she belonged. A place that was hers. A place where she wasn't the distant relative taken in out of kindness.

She thought she'd found that here with Nick.

Nick. Amanda's heart ached anew as she thought of him. She forced him from her mind and concentrated on the very real, practical reasons she'd decided to stay.

While her first inclination had been to return home and never see Nick, the Hastings house or Los Angeles again, Amanda hadn't lost sight of the other issues involved in her decision. It wasn't only *her* life that would be affected.

Finally, she'd decided that there was no sense in letting the less fortunate women of Los Angeles do without the very real need for the refuge she could provide—with Nick's help—just because of her own stubborn pride. Whether she helped women and children in Los Angeles or San Francisco didn't matter.

Of course, there were other advantages to staying. Benefits Amanda couldn't ignore.

If she stayed here she wouldn't have to face her aunt and uncle, answer their many questions. Or the questions of their friends. Gossip would ring through the city for months—years. Amanda didn't want to bring that shame to her family. She didn't want people looking at her, whispering behind her back, discreetly pointing when she entered a room.

And Nick? Did he figure into her decision? Amanda

drew in a breath, willing her head to overrule her heart. She was so emotionally bruised and battered from last night, she didn't know what she felt for him anymore.

"What do you want me to tell him, Miss Amanda?" Dolly asked from across the room.

Amanda turned away from the window. She'd told Dolly what had happened last night. There was no need to keep it a secret—no way to, either. With one look, Dolly had known something was wrong. She'd been supportive and understanding, for which Amanda was grateful.

"Tell him I'll be down shortly," Amanda said.

Dolly opened the door and relayed the message to the butler waiting in the hallway, while Amanda moved to the vanity and checked her appearance. She stopped, wondering why she cared what she looked like in front of Nick. If she was disheveled and baggy-eyed from crying, he deserved to see it. He'd caused it.

Still, before she left, she tucked a loose tendril of hair into place, earning a reassuring nod from Dolly.

Nick sat behind his desk when Amanda walked into the study. Without her wanting it to, her stomach jolted at the sight of him. Frowning slightly, he was studying something amid the clutter of his desk.

He must have sensed her entrance because his head came up as soon as she crossed the threshold, and he lurched to his feet.

"Amanda," he said, coming to her quickly.

He reached for her elbow, but she pulled away, not trusting herself at his touch. Her action displeased him, evidenced by the furrow of his brow, but he didn't pursue it, just gestured to the chair in front of his desk.

Amanda lowered herself into it, straightening her skirt, and he sat in the chair beside her. For a long moment he looked at her, saying nothing. She felt his gaze, warm on the side of her face. She struggled to keep from turning to him.

When she could stand it no longer, Amanda said, "I understand you want to speak with me."

"Yes," Nick said, scooting forward to the edge of the chair. "Amanda, you have to let me explain about that...wager. If you'll just listen I'm sure you'll realize it was all a misunderstanding."

Sincerity warmed his voice as he leaned toward her. Amanda couldn't refuse him.

"All right. Explain, if it will make you feel better."

Nick drew in a breath. "First of all, when Ethan and I made that bet we'd been drinking, and—"

"Scotch?" Her gaze impaled him.

Nick shifted uncomfortably in the chair. "Yes. Scotch. Anyway, we were bemoaning the fact that Aaron had been forced to court Cecilia for over a year, so we thought—"

"That you could do it quickly? Get it over with?"

Nick paused. "Well, yes, but—but we both wanted a wife. I swear, we did."

"One you didn't have to go to the trouble and expense of courting?"

"Yes, but..." Nick rubbed his forehead. "Look, Amanda, I didn't take the bet seriously."

"You didn't run to Ethan after I agreed to marry you? Tell him your good news?"

"No. Of course not."

"Then how did he know we'd gotten married?" she asked.

"Damned if I know," Nick said. "But it was hardly a secret. Lots of people knew. My mother, Aunt Winnie, the reverend, the servants, everyone at my office. Ethan could have found out any number of ways."

Amanda looked away. It pleased her that at least Nick hadn't rushed to Ethan, proclaiming his victory.

"Listen, Amanda," Nick continued, "I'd forgotten all about that bet. I swear I had. Besides, I never really thought I'd find a wife in so short a time. A woman who was perfect for me, as you are."

"That's easy enough for you to say now."

"But it's true. You are perfect for me," Nick insisted. He hopped to his feet. "Wait. I'll show you. I made a list."

Amanda frowned. "You made a list?"

"Yes." Nick lifted his satchel onto his desk and dug through it, tossing papers aside.

Amanda rose from her chair. *"You made a list?"*

"Of course," he said, still digging. He pulled a single sheet of paper from the satchel and presented it triumphantly. "See?"

He held it out, but Amanda refused to take it.

"I compiled it weeks ago, when Ethan and I made the bet," Nick said, coming around the desk again. "I got to thinking about what I wanted in a wife, so I made a list. Look."

He held up the paper in front of her, pointing. "See? Look at the date. Nearly three weeks ago. And—"

"You had it typed?" she asked, frowning and looking back and forth between Nick and the paper.

"Of course. Much neater that way. My secretary typed it." Nick shoved the paper closer. "See the title?"

Amanda leaned forward slightly. "'Evidence of Compatibility.'"

"And you'll see here that I listed all the things that are important to me in a wife. Go ahead. Read them."

Amanda took the paper. "Item number one—enjoys frequent sexual encounters."

"What?" Nick snatched the paper from her hand and looked at it. Then he cleared his throat. "Oh, well, ah, the items aren't in order of importance."

"I'm sure."

"But look here. See the rest?" He held the paper close to her again and ran his finger down the column. "Ten other items, all checked off. That's because of you, Amanda. You met all my qualifications for a compatible wife. So that should convince you that you're the perfect wife for me. You're everything I want. We belong together."

"That's your reasoning?" Amanda asked.

"It makes sense," Nick said. "We're compatible in every way—well, except for item number one. But that's only because we haven't had the opportunity yet to—"

"Enjoy frequent sexual encounters?"

He gave her a little smile. "If you'd like to go for one hundred percent perfection, we could slip upstairs and—"

"That won't happen."

He shrugged. "Just checking. So, anyway, surely this list and my explanation proves how special you are to me. You can see that, can't you?"

Amanda drew in a breath. "Last night I thought I was merely a prize in a wager."

"Yes," Nick said hopefully.

"And now, thanks to your list, you're telling me that I'm also a compilation of statistics?"

"What? No—"

"There's no heart in your list." Amanda pulled the paper from his hand and shook it. "Where is the item that says 'undying love'? Where is it, Nick? Show it to me."

"You're not listening," he insisted.

Amanda gave a disgusted grunt, threw the list at him and stomped out of the room.

Nick stood at his desk, once again watching her walk away from him. At least this time she hadn't slammed a door in his face.

He looked down at the list, which had fluttered to the floor. He picked it up, crumbled it into a ball and tossed it in the trash can.

"Damn it..."

The whole thing made perfect sense to him. He couldn't understand why Amanda didn't realize that. Somehow, she'd twisted his theory and made it into something completely different.

Nick flopped into his desk chair, propped his fingers together in front of his chest and sank into thought.

All right, this idea had been a complete failure. But he hadn't built a financial empire by being discouraged by an initial setback. Time to move on. Time to think of another way to convince Amanda she was perfect for him.

Moments passed while Nick sat at his desk thinking. Where had he gone wrong? Where had he made his first mistake?

Making that bet with Ethan came to mind immediately. Of course, Nick was to blame for it, too. He realized that, and now it would be a cold day in hell before he overindulged in liquor again. Just his luck to have a whole case of it sitting upstairs. Thanks to Ethan.

Ethan. Nick's mood brightened a little at the prospect of beating the tar out of him the next time he saw him.

A few more minutes passed before an idea occurred to Nick. He sat up straighter in his chair. Of course. Why hadn't he thought of it before?

He hadn't courted Amanda. That's what was wrong. Except for the first few weeks she'd been here, he hadn't done that. And that hadn't been his best, all-out effort.

But it wasn't too late. Nick rose from his chair, rubbing his palms together briskly. He'd simply court his wife, sweep her off her feet, charm her, shower her with gifts and attention. That was a surefire way to make her happy. And get her into bed.

What could be simpler?

Nick dropped into his chair, took out a sheet of paper and started a list.

The first item on Nick's list was put into action the very next evening. He arrived home—after spending the day at his office with everyone casting furtive glances at him, wondering why he was there instead of at home in bed with his wife—with a special case tucked inside his satchel. He sent Vincent to fetch Amanda.

When she entered the sitting room off the rose garden, Nick's heart beat a little faster. It was the first time he'd seen her since yesterday in his study.

"Yes?" Amanda asked, standing reluctantly at the doorway.

"Sit down," he said, smiling. When he reached for her arm she pulled away, but he didn't let it trouble him. After all, once she saw what he'd brought her, things would turn around quickly.

Amanda lowered herself onto the settee, and Nick sat beside her. He pushed aside the floral arrangement on the marble coffee table in front of them.

"I bought you something," he said, so pleased with himself that he could barely contain his grin.

Amanda frowned and drew back from him slightly. "What?"

With a flourish, he opened the case, displaying an array of sapphire-and-diamond jewelry—ring, necklace, bracelet, earrings. He placed them on the table before Amanda.

"I chose sapphires because they're blue," Nick said. "Like your eyes."

She looked at the jewels, at him, then at the jewelry again. "You bought this for me?"

"Yes," he said, smiling. "All for you."

Amanda spared him one final look, then rose from the settee. "I have no need for jewelry." She left the room.

A lesser man might have been deterred by yesterday's jewelry failure, Nick thought, as he arrived home. But not him. He passed his hat to Vincent in the vestibule, confirmed that his wife was home and asked the butler to send Amanda downstairs.

Not wanting to return to the scene of yesterday's fiasco, Nick entered the music room. When Amanda appeared, he seated her on the settee beside the piano and grandly presented her with several sheets of paper.

"For you," he announced.

Amanda eyed the papers, but didn't reach for them.

Quickly, Nick sat down beside her. She moved away slightly.

"These are letters of credit from all of the finest shops in the city," Nick said, spreading them out on the table in front of them. "I've made arrangements with the owners. All you have to do is present them, and you can have anything you want. As much as you want. It's yours."

Amanda eyed the letters, then huffed and rose. "I don't want anything," she said, and left the room.

Returning home the following evening, Nick once more sent for Amanda. He awaited her in the dining room. Yes, both his previous attempts to woo her with gifts had failed miserably. But today was different. Today he would succeed. He could feel it in his bones.

When she arrived, Nick seated her at the table, then unfurled a map and spread it before her, anchoring the ends to the table with the silver candlesticks.

He gestured grandly and smiled. "I give you the world."

She looked up at him. "I don't understand."

"The world," he said. "Anywhere you want to go. Just name it."

"Really?" she asked, her face brightening slightly.

Nick's spirits soared. This was the most favorable

reaction he'd gotten from her in days. She'd stayed in her room whenever he was home, refusing to come down to have supper with him. He'd failed with the jewelry and the credit accounts. Now, finally, he was onto something, just as he knew he'd be.

"What would you like to see? Europe? The Orient? New York City?" Nick asked, easing into the chair beside her. "Where would you like to go?"

"My goodness...it's so hard to choose. Why, I'm not sure—wait." Amanda stopped, the wonderment fading from her face. She looked at him, her lips turning down distastefully. "I suppose *you* intend to go along?"

"Well—yes," he said.

"No, thank you." Amanda left the dining room.

"But..." Nick watched her skirt swish out the door, then grumbled under his breath. "Damn it..."

He was just about out of ideas—and patience. He'd tried to do as much for Amanda as a man could possibly do. What more could be expected of him?

She was simply being hardheaded, he decided. Vengeful, spiteful and difficult.

He rose from his chair. Well, he'd had just about enough of it. Amanda was his wife; this was his home. He wanted things done a certain way, as any reasonable man would.

He tugged on his vest. It was time a few changes were made around here. Starting with Amanda.

Chapter Thirteen

Amanda wondered what Nick might tempt her with this time, as she entered the study, summoned by him for the second time today. A new house? A yacht?

She wished with all her heart that he would simply leave her alone. Seeing him, speaking with him, proved more and more difficult. Bit by bit he was chipping away at the emotional barrier she'd put up against him.

Night had fallen, and the great windows in the study were black and featureless. Warm light glowed from the wall sconces and the desk lamp, casting Nick in their pale glow as he sat behind his desk.

The look on his face told Amanda that no gifts would be offered tonight. He was staring at a slip of paper—a telegram, she realized—and seething with anger.

Amanda hurried inside, worried that he'd received bad news. "What's wrong?" she asked, crossing the room to him.

He looked up and got to his feet, struggling to repress his anger.

"What is it?" Amanda asked, gesturing toward the telegram. "Bad news from your mother? Is she all right?"

Nick glanced down at the telegram. "It's nothing," he said, then crushed it in his fist and tossed it aside.

Annoyance rippled through Amanda that he wouldn't tell her the news he'd just received, the reason he was upset. A few days ago—before they were married—she'd come to his study every day and he'd told her all that was happening with him, with his business. He hadn't even spoken of his Whitney project in days.

She waved her hand toward the telegram on his desk. "What's your bad news?"

Nick glanced at the crumpled paper, then grumbled and pulled on the tight muscles of his neck. "It's from my men in Oregon. Danton Moore has been located."

"Has he refused to sell you the tract of land you need for your factory?"

"He's dead," Nick said. "And just why the hell it's taken weeks to locate a dead man, I don't know."

"Will this delay your project?" Amanda asked.

He paced back and forth behind his desk, reminding her of a caged animal. "I'm ready to break ground on the factory, but can't now, of course. Not until I find Moore's heir."

"Your men are searching for him?" Amanda asked.

"Yes. He'll be found in short order."

Nick sounded confident, but Amanda saw the tension in the lines of his face, the stiffness of his shoulders. And suddenly, she wanted desperately to do something to help. Travel north herself. Search for the elusive heir. Secure the property for Nick. Take him in her arms, rub her fingertips against his temples, massage his neck until he—

She flushed slightly, stunned by where her thoughts had gone. How could she still want to help him, after what he'd done to her? What he'd put her through these past few days?

Lost in his own thoughts and problems, Nick continued to pace, one hand shoved into his trouser pocket, the other pulling at his neck. Amanda turned to leave.

"I want to talk to you," Nick called.

She turned back.

"Sit down," he said, seeming to make an effort to push aside his anger at the news he'd just received. "Please."

Amanda eased onto one of the chairs that faced Nick's desk, steeling her emotions.

He sank into his chair and drew in a breath, as if mentally shifting gears.

"In view of our rather unconventional marital... circumstances," Nick said, "I think we need to get a few things straight between us."

She leaned back slightly. "What do you mean, exactly?"

"Rules. Guidelines for conduct."

She glanced at his satchel. "Do you have something typed up?"

He glared at her. "No. But since we're not behaving as a normal married couple, I think we should determine how we are going to behave."

"Good, because I have a request," Amanda said.

Nick eyed her sharply. Obviously, he hadn't expected this. "What sort of request?"

"I want a lock put on the door to my room—the one connecting to the sitting room and your bedroom."

"A lock? A *lock?*" Nick sprang to his feet, his cheeks reddening with anger. "For chrissake, Amanda, do you think I'm the kind of man who would burst into your room and force myself on you?"

Amanda surged to her feet, her emotions boiling in turn. "I don't know what kind of man you are, Nick! I thought I knew—but obviously, I don't!"

Nick swept around the desk and leaned toward her. "What the hell kind of answer is that? Is that what you think of me? That I would do such a thing?"

Her own anger bubbling, Amanda stretched up until her nose was even with his. His emotions were ragged, raw, barely contained. The last shreds of self-control threatening to dissolve. An energy pulsed from him, filling her with it.

"I want the lock," Amanda said.

"No."

"But—"

"No!"

They glared at each other, their breathing hot and ragged. Nick leaned closer. For an instant, Amanda thought he'd try to kiss her. For an instant, she hoped that he would.

She pulled back, broke eye contact and turned her head. Good heavens, what was wrong with her? Why would she even think such a thing?

Tension swirled between them. Finally, Nick

backed away and dropped into the chair behind his desk.

Amanda reined in her wild thoughts and sank into her own chair. "What 'rules' are you suggesting?" she asked, surprised that her voice sounded so unsteady.

Nick moved his head left, then right, attempting to ease the tightness in his neck. He drummed his fingers on his desk and blew out a heavy breath, as if trying to compose himself. Finally, he spoke.

"First of all, I think it would benefit all concerned if we kept our...situation...to ourselves. A lot of gossip wouldn't be pleasant for either of us—or our families."

Thank goodness one of them was making sense. Amanda nodded in agreement. "Yes. Of course, you're right."

"Good," Nick said, and looked relieved. "I also think it's important that we conduct ourselves as husband and wife when in public."

She raised her eyebrow and met his gaze across the desk. "What, exactly, do you have in mind?"

Another wave of warmth arced between them. Amanda felt it wash over her as Nick's gaze burned into her. He shifted in his chair, then huffed impatiently. "For one thing," he said, "I'd appreciate it if when I touch you, you wouldn't recoil as if I'm disease ridden. I'd like us to speak pleasantly to one another. To behave as civilized adults."

"Oh." Amanda's cheeks flushed. Why had she thought he meant something more? Why did she allow him to have this effect on her?

She cleared her throat. "I'm agreeable with that."

Nick's gaze turned cold. "Don't embarrass me by going to your uncle for money."

Her gaze came up sharply to meet his. She looked guilty and she knew it—because she'd intended to do just that.

"You're my wife," Nick said. "I'll see to your needs—as many as you'll permit, anyway."

Heat rushed up Amanda's neck and spilled into her cheeks.

"Are we in agreement?" he asked.

"Yes," she said. "Is there anything else you want to discuss?"

"No. That's it."

"Fine." Amanda stood and walked away, but at the doorway, Nick called her name. She looked back.

"One more thing." Nick rose from the chair. "I'd like you to have your meals with me."

Amanda hesitated. "I don't think that would be a good idea."

He raised an eyebrow at her. "Why not? Don't you trust yourself to be alone with me?"

Her spine stiffened. No, she didn't trust herself—nor did she trust him. Yet he'd thrown the words at her in a challenge. For some reason, Amanda couldn't resist it.

"We'll have meals together," she told him. "As long as you remember that's all we'll have between us."

She left the study, Nick's burning gaze etched in her mind, and wondered why her small victory left her feeling so hollow.

The first light of dawn spread across Nick's room as he lay in his bed. He'd been awake for hours. In fact, he'd hardly slept at all. His thoughts kept straying to the room next to his. Amanda. His wife. The woman who was perfect for him. The woman who wouldn't let him touch her…

He flopped over and stared at the ceiling. He tried to focus his mind on business, specifically the Whitney project and Danton Moore's heir. For a few moments Nick considered his decision to go this far with the project without first finalizing the purchase of Moore's land. Had it been a mistake?

No. He didn't think it was. A calculated risk, certainly, but not a mistake. After all, the land had been vacant for years. No one had shown interest in it—certainly not the Moore family. Actually, they probably considered it a liability, if they even knew about it.

Besides, the site was perfect. Nick had looked at many, had considered a few, but all had problems. The Whitney farm and the tract of land owned by Moore were ideal. Nick wouldn't settle for less.

He pushed his fingers through his hair. He hadn't made a mistake in going ahead with the project. In fact, given similar circumstances, he'd do the same thing all over again.

That decision made, Nick found his thoughts flowing back to Amanda. It was almost impossible not to think of her, given the nearly constant desire he felt for her. A wanting made all the more difficult to bear because he couldn't act on it.

"Damn it…" Nick swore in the silent room. She was the most beautiful, desirable, compatible woman he'd ever met, and he couldn't touch her—even though they were married.

He tried to muster up a little anger toward her, thinking it would ease his discomfort. It didn't.

Somehow, he'd have to change things between them. But how?

He'd tried hard to please her. In fact, he'd tried harder to make Amanda happy than any other woman he'd known in his life. He wasn't sure what else he could come up with to convince…

Nick sat straight up in bed, his heart suddenly beating a little faster. He already knew exactly what she wanted. She'd told him what it was, and already he'd promised to give it to her.

Her women's refuge. That's what she wanted. That's what kept her in the city. That's what would bring them close.

Nick sprang from the bed, pacing and stroking his chin. Yes, the women's refuge. They would build it together. It would take months—longer, if he dragged it out—to construct the refuge. Plenty of time for him to wear down her defenses, prove that they were perfect for each other.

Nick smiled to himself in the quiet room. Why had he been wasting his time offering her jewelry, credit accounts and travel? He already had the one thing Amanda wanted.

His smile widened as he eyed the doorway that led to Amanda's bedchamber. At last, a plan that would work.

Chapter Fourteen

Amanda rose from her bed and slipped into the dressing gown Dolly had laid out. Across the room, her maid stood at the open closet door, studying the garments hanging inside.

A feeling of calm passed over Amanda at the sameness of the situation. How nice to be in familiar circumstances—especially in light of the uncertainty she'd been dealing with for so long now.

Nick. The man managed to upset her no matter what he did. Emotions flared, regardless. Last night in his study she'd been angry with him, then, like quicksilver, she'd wanted him to kiss her. What was wrong with her?

And the dream she'd had during the night hadn't helped, either. In it, she'd found herself standing near the edge of a very high, very steep cliff. She'd been deathly afraid, fearful that she'd fall. Then Nick had appeared, calling to her, urging her to come to the edge.

Amanda shuddered, a chill passing through her as she remembered the nightmare. She wished Winnifred were here to interpret it for her. Though the woman's ideas on dreams seemed far-fetched at times, Amanda desperately wanted to know what this dream meant—other than the obvious, that Nick was trying to kill her.

"I hope you're planning to get out of this house today," Dolly said. "It would sure do you a world of good."

"Yes, I probably should," Amanda said, knowing the maid was right. For days now she'd been holed up in her room, brooding, forbidding herself to cry another tear, trying to decide what she could do.

Finally, after dozens of tries, she'd composed a letter to her aunt and uncle, advising them of her marriage. In it, she'd lied shamelessly, stating how happy she was, then had told them that she and Nick were leaving for an extended honeymoon.

The last thing she wanted was Uncle Philip and Aunt Veronica traveling to Los Angeles to visit and celebrate the marriage. It was difficult enough to hide her true feelings in the letter. Amanda couldn't manage it in person.

Another wave of dread washed through her. What would happen when Nick's mother and aunt returned from San Diego? They would see immediately that something was wrong. How could she hide the truth from them?

By focusing on building her refuge, Amanda decided. Her dedication to that cause could mask most anything. She'd force herself be civil to Nick, yet not get close. Somehow, she'd learn to control her feelings around him. The reason she'd decided to stay—the main reason, anyway—was to build her shelter. It had been her dream for so long and now it was coming true.

Amanda drew herself up, mentally mapping out her strategy. She'd have to learn to function in Nick's presence. Forget how she felt about him. Treat him as a friend. He'd said they should behave like civilized adults, and he was right. If she could manage that, she could maintain appearances. Keep the truth of their relationship between the two of them, out of the mouths of gossips, and get her refuge built.

And, just as importantly, she could find some joy in her life again. She was tired of moping around, being upset and having nightmares. She was tired of letting Nick control so much of her life.

"You're right," Amanda said, turning briskly to Dolly. "I'm going out today. Immediately."

Dolly smiled. "Good. What are you going to do?"

"Get started on my women's refuge," Amanda declared with a decisive nod.

"Well then, you'll need something businesslike to wear today." Dolly eyed the dresses in the closet. "How about—"

A knock sounded at the door.

"The dark-blue one," Amanda called, walking to the door and opening it. "With the cream-colored—"

She gasped as Nick towered over her in the doorway. A few seconds passed while she just stared. She'd expected one of the servants—not him.

"Good morning," he said.

Amanda gulped and clutched her dressing gown closed.

"Yes...good morning," she answered, unable to ignore how handsome he looked in his gray suit and maroon necktie—and the way it made her stomach quiver.

"Are you free this morning?" Nick asked.

An unexpected tremor of regret passed through Amanda. Her intention to start work on her refuge had seemed so exciting only moments ago that she couldn't wait to begin. Now, suddenly, it hardly seemed appealing at all.

"Actually," Amanda said, refusing to give in to those feelings, "I have plans."

"I see," Nick said. "Could you change them? I'd like us to get started on your refuge."

Amanda opened her mouth to protest, then realized what he'd said. A little smile spread across her lips. "That's exactly what I'd planned to do this morning."

Nick smiled in response. Briefly, Amanda wondered if she should be concerned that they were thinking alike.

"But don't you have work at your office today?"

He shrugged. "Nothing that can't wait."

"I'll get ready, then," Amanda said.

"Take your time," Nick said. His gaze dipped, resulting in the tiniest hint of a grin. "You're worth waiting for."

He left, and Amanda stood in the doorway, watching him disappear down the stairs. Excitement tickled her stomach. Excitement at beginning work on her refuge, Amanda told herself, stepping into her room again—*not* at spending the morning with Nick.

Nick was waiting in the foyer when Amanda descended the staircase. He glanced up and smiled appreciatively as she joined him, and Amanda was glad she'd dressed in a mauve shirtwaist instead of the dark-blue dress she'd considered earlier. They went outside together and boarded his waiting carriage. Nick took the seat across from her.

"There are several locations in the city that might accommodate your refuge," Nick said, as they got under way. "I've instructed my driver to take us to each so you can see them. After the lot is selected, we'll commission an architect to get started on the plans."

Amanda nodded. "I'll meet with Aurora Chalmers right away. Your mother introduced us last week. She's heavily involved in all sorts of community activities, according to Constance, and absolutely lives for the opportunity to get her name in the newspaper. I'm going to speak with Mrs. Chalmers about hosting the first fund-raiser for the refuge."

Nick frowned. "Why? I told you I'd build it for you."

"The refuge will be an ongoing project. It will never make money. I can't expect you to fund it forever," Amanda said. "If I can get Mrs. Chalmers's support, other women will host events, too."

"Are you hosting something yourself?" Nick asked.

Amanda glanced away. Outside, the city rolled by, bathed in hazy morning sunlight. "No."

"Why not?" he asked.

She shrugged and turned back to him. "It doesn't seem right, planning an event in your mother's home."

"But it's your home, too," Nick said. He sat forward. "Amanda, I want you to feel comfortable here. If there's anything you need or want, all you have to do is ask."

She gave him a quick smile. "I'll keep that in mind."

"Listen, I'm serious about this," Nick said, sitting back. "If your room isn't decorated to your taste, change it any way you'd like. If the menu doesn't suit you, all you need do is advise the cook. Feel free to select a sitting room downstairs and make whatever modifications necessary to please you."

Amanda shook her head. "I don't feel right about doing any of those things."

"Why not? You're my wife."

"Not...completely." She met his gaze for only a few seconds before her cheeks colored and she looked away.

Nick folded his arms across his chest. "Because we're not...enjoying frequent sexual encounters?"

Amanda's cheeks heated. "Yes."

"If your guilt over your decision weighs too heavily on your conscience, we can change that situation. I'm at your disposal. At any given moment. Day or night."

"Is there no end to your generosity?" she asked, and raised her brows.

Nick shifted on the seat, then pointed out the window. "Here's the first lot."

Amanda gazed outside at the vacant, weed-choked piece of land as the driver brought the carriage to a halt. Nearby were several warehouses, most with broken windows.

"Not the best area of town," Nick said. "But

there's a factory just down the block that could employ the women. I believe that was one of your criteria.''

Amanda craned her neck. ''Where?''

''There.'' Nick pointed out the window. ''On the far side of that last warehouse.''

''Oh, yes,'' she said, following his finger. She studied the area for a moment, then turned back to him. ''I'm not sure women will feel comfortable in this neighborhood.''

Nick gazed at her for a moment, then nodded. ''I think we'll find something better. We'll keep looking.'' He rapped on the roof of the carriage and they drove away.

The second and third lots they looked at each offered a few of the things Amanda wanted for her refuge, yet neither was ideal.

''Nice,'' she said, as they pulled away from the third one. ''But it didn't...feel right.''

''There are plenty more to look at,'' Nick said, seemingly unperturbed by her reaction to the lots, or the amount of time it was taking to look at and discuss each of them. He favored her with a secretive smile. ''I think you'll like the next one. If not, we'll keep looking. As long as it takes.''

Amanda nestled back into the seat, feeling the same contentment to keep looking that Nick displayed. How comfortable she'd felt in his presence this morning. A welcome change, after what they'd been through.

The tension Amanda had carried deep inside her since their wedding night eased a bit. The man sitting across from her was the man she'd loved all these years. This was the Nick of old—not the man who'd considered her a prize in a wager, the man who'd married her without loving her. Now, at this moment, being with Nick had never felt so right.

"Here we go," he said, gazing past her out the window.

Anticipation grew in Amanda. "Where?"

"There." Nick slid onto the seat beside Amanda, leaned across her and pointed. "See?"

Craning her neck, Amanda saw the vacant lot. It was situated on a corner, across the street from a church. The lot was considerably bigger than the others they'd looked at. Farther down the block were several stores and shops.

"There's a school nearby," Nick said, as they gazed out the window together and the carriage drew to a stop. He pointed again. "And around the corner are a number of companies where your women can find work. The lot itself is big enough that we could build a playground for the children."

"Oh, Nick..." Amanda's heart thumped a little faster. She turned to him. His face was inches from hers.

He didn't back away. Instead, he leaned a bit closer and stretched out his arm across the seat back, encircling her shoulders.

"What do you think?" he whispered, gazing into her eyes.

"I—I think it's...perfect...." Amanda breathed.

"Perfect..." Nick touched his finger to her cheek and drew it along the line of her jaw, lifting her chin as his gaze locked with hers.

Amanda's breath caught, and she became suspended in the moment with Nick.

"Yes," he said, his voice low and seductive. "Absolutely perfect."

He leaned in and kissed her. Amanda gasped as he took her lips with his. Warm. Smooth. Luxurious... His arm tightened around her shoulders. His palm cupped her cheek. Tilting her head back ever so slightly, he deepened their kiss until her lips parted.

He slipped his tongue inside her mouth. Amanda's senses reeled at the intrusion—the delight. He pressed deeper.

Their kiss lengthened. Groaning, Nick pulled his lips from hers and made his way down her jaw to the hollow of her neck.

Amanda moaned, lost in the feel of his hot mouth on her flesh. How easy it was to be lost...with Nick. Just as she had on that snow-covered mountain ten years ago, Amanda let go, drinking in what he offered. How easy it was to love him. How easy it was to forget what he'd done. To forgive him, as if it had never happened.

He claimed her lips again, then eased her backward onto the seat.

"Amanda..." His breath was hot and moist on her face as he pressed closer.

She tried to speak, but nothing came out, just a gasp as Nick's hard body snuggled against her. His leg eased between hers. Something hard dug into her thigh. His hand cupped her breast.

"Amanda..." He panted against her cheek as he kissed her greedily. "See? See how perfect we are for each other? If you'd just give us a chance..."

A few seconds passed before his words invaded the fog of passion enveloping Amanda. "Wh-what?" she stammered.

He pressed his mouth to her throat. "Please, Amanda. Give us a chance."

The warm haze shattered. Anger took its place.

"But you don't love me," she declared, struggling to sit up.

Nick groped with his lips as she wiggled beneath him. "Amanda...please..."

"*This* isn't love!" She lurched upward with every ounce of strength she possessed. Nick toppled to the floor.

"Ouch—damn it. What the hell?" He gazed wildly at her through his own fog of passion.

In a flurry of skirts, arms and legs, Amanda sat up, glaring at Nick. "You liar! You filthy liar! You lured me out here today just so you could do *this!*"

Nick grimaced and rubbed the elbow he'd banged on the floor. "That's not true."

"You don't care about my refuge! You don't care about anyone but yourself! I can't trust you at all!"

Anger twisted Nick's face. "Damn it, Amanda, that's not true!" He sprang to his feet and cracked his head against the roof of the carriage. "Son of a—"

"Stay away from me!" Amanda grabbed the door handle.

Nick's eyes blazed as he held his head. "Don't you dare leave this carriage until I—"

She bolted out the door.

"Amanda!" Nick bellowed her name as she hurried down the sidewalk. She didn't stop. She didn't look back. Fueled by her anger, Amanda didn't care what Nick—or anybody—said.

Footsteps pounded the sidewalk behind her, then Nick bounded in front of her, blocking her path. Fury flared his nostrils and narrowed his eyes. He pointed a finger at her.

"I forbid you to do this! Get back into the carriage!"

"Never!" Amanda drew herself up.

Nick glared at her for a long minute, then pulled in a breath, harnessing his anger. "Look, Amanda, I'm sorry. I didn't mean for that to happen. Things just—"

She jerked her chin and looked away.

"Listen to me!" Nick demanded. "I'm sorry! I'm sorry for everything! I'm sorry about the wager, and the Scotch, and for hurting you! If you'd just stop being so damn pigheaded, things would work out for us!"

She gasped and pressed her fingers to her lips, staring at him in disbelief.

Nick stared back, realizing a stunned second later exactly what he'd blurted out.

"I didn't mean—"

She spun away. "Leave me alone."

"For chrissake, Amanda—" Nick went after her and caught her arm "—I didn't mean—"

"Stay away from me. I don't want anything from you."

His eyes narrowed. "You sure as hell want that refuge, don't you?"

Amanda gasped. "I knew it. You never really cared about my refuge."

"Amanda—"

She jerked away from him. "I'll build it myself. You're to have nothing to do with it from now on."

"You can't—"

"Yes, I can! I'll find a way."

Her words penetrated his anger. Nick pulled in a calming breath. "Get in the carriage, Amanda. We'll go home and discuss this."

"I'm not going anywhere with you." She spun around and started walking.

"Christ..." Nick hurried after her. "See? You're being pigheaded again. Damn it, Amanda, you don't even know where you're going—much less how to get home."

"I'll figure it out! Just leave me alone!"

"Like hell I will." Nick scooped her up and headed for the carriage. Amanda screamed and kicked her feet.

The driver up top gaped openmouthed at them. Conveyances on the street slowed. Pedestrians stared.

Nick dumped Amanda into the carriage and slammed the door. "Take her home!" he shouted to the driver. "And don't stop for anything!"

The driver whipped around, shook the reins, and the carriage lurched forward.

Standing on the street, Nick watched them disappear around the corner. He grumbled a curse, catching his breath. Gradually, he became aware of passersby staring.

Embarrassment crept up the back of his neck, burning his ears. He straightened his shoulders, tugged down on his jacket sleeves, executed a sharp turn and started walking.

His office wasn't far away. He'd go there. He sure as hell didn't trust himself to go home right now.

He had just about run out of plans. Everything he tried alienated Amanda further. Still, there had to be something he could do—and when it came to him, he intended to pounce on it.

Nick trudged through the streets. Amanda—his wife—had caused him to make a public spectacle of himself. His head ached. His elbow hurt.

He muttered another curse, shoved his hands in his trouser pockets.

And still he wanted her.

Chapter Fifteen

Aurora Chalmers lived around the corner from the Hastings residence on St. James Place. Amanda arrived precisely on time and was escorted to the parlor off the flower garden by the Chalmerses' butler.

She'd visited the Chalmers home once before when accompanying Constance and Winnifred there for tea. Receiving an invitation to return was an unexpected surprise. One Amanda couldn't refuse.

Constance had told her about Aurora Chalmers's dedication to promoting worthwhile events and projects in the city. If anyone could launch the women's refuge successfully, Amanda knew it was this woman.

"Good afternoon," Mrs. Chalmers called in greeting from the settee. She was elegantly dressed and perfectly groomed. "Do join us."

Amanda settled beside Aurora, surprised to see Julia Prescott and her aunt, Marilyn Givens, seated in chairs across the marble-topped table. She'd met them both at Cecilia's wedding reception, then seen Julia at a restaurant with Ethan Carmichael a few weeks ago. It flashed in Amanda's mind to wonder whether

Julia had simply been Ethan's attempt to win the wager with Nick, or if Ethan was truly interested in her.

Primly folding her hands in her lap, Amanda wasn't sure whether she should proceed with her real purpose for coming here today. She'd hoped to have Mrs. Chalmers all to herself, to propose her refuge and gauge her reaction to it. With others present—witnesses—a failure could mean the end of her fund-raising attempts.

The ladies chatted easily as refreshments were served. They sipped tea and ate delicate pastries.

"How are Constance and Winnifred?" Mrs. Chalmers asked, setting her teacup aside.

"Quite well," Amanda said. Really, she didn't know how they were doing, but didn't dare say so. If Nick had received word from them, he hadn't shared it with her. "They're enjoying San Diego very much. Marvelous weather."

"San Diego?" Marilyn Givens, a robust woman with graying hair, set down her teacup. "Seems the place to go. Why, just yesterday I heard that Mr. Osborne was there, too."

"Charles Osborne?" Amanda asked. She remembered him from the wedding reception—the older gentleman with a rigid stance, white hair and bushy mustache, who had taken a liking to Constance.

"Yes, that's him," Mrs. Givens said. She turned to Julia. "We really must get down there soon."

"Yes, Aunt Marilyn, we should," Julia replied, though Amanda thought she didn't seem all that anxious to go.

"So tell us, dear," Mrs. Chalmers said, turning to

Amanda. "How do you like living in our fair city? Are you getting acquainted? Enjoying yourself?"

Mrs. Chalmers stared intently at Amanda, as did the other two women. Now was the moment, she knew. Now was the time to announce her plans. She'd lain awake most of the night preparing what to say. Several times she'd changed her mind, because now, since Nick wouldn't be paying for the land on which the refuge would be built, she needed financial support more than ever.

Of course, Nick hadn't refused to pay for the land. But she couldn't imagine him doing so now, after what had happened two days ago in the carriage. Besides, Amanda didn't want his help. Not when his intentions were so blatantly insincere. When he only used the refuge as an excuse to further his own cause.

A flush of heat warmed Amanda and she pushed it away, busying herself with her cup and saucer and hoping the ladies wouldn't notice. Last night as she'd paced the floor of her room, rehearsing her speech for Aurora Chalmers today, Amanda had considered returning to San Francisco. Perhaps she should force herself to endure all the gossip and just go home.

But she couldn't bring herself to do it. She wanted to build her refuge. Women—though they didn't know it yet—were depending on her to improve their lives and the future of their children.

And besides that, she'd given her word that she would stay. She'd made a deal with Nick.

Nick…

Everything the man had said and done since their wedding night told her that he didn't really, truly love her. Yet she couldn't force herself to leave.

Around dawn, when she'd ventured into the adjoining sitting room, she'd heard him stirring in his bedroom. A little ache had throbbed in her chest as she'd thought of him there, alone. Later, when she heard his footsteps in the hallway, she'd almost opened the door just to see him, talk to him.

But what could she say? What could Nick say that would ease the tension between them? Another lie? Another hurtful remark?

Finally, Amanda had crawled under the coverlet, closed her eyes and forbidden herself to cry.

"Actually," she said now, aware that the women were still staring expectantly at her, "I'm learning my way around the city, beginning to feel at home. So much so, in fact, that I've decided to start a project here that I'd intended to implement in San Francisco."

"Oh?" Mrs. Chalmers's brows rose. "What might that be?"

"I'm going to open a refuge for women who have lost or been abandoned by their husbands."

A long moment dragged by in silence. Amanda watched Mrs. Chalmers, holding her breath. Marilyn Givens watched, too, waiting for the woman's response, surely intending to adjust her own accordingly.

Finally, Mrs. Chalmers sat a little straighter and announced, "An outstanding idea!"

"Why, yes it is," Mrs. Givens declared. "Tell us more."

Amanda managed to hold in her huge sigh of relief, and laid out her plan, detailing the type of building she'd need, the funds she wanted to raise through community involvement, and what she hoped to provide for the women and children who sought help.

"And so," she said, "if you're pleased with this idea, I'd like to offer you, Mrs. Chalmers, the opportunity to host the premier fund-raising event."

"Of course!" Mrs. Chalmers opened a small drawer in the table beside the settee and pulled out a tablet and pencil. "We'll do a series of events."

"A bingo tournament is always fun," Mrs. Givens offered.

"Excellent," Mrs. Chalmers said, writing it down. "An auction works well."

"Musical performances," Julia suggested.

"All culminating in a grand ball—hosted by myself, of course," Mrs. Chalmers said. "And we'll keep the newspaper informed each step of the way. Coverage at every event."

"A ground-breaking ceremony would draw attention," Mrs. Givens ventured.

"Certainly," Mrs. Chalmers declared. "We will invite the mayor and other dignitaries. *Everyone* will be there." She made a final note, then laid her tablet aside and turned to Amanda. "You'll handle the details of actually constructing the refuge, of course."

"Of course," Amanda said.

Mrs. Chalmers leveled her gaze at Amanda. "And you're up to the task?"

A tremor of self-doubt waffled through Amanda at Mrs. Chalmers's harsh look. But she refused to let those troubled feelings show in her expression.

"Certainly, Mrs. Chalmers."

A moment dragged by while the woman gazed at her, judging her, assessing her.

"Excellent," the dowager finally said.

She rose from the settee. The other women rose, as well, exchanged goodbyes and thank-yous, and headed for the door.

"Mrs. Hastings?"

Amanda hung back as Julia and her aunt disappeared outside.

Mrs. Chalmers gave her a thin smile. "It would be...unfortunate...if, after all this preparation, your project never came to fruition."

A warning. Clear, distinct, veiled by a pleasant expression, but a warning, nonetheless. Amanda knew she dare not fail. It would mean the end, socially, not only of herself, but of the Hastings family. Mrs. Chalmers would see to it.

"I'm committed to this project," Amanda said. "I will see it through. You needn't worry."

Mrs. Chalmers nodded slowly. "I'll count on that."

"Please do." Amanda gave her what she hoped was a confident nod, and left the house.

In the driveway, Julia and her aunt waited as their carriage approached.

"Julia," Amanda said, "please give my regards to Ethan."

The young woman glanced down at her handbag. "Actually, I haven't seen Ethan lately."

Anger spiked in Amanda. So her suspicion was true. Ethan had called on Julia in an effort to win the wager with Nick. And now that Nick had won their bet, Ethan had no further use for Julia. He'd used her, just as Nick had used Amanda.

She was tempted to tell Julia about the wager.

Surely Julia wondered why Ethan had given her the rush, then suddenly lost interest.

Still, blurting out such information while standing in a driveway with Marilyn Givens as a witness wouldn't do Julia any favor. Besides, Amanda had promised Nick she would keep the circumstances of their marriage to herself.

"Well, then," she said, changing the subject. "Perhaps you'll have some free time to contribute to the refuge project? I could certainly use your help."

Julia smiled easily. "I'd enjoy that."

"Wonderful," Amanda declared, and waved as the two women climbed into the carriage and drove away.

Amanda walked to the street and headed home. At long last, her project was moving forward. Her dream would come true. Yet instead of happiness, a huge knot twisted in her stomach.

Aurora Chalmers, the most prominent socialite in the city. Fund-raising events at all the best homes. A ground-breaking ceremony. The mayor. Dignitaries. Newspaper coverage.

Mrs. Chalmers had put her faith in Amanda to complete the refuge. She'd also put her own name and considerable reputation on the line. If the project failed—if Amanda didn't follow through, didn't get the refuge built—the gossip about a potential divorce from Nick would pale in comparison. She'd never be able to show her face in the city again. She'd be ruined, and she'd drag Mrs. Chalmers and the Hastings family reputation down with her.

The knot twisted tighter in Amanda's stomach as

she stopped walking and gazed back at Aurora Chalmers's house. She dare not fail. No matter what, that refuge had to be built.

When Amanda arrived home and Vincent greeted her in the vestibule, her first instinct was to ask if Nick was home. During the walk from Mrs. Chalmers's house around the corner, she'd managed to push aside her concern about falling on her face in front of the entire city of Los Angeles, and instead get angry at the way Ethan had shamelessly used Julia. And now, arriving home, she wanted to confront Nick about it.

"Mr. Hastings has not arrived yet," Vincent said.

"Thank you," Amanda murmured as she headed upstairs.

Before they were married and their relationship had fallen to pieces, Nick had come home early. Now he seldom did. Really, Amanda couldn't blame him. What was there to come home to?

In her room, she stopped at the mirror, unpinned her hat and laid it aside. The windows stood open and a cooling, late-afternoon breeze blew in.

"Well, how'd it go?" Dolly asked, coming through the door. "That Miz Chalmers lady loved your idea, didn't she?"

The knot in Amanda's stomach grew and the vision of social ruination flashed before her eyes. Determinedly, she ignored it.

"Yes, she did," she replied, managing a smile. "The refuge project is off and running."

"That's good. If you ask me—" Dolly stopped and eyed the bed. "Well, now, what's this? Looks like you've had yourself a visitor while you were out this afternoon.''

Amanda walked to the bed. Atop the coverlet lay the jewel case Nick had offered her, the letters of credit and the map rolled and tied with a red ribbon. Beside them was a sealed envelope.

A little grin spread across Dolly's face. ''Well, looky here at all this. Does it mean things are, you know, *normal* with you and Mr. Nick now?''

Warmth heated Amanda's cheeks at Dolly's suggestion. ''No,'' she said. ''Nothing has changed.''

''Oh,'' the maid said, sounding disappointed. ''If'n you don't mind me saying so, Miz Amanda, this thing of you two being separated don't do nobody any good. A man—especially a man like Mr. Nick—well, he's not gonna wait around forever, if you get my meaning.''

Amanda gasped and turned to Dolly. She hadn't considered such a thing. She'd been so upset, so confused, so hurt over everything that it had never occurred to her that Nick might seek companionship elsewhere.

And suddenly, Amanda couldn't bear the thought. Pictures, images flashed in her mind. Nick, with another woman?

''Oh, Dolly, no. Do you think so?'' Amanda asked.

She nodded sadly. ''Yeah, I think so.''

A heaviness enveloped Amanda's heart. Yet what could she do? Nick didn't love her—not really. He'd considered her merely a prize in a wager. He thought because she represented his idea of the ''perfect'' wife that should somehow be enough.

How could she give herself to him under those circumstances? How could she pour out her love for him in the most intimate way when he didn't feel the same as she?

"Every time Nick leaves the house, I'll wonder where he's going and what he's doing," Amanda said. "How can I live like that, wondering if he's...been with another woman? How can I tell? How can I know for sure?"

"Well," Dolly said, "for one thing, he'll be smiling."

Amanda's cheeks colored, yet she knew Dolly was right. She couldn't remember anything but a sour expression on Nick's face since their wedding day.

"There must be some way to know for sure," Amanda said.

Nick had mentioned the Pinkerton Detective Agency. The idea of having Nick followed slipped into Amanda's thoughts.

Dolly gestured to the items lying on the bed. "Maybe you don't have nothing to worry about, after all. Seems he's still interested in you. Still trying to get on your good side, tempting you with nice things."

Amanda looked hopefully at the gifts and felt her spirits lift. Yes, maybe that was true.

"What's in the envelope?" Dolly asked.

Amanda opened it and drew out the packet of papers it held. She studied them for a moment, trying to decipher the official language, then realized what it was.

Her heart tumbled.

Nick had bought the land for her refuge.

Chapter Sixteen

The silence of the house, the lonely ticking of the mantel clock, weighed heavily on Amanda as she sat on the leather settee in the corner of Nick's study. It was late. She'd eaten supper alone. She'd come to his study and switched on a single lamp. And waited.

He wasn't home yet. Never could she recall him coming home this late. A knot of worry rose in her throat. Why? Why was he so late? Where was he?

Working. Surely he was working.

Amanda clung to that thought, too fearful to believe that what Dolly had suggested might have actually happened. Nick, with another woman.

She banished the possibility from her mind. No, she mustn't think such thoughts.

Amanda drummed her fingers on the arm of the settee. Sooner or later, Nick would arrive home. He always came to his study first. When she saw him, she'd know the truth of where he'd been tonight, know if what Dolly had suggested was correct. She'd know by the expression on his face.

A sudden commotion caught her attention. Amanda

sat forward on the seat, her heart thumping hard. Nick was home. Would he walk into the study wearing a smile?

A moment later he entered the room with long, striding steps. His shoulders were hunched, his brows drawn together. Scowl lines cut into his forehead and cheeks.

Amanda breathed a little easier. No smile.

She rose from the settee. "Good evening."

Nick's head came up sharply as he stepped behind his desk. He squinted at her in the dim light. Still no smile.

"Is something wrong?" she asked, walking forward.

"Damn right something's wrong. My employees are incompetent. Danton Moore's heir has disappeared off the face of the earth. My whole project is in jeopardy." Nick slammed his satchel on the desk, ripped it open, pulled ledgers out and smacked them down one by one. "And I'm so damned randy I can hardly see straight, and my wife won't let me touch her!"

Amanda gasped softly.

Nick stopped abruptly, then gazed off thoughtfully for a moment. He looked at Amanda. "Did I say that out loud?"

She smiled. "Yes."

"Oh." He straightened the stack of ledgers. "Well, sorry."

Even if he hadn't said it aloud, Amanda would have known of his distress. Though it was cool outside now, Nick seethed with heat and sweat. Tension radiated from him. Tightly contained power exuded from his every movement. He was a man boiling in his own skin.

And for some reason, that made Amanda suddenly boil, too. She tingled in places where she shouldn't. Things ached, tightened.

She should leave. She should turn and walk out of this study and away from Nick. Yet she couldn't. Something inside her made her stay. Like a moth, dancing with a flame.

"I don't want you involved with my refuge project," Amanda said. "I told you that."

Actually, she'd screamed it at him on the street outside of the carriage.

Nick's gaze came up, hard and taut. "I got you the lot. Bought and paid for. It's done. And that's that."

"I didn't expect it," Amanda said, softening her voice. "Not after...what happened in the carriage."

Nick winced, as if remembering the two of them rolling around in the carriage caused physical pain. He shuffled the ledgers around needlessly.

"Anyway," Amanda said, "I certainly appreciate it. It's incredibly generous of you. How can I thank you?"

"Damn it," he whispered, rubbing his forehead. "Don't tease me, Amanda."

She gasped, realizing how he'd interpreted her comment. "I'm sorry. I didn't mean—"

Nick waved away her words, then flopped into his chair, looking weary and anxious and ready to explode.

"Anyway," Amanda said, pushing on, "I spoke with Mrs. Chalmers. She's very supportive of the refuge and has some wonderful fund-raising ideas."

Nick shuffled the ledgers again. ''Have you selected an architect yet?''

''No,'' Amanda said. In fact, she hadn't even thought about it.

''I can recommend Avery and Sons. They're designing my factory. Their office is in the Bradbury Building on the floor just below mine,'' Nick said, and seemed to struggle to remain calm. ''You'll need a banker, and an accountant to keep track of the money.''

''I'll make all the necessary arrangements,'' Amanda said, though she hadn't realized she'd need a banker or an accountant, and didn't have the slightest idea where to find either. ''As I said, I'll handle the refuge myself.''

Nick's expression soured further, but he didn't say anything.

''I spoke with Julia Prescott today,'' Amanda said, glad to change the subject.

Nick's gaze met hers, the hunger in his eyes undeniable. An unexpected throbbing pulsed through Amanda. She pushed on, refusing to acknowledge it. ''Did you know Ethan is no longer calling on her?''

Nick's hunger turned to anger. ''I haven't spoken with Ethan in a long time.''

''Julia seemed hurt by his sudden lack of attention.''

''Did you tell her about...?''

''The wager?'' Amanda shook her head. ''I wanted to. But I didn't. You and I agreed that we'd keep it to ourselves.''

Nick nodded, as if pleased that she'd done as he'd asked.

Tension stretched between them in the quiet room. Amanda couldn't think of anything else to tell Nick, couldn't think of a reason to stay.

"Well," she said, backing toward the door. "Good night."

"Amanda." Nick pushed himself to his feet.

She turned back. In the dim light she saw desperation flash across his face.

"I'm sorry," he said yet again, and touched his palm to his chest. "I'm sorry about the wager. I'm sorry that I hurt you. I'm sorry that I made you feel as if you aren't important to me."

Amanda's heart melted a little as she saw the sincerity in his expression, heard the warmth in his words. He'd said them before, shouted them at her that day in the carriage. But now, at this moment, they sounded genuine.

"You are my perfect wife. Everything I want," Nick said. "I can say that without hesitation."

"But can you say that you love me, Nick?" she asked softly. "Can you honestly say that's what you feel for me?"

He sighed wearily and his shoulders slumped. "Amanda, please..."

Her chin went up a notch. "You can't say it, can you?"

"Why won't you give our marriage a chance, Amanda?"

"What you mean is why won't I hop into bed with you."

"If you'd just let us become husband and wife in the true sense," Nick said, "we could put all this behind us and get on with our lives."

"And spend the rest of my days pretending that my husband loves me?" Amanda shook her head. "No, thank you."

"Love isn't all it's cracked up to be," Nick insisted. "Better that we're compatible. Better that we have common interests. Better that we can carry on a conversation over the supper table every night."

"I grew up in a home where I was made to fit in. Made to conform. Where I was made 'compatible' with my cousins." Amanda gulped, tears suddenly filling her eyes. "But no one loved me, Nick. I had to pretend it was all right, that it was enough. But it wasn't. I won't do it anymore. And I certainly won't accept it from the man who is my husband."

She walked out of the room, and Nick nearly went after her. He wanted to. With all his heart he wanted to. He wanted to hold her and kiss her, and make her understand why he felt the way he did. Show her that his way was the right way.

He didn't, though. Nick shook his head, cursing under his breath, then dropped into his chair.

He ached, positively ached for her. He tossed and turned at night, couldn't sleep, couldn't concentrate on work—all for wanting his wife. His wife!

Nick fumed silently. If he didn't do something soon, he couldn't guarantee what might happen. She'd asked for a lock on her bedchamber door, fearing that he would burst in and force himself on her. At first he'd been insulted that she'd think such a thing of him. Now, as the days and weeks wore on, Nick thought she was right to be concerned.

He shifted in the chair. Hell, maybe that's exactly what he should do. After all, once they'd made love,

Amanda would see how wonderful it was. How it would bind them together. Seal their marriage.

Nick pushed himself out of his chair and paced across the room. He wasn't about to give up on his marriage. He certainly wasn't going to turn loose his truly perfect wife. Still, if Amanda didn't come to her senses pretty soon, he didn't think he could bear it. He'd never wanted a woman so badly in his life.

He needed an outlet. His body was tense and tight, aching everywhere.

Nick stopped abruptly. He nodded to himself in the silent house.

Yes, he knew exactly what he could do.

"Nick, old boy, what are you doing out at this hour of the night when you've got that pretty new wife—*woof!*"

Ethan reeled backward as Nick drove his fist into his stomach, stumbled over a footstool and sprawled across the settee in the billiard room. As he wheezed and gulped air, Nick stood over him, waiting for him to get up so the two of them could go at it in earnest. Nick was taut and ready, anxious for the confrontation. That's what he'd come to Ethan's house for.

But Ethan didn't attempt to rise from the settee. When he'd caught his breath, he looked up at Nick, dumbfounded. "What—what the hell was that all about?"

"You know damn well what it was for," Nick insisted, his hands still curled into fists.

Dazed, Ethan just stared at him. "What's wrong with you? Have you lost your mind?"

Nick relaxed a little, disappointed that Ethan didn't

intend to get up and fight him, disappointed that punching him in the gut hadn't made him feel any better.

"I'll get you a drink," he murmured, and went to the sideboard. He filled a glass from the crystal decanter and carried it to Ethan.

Ethan eyed him suspiciously for a moment, then rose from the settee and accepted the glass. He sipped. "You're not having something?"

Nick cringed. After what had happened the last time he and Ethan drank together, he never intended to lift a glass with his friend again.

"I want you to leave Julia Prescott alone," he said.

Ethan eyed him over the rim of his glass. "I'd think you'd have enough on your hands with your own wife instead of worrying about what I'm doing."

"Oh, yeah," Nick said. "And thanks a whole hell of a lot for sending that case of Scotch."

Ethan spread his arms. "I was paying my debt. You won fair and square, and—oh, God."

Nick nodded slowly as Ethan realized what had happened. "Amanda got the Scotch. And your note."

Ethan slapped his palm across his eyes and shook his head. "I guess I deserved that punch in the gut."

"Damn right you did," Nick said, flexing his fingers.

"But what has this got to do with Julia Prescott?"

"You've hurt her with your sudden lack of attention. You don't love her, you don't care about her," Nick said. "She was just your attempt to win the wager."

Ethan uttered a bitter laugh. "You, of all people, have no business giving me advice."

"Amanda saw you with Julia a few weeks ago. You acted as if you cared about her. But you don't."

Ethan grunted. "At least *I* didn't actually *marry* her."

Nick's temper flew once more and the desire to punch Ethan again nearly got the best of him. But what his friend had said was true.

"I care for Amanda," Nick said. "She's the perfect wife."

Ethan raised an eyebrow. "Yes. I can see how happy you are."

Nick waved away his sarcasm. "We'll be fine. She just...just needs more time."

"You could do what your father did," Ethan said softly.

Old, time-worn anguish twisted in Nick's stomach, driving his temper up again. "No."

Ethan shrugged. "It's not so big a deal, you know. Lots of men—"

"No," Nick insisted. "Amanda will make a good wife. She'll see that, eventually, and everything will be..."

"Perfect?" Ethan shook his head. "You and your pursuit of perfection. For God's sake, Nick. Just like that damn Whitney project. You don't know when to let go."

Nick drew in a determined breath, refusing to address the accusation. "Everything will be fine with Amanda and me," he said.

He left Ethan's house without another word, without the feeling of satisfaction he'd hoped for when he arrived. If anything, his situation seemed more difficult than before.

Ethan was his friend. They'd known each other for years. Yet Nick didn't like to think that he might be right about something.

Such as his Whitney project.

Or Amanda.

Or that he should do as his father had done.

The streets were quiet as Nick walked. It was dark. Trolley service had stopped for the night. Only an occasional clip-clop of hooves broke the silence. Streetlamps and windows glowed yellow as he passed, heading home.

Home. Home to his wife, who wouldn't let him touch her. Nick had thought that punching Ethan in the gut would somehow make him feel better about things. Or at least work off some of his pent-up energy. Instead, now his hand hurt—on top of all his other discomforts.

Having a wife was a hell of a lot more difficult than he'd imagined.

Nick drew in a deep breath, clearing his thoughts. Amanda was certainly worth all the troubles they were having now. She would come around, just as he'd told Ethan. Soon, something would happen, something that would convince her he was right—that becoming husband and wife in the true sense was the best thing they could do. The only thing, in fact, that would get their marriage on course again.

Nick rounded the corner onto West Adams Boulevard. His feet dragged to a stop as he saw the carriage in his driveway. His shoulders sagged.

Aunt Winnifred and his mother were home.

Great. Just what he needed. Two more women to contend with.

Chapter Seventeen

So here it was. Her very first opportunity to make a complete fool of herself in front of everyone who mattered in the city of Los Angeles.

Amanda drew in a deep breath as she sat on her vanity bench and gazed into the large, oval mirror in front of her. Tonight, only an hour from now, Aurora Chalmers would host the premier fund-raising event for the women's refuge. She'd informed Amanda that nothing less than a ball was called for, under the circumstances. She'd deliberately kept the reason for the occasion a secret, forbidding Amanda, Julia Prescott, Marilyn Givens and everyone else connected with it from telling anyone about the refuge. Drama, Aurora had insisted, would intrigue her guests.

Amanda hadn't argued. In fact, she'd thought it an excellent idea. Now, however, with the event upon her, her stomach was in a knot and her hands were shaking.

If things didn't go well tonight, the whole project could be lost. And she—as well as Aurora and the

Hastings family—would be the topic of gossip for months.

Gazing into the mirror, Amanda once again questioned her decision to exclude Nick from the refuge project. She'd told him not to involve himself, and forbidden him to have a role in it. After all, he only feigned interest as an excuse to get closer to her.

But now, facing the myriad of decisions that had to be made to get the project going, Amanda wished she could go to him for advice, or at least talk to him about her fears.

She'd been tempted to do so many times. Never had she handled a project of this nature. Amanda wasn't certain exactly what should be done, or when. Nick knew all these things. He could help her easily.

But Nick was burdened with his own problems. She was reluctant to add to his concerns. From what she could gather, his Whitney project was still stalled as the search for Danton Moore's heir continued, the costs piling up with each day of delay.

Yet those weren't the only reasons she hesitated to seek Nick's counsel. Amanda took a hard look at herself in the mirror. She'd been called beautiful at times, though she didn't see it herself. Yet he seemed positively enthralled with her.

His desire for her exuded from him as if it were a living energy. He seethed with it. Every time he looked at her, Amanda felt it. It was so distracting they could hardly look each other in the eye.

Constance and Winnifred's return from San Diego had helped a little. The two women had been full of conversation about their trip—friends they'd seen, people they'd met. Winnifred had spoken of returning there soon.

Constance had talked mostly of Charles Osborne. Just how the man had ended up in San Diego so soon after she and Winnifred arrived was never made clear. Constance didn't seem to care, in any event.

Nick and Amanda had hardly spoken in days. She'd thought that staying away would make things easier, but that hadn't happened. If anything, Nick seemed to want her more.

Yet the sickening question was never far from Amanda's thoughts: how much longer could she deny him and still expect him to be interested?

"You know what?" Dolly mused, coming out of the closet carrying Amanda's evening gown. "I wouldn't be surprised if we didn't have us another wedding in this house."

Amanda turned on the vanity bench. "What do you mean?"

"That Miz Constance," Dolly said, hanging the gown on the hook near the dressing screen. "Way I hear it, she's plum taken with that Mr. Osborne fella."

"Yes, she certainly seems to be," Amanda agreed.

Dolly stepped back, looking the gown up and down. "You're gonna be the prettiest thing at the ball tonight, you mark my words. Mr. Nick won't be able to take his eyes off of you. And neither will any other man in the room."

Amanda cringed at the thought. Just what she needed—more men in her life.

She reached for her hand mirror to check her hair. Dolly had sculpted it for her, shaping it into a mass of intricate curls atop her head, held in place with strategic combs and hidden pins.

Amanda's gaze caught on the bottle of Scotch sitting on her vanity—from the case that had been delivered on her wedding night. She'd kept this one bottle, telling Nick it was to remind her of her hurt and his betrayal.

A surprising surge of warmth passed through Amanda as she recalled Nick's reply—that she would use the Scotch in a toast the night she welcomed him into her bed. Honestly, the gall of that man.

Amanda laid the mirror aside and opened the jewelry case Dolly had left there for her. Sapphires. The set Nick had given her. One of his attempts to soften her feelings toward him.

Lifting the bracelet from its velvet nest, Amanda watched the sparkles as the gems caught the light. The set was beautiful. She couldn't deny that.

Never had she owned anything so grand. Uncle Philip had been restrained in his generosity. After all, she wasn't his child. He couldn't be expected to treat her as he did his own daughters.

Amanda decided to wear the sapphires tonight for the fund-raising ball. They would look marvelous with the ivory gown she'd selected. Nick had been right—they did set off the color of her eyes.

Without wanting to, Amanda's gaze ventured once more to the bottle of Scotch. Would Nick prove right about it, too? Would they drink a toast the night she welcomed him into her bed?

Amanda rose from the vanity bench. No, she didn't

see how that would ever be possible. Nor could she envision Nick wearing a big, silly smile because of her.

The formal ballroom in Aurora Chalmers's home was situated on the main floor. Reputed to be one of the most spectacular in the city, the ballroom boasted a domed yellow ceiling, with yellow-and-brown marble on the floor and door trimmings. The walls were bronzed and decorated with ivory Greek miniatures. A dozen stained-glass skylights and a like number of carved pillars enhanced the immense room. Hand-chiseled figurines at the base of the dome were gilded in gold, as was the fountain on the south wall. An orchestra played softly, and servants moved silently as they attended the guests and the refreshment tables.

It was a spectacular setting in which to launch the women's refuge project, Amanda agreed, as she moved through the crowded room alongside Julia Prescott, whom she'd run into in the vestibule. A spectacular setting to become the laughingstock of the city.

"Quite a turnout tonight," Amanda said as they stopped at the edge of the dance floor. Julia wore a teal gown this evening, dramatically emphasizing her blond hair and pale skin.

"No one would refuse Aurora's invitation," Julia said. "You're fortunate she's supporting your cause."

"Yes, very fortunate," Amanda agreed, though with her stomach knotting, she didn't feel fortunate at the moment.

"Will Mrs. Chalmers make the formal announcement?" Julia asked. "Or is she giving you the privilege?"

''I'll do it.''

Julia uttered a little laugh. ''Really? How unlike the woman to relinquish a moment in the spotlight.''

Or perhaps she just wanted a little distance from the project, Amanda thought. At any rate, later in the evening, Mrs. Chalmers would call for her guests' attention, introduce Amanda and let her explain the refuge. Afterward, hopefully, the guests would dig deep into their pockets to get the project rolling.

''Oh, dear,'' Julia murmured. She halted quickly, ducked her head and turned away. ''There's Ethan.''

Amanda saw him standing nearby, scanning the crowd. Was he looking for Julia? Or was he hoping to spot her so that he could head in the opposite direction?

''Is he coming this way?'' Julia asked, keeping her head averted.

With a watchful eye, Amanda kept track of Ethan as he moved among the guests, talking and nodding. Finally, he headed across the room, away from them.

''He's gone,'' Amanda reported in a low voice.

Julia turned to face the dance floor once more, her expression troubled. Yet she didn't say anything, offered no comment on Ethan's apparent lack of attention. Obviously, he hadn't asked to escort her to tonight's ball. Perhaps that summed up his feelings.

Yet Amanda was annoyed by Ethan's conduct. She'd arrived by carriage with Nick, Constance and Winnifred, and had seen Julia immediately upon entering the Chalmers home. Amanda had been glad to escape the carriage. Nick was silent and sullen, his mother and aunt chatty and excited about the ball.

Julia had provided Amanda with an easy escape from all three of them.

So she knew for certain that Ethan had not approached Julia tonight. Not once. It irritated her, and her opinion of him dropped lower, though she hadn't thought that possible.

"Please, excuse me," Julia murmured, and hurried away.

Amanda watched her weave through the crowd, and was tempted to go after her. Had she seen tears welling in Julia's eyes?

"What's wrong?"

A tremor passed through Amanda at the sound of Nick's voice speaking softly at her shoulder. She turned. His brows were drawn in concern, and he must have seen the expression on her face, Amanda realized, and known something was troubling her. Her heart tumbled.

How handsome he looked. Easily the best-looking man in the room, he was turned out splendidly in white tie and tails.

"Julia," she said by way of explanation, and nodded her head across the room to where she'd disappeared. "She saw Ethan and was upset."

"That troubles you?" Nick asked.

"Of course. I can't help but think that if she knew the truth behind his initial interest in her, his lack of attention now wouldn't be so difficult for her."

"If you'd like, I'll take Ethan out back and shoot him."

Amanda gasped, then gazed up at Nick and saw the tiniest hint of a smile on his face. The first—the only—smile she'd seen in days.

"Tempting," Amanda said. "But you can't really do that."

"Still, I'd enjoy it."

They laughed together softly. Amanda reveled in the moment. Just she and Nick, sharing a private moment.

"I see you're wearing the sapphires tonight," he said, his gaze dipping to her necklace.

His gaze actually dropped lower than her necklace, to the gown's plunging neckline. Somehow, that pleased Amanda.

She touched the jewels. "Thank you for them. They're lovely."

"You make them lovely," Nick said, his voice deep, yet somehow soft, tugging her toward him.

He inched closer until his sleeve brushed her arm. Fire raced across Amanda's flesh. She gazed up at him, sure that she saw those same flames reflected in his eyes.

The music and voices around them seemed to fade, the guests disappear. Suddenly, only the two of them existed in the room, the world, the universe.

"Amanda," Nick said, his voice thick.

"Yes?" she answered, leaning closer, surprised that her own voice sounded similar.

"Amanda, I—"

"What did you dream last night?"

Winnifred, decked out in a gold brocade evening gown, pushed her way between them, jostling Amanda and causing Nick to step sideways. Yet a long, lingering look held them together until Winnifred spoke again.

"Tell me," she insisted, looking back and forth

between them. ''What did you dream? I must get caught up since my trip. Amanda, you go first.''

A few seconds passed while Amanda tried to focus her thoughts. She looked at Winnifred, but knew from the prickling of her skin that Nick's hot gaze still touched her.

''Well, let me think.'' She pressed her fingertips to her temple, trying to come up with something to share with Winnifred, knowing the woman wouldn't leave until she did. Amanda considered telling her about the dream that had come to her so often lately, the one in which Nick was trying, apparently, to push her off a cliff. Yet this wasn't the time or place, especially with him standing close by.

''I dreamed about the railway station again,'' Amanda lied. ''You interpreted that for me already.''

''Oh,'' Winnifred said, sounding disappointed. She turned to Nick. ''What about you?''

He glanced at Amanda. ''Actually, Aunt Winnie, I dreamed of nothing last night.''

''Impossible,'' she declared. ''Everyone dreams, every night. Perhaps, Nick, you simply don't want to tell me about it here and now? Understandable.''

''No, really, Aunt Winnie, it was nothing.''

''Was it embarrassing?''

''No—''

''Were you frightened?''

''Of course not.''

''Was it the result of a sexual experience?''

''I should be so lucky,'' Nick murmured. He pushed past his aunt and latched on to Amanda's arm. ''Excuse us, Aunt Winnie, I'd like to dance with my wife.''

At the edge of the dance floor, Nick looked down at Amanda. "You don't mind, do you?"

She smiled. "No, not at all."

How nice it felt to be in Nick's arms as they swayed among the other couples. Though they barely touched, as propriety dictated, a warmth radiated from him, seeping into her every pore. Amanda didn't know how he stood it, being so hot all the time.

"Your mother seems to be enjoying the evening," Amanda said, as Constance swept past in the arms of Charles Osborne. "They make a handsome couple. Don't you think?"

"No, not especially," Nick grumbled.

"You still don't like Charles Osborne, do you?"

"Something about that man bothers me," he said. "I can't put my finger on it."

"You hardly know him," Amanda pointed out. "Perhaps you should get better acquainted."

Nick didn't answer. Yet from the look on his face, Amanda suspected that Charles Osborne hadn't left Nick's thoughts completely.

"Are you enjoying the ball?" he asked after a moment.

"Well...yes," Amanda said, trying to hide her discomfort, but failing miserably. Even she could hear the telling tone in her voice.

"What's wrong?" Nick asked. "Your project is under way. I thought you'd be thrilled."

She managed a small smile. "Just a little apprehensive over the whole thing, I suppose. The newness of it."

"Everyone is nervous their first time," Nick said.

"What should I do?"

Nick's hand tightened on her back, easing her a little closer. "You should just let go and enjoy it."

"But what if I get into it and realize I don't like it?"

His thumb rubbed little circles against her palm. Even through the fabric of her glove, his touch sent ripples up her arm.

"Oh, you'll like it, Amanda. I know the kind of woman you are. Once you have a taste, you'll never want to stop."

Nick gazed at her with such intensity that Amanda's stomach fluttered. For an instant, she wondered if they were still talking about the women's refuge.

The music stopped and the crowd quieted. Aurora Chalmers moved into position in front of the orchestra. The guests edged along the perimeter of the dance floor.

Mrs. Chalmers called the room to attention, and with dramatic flair worthy of the world stage, announced the reason for the ball. It seemed, as Julia had predicted, that the woman couldn't resist making the announcement herself. A gasp and an enthusiastic round of applause broke out.

Mrs. Chalmers continued. "And now, to give you the details, is the woman who originated the idea, the woman who will bring this worthwhile project to fruition, Mrs. Nick Hastings."

Another round of applause broke out. Amanda's stomach fluttered as Nick took her arm and escorted her across the empty dance floor to stand beside Mrs. Chalmers. For a moment—a private moment—he gazed into her eyes, then gave her a wink and stepped aside.

His strength filled her. His presence a few steps away infused her with confidence as she thanked Mrs. Chalmers for her support and for the lovely evening she'd provided. Then Amanda told the guests of her vision for the refuge. She didn't tell them her reasons for wanting the refuge, but the emotions of her own personal tragedy filled her voice.

When she announced that her own husband had generously donated the land on which to build the refuge, applause broke out again. Amanda looked at Nick and saw what she thought was pride gleaming in his eyes. A final round of applause filled the ballroom as Amanda concluded her remarks with a request for the support of the guests.

Nick approached her and took her arm. Mrs. Chalmers smiled at her. Every eye in the room was on Amanda. And all she could think was that now she couldn't possibly go back. No matter what, she couldn't let this project fail.

The ball lasted until the wee hours of the morning. Most of that time Amanda was surrounded by guests asking questions about the project, pledging their support. To her surprise, Nick stayed at her side the whole time.

What a comfort it was having him there. Along with the heat he always seemed to generate, there was a strength about him that gave her courage, made her feel stronger. One thing she'd always known about Nick was that he was a man who, somehow, would always make things work out all right.

Nick and Amanda were the last guests to leave.

Standing in the doorway, Amanda took Mrs. Chalmers's hand.

"Thank you so much for this lovely evening," she said, "and for the opportunity to get this project under way."

The older woman nodded. "I know you won't fail me, Amanda."

No, Amanda thought. She wouldn't dare.

When they arrived home, the house was silent. Constance and Winnifred had left the ball earlier and retired hours ago. Nick walked with Amanda to the door of her bedchamber. He lingered, and for a moment she thought that he might—

What? Kiss her? Hold her? Ask if he could come inside?

Amanda didn't know where those thoughts had come from. She'd made it perfectly clear to Nick that she wanted nothing to do with him on an intimate level. Yet tonight, being with him at the ball had been wonderful.

He gazed at her for a moment, then simply nodded and walked down the hallway, disappearing into his own bedchamber without saying a word.

Disappointment tightened Amanda's heart. She went into her room, but admonished herself for having that particular emotion. What did she expect? Nick was only doing what she'd told him to do.

"Well, Lordy, Miz Amanda, you must have had quite a night," Dolly said, rising from the chair in the corner of the room. She looked sleepy, as if she'd napped there while waiting for Amanda to return home.

"It was wonderful. I'm certain the project is off to

a good start.'' Amanda peeled off her gloves and presented her back for Dolly to unfastened her gown.

''You're going to have money pouring in right away,'' Dolly said.

Amanda stepped out of the dress and kicked off her slippers. ''It will be arriving by wheelbarrow first thing in the morning,'' she predicted.

''Good. That's real good, Miz—''

A quick knock sounded on the door to the sitting room. It opened and Nick stepped into Amanda's bedchamber. His jacket was off, his necktie hung loose and his collar stood open. Amanda grabbed her dressing gown and yanked it on.

Nick just stood there for a moment, watching her. Then, slowly, he stepped farther into the room.

''I'd like to speak with you, Amanda,'' he said, the rich timbre of his voice filling the room.

Amanda's heart thumped in her chest and her stomach fluttered uncontrollably. Nick had never come into her bedchamber. Never once.

She exchanged a look with Dolly. The maid raised her brows.

''That will be all, Dolly,'' Amanda said, trying to keep her voice from trembling.

''Yes, ma'am.''

Dolly gave her one more glance and left the room, leaving her alone with Nick.

Chapter Eighteen

What the hell was he doing in here?

Nick drew in a breath, mentally berating himself for walking into Amanda's bedchamber. He should have stayed in his own room. Yet somehow he couldn't.

Not after tonight. Not after holding Amanda in his arms on the dance floor, teased by her scent, enjoying the view of her rounded breasts pushing up out of her ball gown.

Moments ago, undressing his own room, Nick had forbidden himself to step one foot into Amanda's bedchamber. She didn't want him there.

Then his pride had gotten the best of him. Hell, this was his house and she was his wife. His wife, for chrissake. He could go into her bedchamber if he wanted to.

Now, standing across the room from her, he knew it was a mistake.

Amanda had wrapped herself in her dressing gown, covering herself completely. Actually, more of her—a great deal more—of her tantalizing flesh had been revealed when she'd worn the ball gown earlier this evening. But somehow, knowing that only the thin dressing gown covered her and that she wore only her undergarments beneath was more tantalizing. His body's reaction was swift and strong.

"Did you…want something?" Amanda asked, still holding on to the sash of her dressing gown. Her cheeks flushed at her choice of words. Nick's desire for her pumped harder through his veins.

"I had something to tell you," he said, trying not to sound desperate. He walked nearer. "I spoke with Ethan tonight about Julia."

"You did?" she asked, seemingly relieved to have a topic of conversation to concentrate on. Amanda let go her death grip on her sash and ventured closer.

"Seems it wasn't Ethan who called things off between them," Nick said. "It was Julia."

"Julia?" Amanda frowned. "But how can that be?"

Nick moved slowly across the room, stopping within a few feet of her. He pulled in a deep breath. Lord, she smelled wonderful. And her hair. All done up atop her head. His fingers itched to pull it free of its pins, see those long, lovely tresses curl around her shoulders, her waist, her—

"Nick?"

"Hmm?"

"Julia and Ethan?"

"Oh. Yes, of course." He rubbed his forehead. "Well, anyway, Ethan admitted that he began seeing her only because of the wager. But then he realized that he was genuinely interested in her. Only by then, Julia wanted nothing to do with him."

"But why? What happened?"

Nick shrugged. "Ethan didn't seem to know."

"Did she find out about the wager, somehow?"

"I don't know how she could have," Nick said. "And if she had, I doubt she would have hesitated to make Ethan aware of it."

"That's true," Amanda mused. "What is Ethan going to do about the situation?"

"Respect her wishes," Nick told her.

Actually, when he'd happened upon Ethan on the side portico of Mrs. Chalmers's house tonight, having a smoke, Ethan hadn't hesitated to make his feelings known on the subject. If Julia didn't want anything to do with him, that was fine. "To hell with her," had been Ethan's exact words. He'd gone on to proclaim that there were dozens of other women available and he could have whomever he chose.

Nick didn't see any need to relate that portion of their conversation to Amanda.

"Well," Amanda said, "I suppose that settles things between them."

She drew in a deep breath and lapsed into thought. All Nick could think was how delightful it was to see her breasts rise and fall beneath her dressing gown. How beautiful she looked even when frowning and worrying about her friend.

A few more moments passed. Nick didn't want to leave her room. Just being close, seeing her, reveling in the intimacy of this moment was something he couldn't let go of, though he'd already said everything he'd come to say.

"I'm going to contact the Pinkerton Detective Agency about Charles Osborne. Something about that man isn't right,'' Nick said. He hadn't intended to tell Amanda about his plan to have the man investigated. But it was as good an excuse to stay in her room as he could think of at the moment. In his current condition, his thought processes seldom performed well.

Her gaze rose and she stepped even closer. Nick's breath came a little quicker.

''You can't do that,'' she said.

Inches. She stood merely inches away. If he leaned forward, took one tiny step, he could touch her. Nick's body pulsed, aching to do just that.

''I think I should,'' he insisted.

''But why?''

If he reached out, just slightly, he could touch her. Her neck was the only exposed flesh, but it looked delightful. Somehow, it called to him. Urged him forward.

Amanda frowned up at him. ''You can't do this. You can't have Charles Osborne investigated. If your mother found out she'd be furious. And rightly so.''

Nick reined in his runaway thoughts and forced himself to focus on their conversation. ''She'd be more upset if Osborne turns out to be a fraud, merely after her money.''

''But you don't know that. Really, you hardly know anything about him. And besides, it's none of your business.''

''Of course it's my business. She's my mother.''

Amanda shook her head. ''You'll regret this if you go through with it. You'll only end up hurting a lot of people.''

Nick shoved his hands into his trouser pockets. ''I seem to be doing that often these days.''

Amanda glanced away.

"I'm sorry," Nick said, and he'd never meant anything more in his entire life. "I'm sorry about everything. If only you could find it in your heart to forgive me, Amanda. If only..."

He reached for her. His palms brushed her arms. Amanda gasped softly and backed away, out of his grasp.

Nick's shoulders slumped. Frustration filled him. Desire nearly overcame his good sense. He wanted to take her in his arms, hold her, kiss her, show her—finally—the delights of being his wife. Show her all night long.

"Amanda," Nick said, taking one step toward her. "Won't you just give us a chance?"

"But why?" She crossed her arms across her stomach and held her shoulders rigid. "Nothing has changed, has it?"

Nick just looked at her for a long, aching moment. "Amanda..."

"I think you should go," she said, and turned away.

He didn't. Not for a long, tense moment. Finally, he left her room, slamming the door behind him.

"Gracious, so much money," Julia said, leaning sideways to look at the figures tallied on Amanda's tablet.

Amanda glanced out the window of the hansom cab as they passed through the streets of Los Angeles. She'd invited Julia to accompany her this afternoon to tend to the business of getting the women's refuge under way, and was glad that her friend had accepted.

Now, with the project going forward, Amanda was as nervous as ever about its completion.

''Everyone in the city has been incredibly generous,'' Amanda said, gesturing to the tablet of figures.

''Where are you keeping the money?'' Julia asked.

''Nick said I should see a banker, and find an accountant to keep track of it all,'' Amanda explained. ''Right now, I'm keeping the money in a hatbox on the top shelf of my closet.''

Julia gave her a sideways look, and they both giggled.

Amanda had been overwhelmed at the generosity of people of Los Angeles. The morning after Aurora Chalmers's ball, the cash had begun to roll in. Donations, each one seemingly larger than the last, arrived at the Hastings home. Amanda hadn't known exactly what to do with it, except to keep a log of who had given how much so that appropriate thank-you notes could be written. Her hatbox had seemed as good a place as any to keep the money.

But now, days later, there was simply too much money to keep in her closet. She intended to turn it over to a banker, as Nick had suggested. There were expenses to meet so that construction could begin on the refuge.

''The first thing we'll need is an architect to design the building,'' Amanda said, consulting one of the many lists she'd written. ''Nick suggested Avery and Sons. That's where we're going now. We have an appointment.''

Moments later, the hansom cab pulled over to the curb in front of the Bradbury Building at the corner of Third and Broadway, and Amanda and Julia climbed out. The Bradbury Building was one of the most sought-after office buildings in the city, only blocks from the fashionable homes on Bunker Hill.

Amanda leaned her head back, gazing up at the tall building's facade of brown brick and sandstone terra-cotta, then led the way inside.

The interior court was flooded with light from the glass roof five stories overhead. Offices opened on to balconies surrounding the court. The walls were gleaming yellow brick. The marble staircases at either end boasted ornately designed railings of wrought iron and polished wood. Two birdcage elevators rose toward the roof.

"Nick's company is housed here, isn't it?" Julia asked. "Will we stop by and see him?"

Amanda wasn't certain Nick would welcome a visit from her. Had their relationship been a more normal one, he might. But her showing up at his office might give him the idea that things were improving between them. And they weren't.

The night Nick had suddenly appeared in her bed-chamber after the ball, Amanda had been tempted—goodness, was she tempted—to give in to him. To be his wife completely.

But doing so made no more sense that night than it had when they were first married. Nick didn't love her. He considered her a "perfect" wife, but no more.

If she went ahead and allowed him to take her to his bed, what would that prove? Nothing. She wouldn't believe he loved her. Only that he desired her.

And she'd known that for a long time, anyway.

"Nick's not in his office today," Amanda lied.

She consulted the directory and led the way to the third floor and the firm of Avery and Sons. A receptionist showed them into a small conference room, and soon Mr. Avery, a white-haired gentleman with a full beard, joined them. He smiled broadly as Amanda introduced Julia.

"Of course, of course," Mr. Avery said, taking a seat on the opposite side of the table. "So pleased to meet you both. And may I say, Mrs. Hastings, that your husband's business is highly valued at this firm, and we're delighted—just delighted—to be of service to you."

"Thank you, Mr. Avery," Amanda said, and felt a little guilty that she'd used Nick's name when she'd made the appointment, yet refused to let Nick himself have anything to do with the project. "I'd like to discuss the building of a women's refuge in the city. You've heard of it?"

"Of course," Mr. Avery said, looking pleased with himself. "Just the sort of project this firm takes great pride in working on. Yes, just the sort of thing."

"Good," Amanda said. "I'd like to get started immediately."

"Of course." Mr. Avery planted his palms on the table top and levered himself out of the chair. "I'm going to turn this over to my son, Donald. Razor-sharp, that boy. Just what this project needs. If you ladies will excuse me?"

He disappeared out of the room, leaving Amanda and Julia alone. Amanda hadn't been sure what type of reception she'd get from Avery and Sons. After all, a woman almost never approached such a firm for any reason. She was pleased that Mr. Avery was taking her seriously. Of course, it didn't hurt that she was married to Nick, the man who was lining their pockets due to his Whitney project.

Amanda wondered if Mr. Avery had read about the women's refuge from the newspaper accounts. Aurora Chalmers's ball had received extensive coverage.

She wondered, too, if Nick had visited Mr. Avery and explained the situation. Had he paved the way for her, making this visit easier, even though she'd told him on several occasions to keep clear of her project?

Her thoughts wandered to the offices on the floors above and below Avery and Sons. Nick was in the building somewhere. She could imagine him in his office—self-assured, comfortable, completely at ease discussing a business venture and an expensive project.

Certainly he wouldn't be perched on the edge of his chair, desperately clutching anything he could get his hands on, as Amanda was now. Deliberately, she loosened her grip on her handbag.

"Excuse me, Mrs. Hastings?"

Amanda and Julia both turned as a young man ventured into the room. He appeared to be barely out of his teens, with a slight build, blond hair and wire-rimmed spectacles that magnified big blue eyes. The face of an angel. Almost too pretty, too innocent-looking to be male.

This was Mr. Avery's razor-sharp son, Donald?

"Yes, I'm Mrs. Hastings," Amanda said, then introduced Julia.

He glanced out the door, then eased a step farther into the room and pushed his fingers through his bangs, sweeping them off his forehead. He wore trousers and a white shirt that were both a little too big, but clean and tidy.

"Excuse me for butting in like this, ma'am," he said. "My name is Clifford Sullivan. I heard about the project you're working on, Mrs. Hastings, the one for the women and children, and I just wanted to tell you how much that's going to mean to a lot of people in this city."

"Thank you," Amanda said. "That's very kind of you."

"No, ma'am, it's not kindness. It's the truth," Clifford said, gazing at her earnestly. "You see, my father passed away three years ago and it's been real hard for my mother to take care of things. I've got seven younger brothers and sisters."

"Eight children?" Amanda asked. "How old are you, Clifford?"

"Twenty-three, ma'am."

"Really? You look much younger."

"Yes, ma'am. I hear that a lot." Clifford grinned and big dimples appeared in his cheeks. "I was real lucky to get this job here with Mr. Avery."

"What do you do here?" Julia asked.

"I work in the bookkeeping department," Clifford explained, and squared his shoulders. "I'm beholden to Mr. Avery for giving me the chance and for training me. I take every cent I earn and give it to my mama to help out with the younger kids."

"Still, it must be very difficult for your family," Amanda said.

"Yes, ma'am. My mama, she works hard. She scrubs floors and washes dishes at a restaurant here in town. My brothers work, too, even though my mama wants them to go to school instead.'' Clifford glanced out the door and began backing toward it. ''I've got to go, Mrs. Hastings. I just wanted to tell you thank you, and say that I'd be proud to help with your project, any way I can.''

Clifford flashed another brilliant smile, then hurried out the door seconds before another man entered. This one, Amanda knew, was Donald Avery. Tall, with slightly graying hair and a build similar to his father, he strode inside.

''Before we get started,'' Amanda said, ''could you tell me something about Clifford Sullivan? Is he a good worker?''

Donald Avery nodded thoughtfully. ''He's been with us for nearly a year now. Learns quickly. Reliable. Always on time. Hard worker.''

''Good,'' Amanda said. ''Now, I suppose we should get down to business?''

Nick came home smiling.

A little tremor of fear passed through Amanda as she stood in the dining room when he walked in, grinning broadly.

Dread knotted her stomach. Could that smile mean what Dolly had suggested? Had Nick been with another woman today?

''Good evening,'' he called out.

Amanda summoned her courage. ''You seem happy. Did something...happen?''

''Actually,'' he said, his smile widening, ''something wonderful happened.''

Amanda gulped. ''What?''

''I've found Danton Moore's heir.''

Relief weakened her knees. "Oh, Nick, that's wonderful. Where did you find him?"

"It's a woman, actually. Charlotte Moore. Danton's daughter and only surviving heir. She lives near here."

"And she's agreed to sell you the property?"

"My attorney will speak with her tomorrow morning." Nick nodded confidently. "The deal will be completed by noon."

Amanda wished she could go to him, throw her arms around him, share the moment, share his success. He'd worked and worried, endured disappointment and financial hardship, and finally his Whitney project would get under way.

Nick pulled out Amanda's chair, seating her. "Where are Mother and Aunt Winnifred?"

"Your aunt is dining with the Wades this evening," Amanda said, "and your mother is out with Charles Osborne."

Nick nodded and took his own chair as the servants slipped quietly into the room and began serving supper. Amanda was pleased that not even mention of Charles Osborne's name dimmed Nick's good mood.

"How is your refuge coming along?" he asked, opening his napkin with a snap.

Though she'd insisted he not involve himself with her project, Amanda saw no need not to tell him what was going on with it, if he asked. And she didn't want to spoil their current rapport with an argument.

"The money continues to roll in. I'm surprised every day by the city's generosity," Amanda said. "I set up an account with Mr. Rayburn at the California Bank and Trust."

"Rayburn?" Nick frowned for the first time. "I wish you'd gone to my banker, Amanda. I told you—"

"Thank you, anyway," Amanda said, cutting him off. "Mr. Rayburn and I are getting along quite nicely, and the bookkeeper I hired is working diligently."

"That Sullivan boy?" Nick asked, pausing over his soup.

Amanda had known from the beginning that Nick hadn't been happy when she'd offered the job of bookkeeper to Clifford Sullivan after she'd met him at Avery and Sons. Clifford had been thrilled—with the salary, as much as the opportunity to help with the project. Nick, however, hadn't thought much of her selection.

"Donald Avery has come up with some wonderful ideas for the design of the building," Amanda said, turning the conversation to something more pleasant. "Julia and I met with a decorator today and got an estimate on furnishings."

"When's the ground-breaking ceremony?" Nick asked.

"In two days," Amanda said, and a nervous knot in the pit of her stomach tightened. She laid her spoon aside, ignoring the soup. "Mrs. Chalmers arranged for the mayor to be there, along with almost everyone of consequence in the city."

"Newspaper coverage?"

"Of course. You know Aurora Chalmers," Amanda said. "She has the presentation well orchestrated. I'm to give a bank draft to Mr. Avery to cover his services, he will present me with the blueprints, then we will break ground."

Nick frowned. "You haven't paid Avery anything yet?"

"No," Amanda said, the knot in her stomach drawing tighter. "Should I have?"

"That's the way it's usually done. A portion of the fee up front to cover the initial work," Nick said. "Avery has already done a great deal on your behalf."

Amanda pressed her lips together, not wanting to admit to Nick that she hadn't known such an arrangement was customary. Perhaps Avery hadn't asked her for payment fearing he might offend her and lose this high-profile project. Still, she was a bit embarrassed at not knowing the workings of business.

Nick shrugged. "No matter, as long as you pay him everything you owe at the ceremony."

"You'll be there, won't you?" Amanda asked.

Nick looked up from his plate. "Do you want me there?"

In that instant, Amanda couldn't imagine standing at the ground-breaking ceremony without Nick at her side. Just seeing him, having him near, gave her strength. And surely she'd need every ounce she could get at the ceremony.

"I'd like it very much if you were there," she said.

A smile wider than the one he'd worn into the dining room spread over Nick's face. "If it makes you happy, Amanda, I will certainly be there."

He reached over and gave her hand a quick squeeze. "Seems things are working out for the both of us."

She smiled. Yes, it was true. Nick had his Whitney project going forward at last, and her refuge was proceeding.

How nice that at least this much of her life was going well. She'd worried endlessly that the refuge project would fall apart. That she would look bad and shame Nick's family in the process. But that hadn't happened.

Amanda smiled to herself. Nothing could go wrong now.

Chapter Nineteen

How could everything have gone so wrong?

Amanda gulped and gazed across the wide, walnut desk at Mr. Rayburn. Around them, the business of the California Bank and Trust went on as if nothing was amiss. As if everything were in its proper place.

As if the world hadn't suddenly come crashing down around Amanda's shoulders.

"I—I don't understand," she said, pressing her lips together and swallowing with difficulty.

Truly, she didn't understand anything that was happening. The ground-breaking ceremony was scheduled to begin in only an hour. She'd stopped by the bank to have a draft prepared to present to Avery and Sons, only to be told by this dreadful Mr. Rayburn that she no longer had any money in her account. How could that be?

"There should be thousands of dollars in the account," Amanda said, her heart pounding frantically. "How could it just disappear?"

Mr. Rayburn shifted his considerable weight and drew in a tired breath. "As I've already said, Mrs.

Hastings, the funds were withdrawn earlier this morning. By your bookkeeper.''

Amanda's head spun. ''But Clifford would have no reason to withdraw any money. Why would you give it to him?''

Mr. Rayburn's gaze sharpened and he drew himself up. ''I resent your implication, Mrs. Hastings, that this bank has somehow misappropriated your funds. Sullivan presented proper documentation, and the transaction was cleared by me personally.''

''But Clifford was only supposed to keep track of the money,'' Amanda said, and heard the desperation in her voice. ''He wouldn't—''

''Perhaps you should speak with him,'' Mr. Rayburn suggested, none too politely. He pointedly glanced at the clock on the wall. ''Now, if you'll excuse me, Mrs. Hastings, I have business to conduct.''

''But—''

''Good day.''

''But....'' Amanda watched as Mr. Rayburn rose from his desk and walked away. She sat there alone, perched on the edge of her chair, clutching her handbag, too stunned to move.

The donations for the women's refuge were gone? All of the money had vanished? Withdrawn this morning by Clifford Sullivan?

A thread of hope wound through Amanda's thoughts. Perhaps Clifford had misunderstood her intentions. Perhaps he'd thought *he* was to come to the bank and have the draft prepared. Could that be what had happened?

Yet if that were true, why would Clifford have emptied the account? A sickening knot formed in

Amanda's stomach as she desperately searched for a reasonable answer.

She glanced around, aware now that people in the bank had started to stare at her. Tellers behind their bars, customers going about their business—people, presumably, with actual money still in their accounts—all cast curious glances her way.

Reaching deep inside for strength, Amanda rose from the chair, head high, and left the bank. Outside on the street, she got her bearings. The Bradbury Building was in the next block. She'd go there, confront Clifford Sullivan and get this straightened out.

When she arrived, the receptionist asked her to take a seat and wait. Amanda couldn't sit. She paced, trying not to wring her hands. When dear old white-haired Mr. Avery finally appeared, she nearly ran to him.

"I'd like to speak with Clifford Sullivan," Amanda said, and managed to sound calm.

Mr. Avery frowned. "Young Sullivan isn't with us any longer. He came by this morning, cleared out his desk and resigned."

Breath left Amanda in a sickly wheeze. Her head spun. "But—but where did he go?"

"Left town, he said." Mr. Avery's frown deepened. "Is there a problem, Mrs. Hastings?"

Was there a problem? Amanda nearly screamed at Mr. Avery. Yes, of course there was a problem. At this very moment dignitaries from all over the city were assembling for the ground-breaking ceremony. Chairs were set up, floral arrangements in place. Shovels with big red bows stood at the ready. Newspaper reporters, wealthy contributors, Aurora Chalmers, the *mayor*—all were waiting for Amanda to arrive and present a draft to Avery and Sons so construction could begin.

"Mrs. Hastings?" Mr. Avery asked again. "Is something wrong?"

Amanda pulled in a breath, steadying herself. She couldn't—absolutely couldn't—let anyone know of this debacle.

She forced a smile. "Everything is fine. Perfectly fine."

"Good, then. I'll see you at the ground-breaking ceremony in a little while."

"Certainly. Well, until then." Amanda held her smile in place, gave him a demure nod and left the office.

Once outside in the hallway, she braced her hand against the wall to keep herself upright. Clifford Sullivan, the sweet young man with the angelic face, had stolen every dime of her refuge money and left town with it. She could hardly believe he'd done such a thing. He'd held a position of responsibility at Avery and Sons for nearly a year. And, suddenly, he was untrustworthy?

Yet the facts were clear.

Now what was she to do?

She owed money to Avery and Sons for the work they'd already done. She'd placed orders for carpets, draperies and furniture with several businesses in town, promising them payment in full immediately after today's ceremony.

How would she pay for it?

And what would people say about her if she couldn't pay at all?

Visions of the entire city of Los Angeles turning against her flashed in Amanda's mind—her worst fear come true. Lately, she'd even dreamed something like this would happen. Public humiliation—for herself and Nick's family. A nightmare only marginally more horrid than the recurring one in which Nick tried to lure her off a cliff.

Amanda forced her fears aside and straightened her shoulders. No. No, she wouldn't let this happen. Somehow, some way, she'd get her hands on the money she needed to pay her debts and keep the refuge going.

Who could she turn to? Uncle Philip popped into her mind. Yes, Uncle Philip. He'd come to her aid.

Amanda's excitement waned as she realized that asking him for money would necessitate telling him everything that had happened. And still, after enduring all that humiliation, it would be days before she actually received the money from him. She needed it in a matter of moments.

Aurora Chalmers? No, never. Amanda dismissed the idea as quickly as it had sprung into her head. She couldn't admit to the woman that she was a complete failure. Mrs. Chalmers would surely withdraw her support and the refuge project would be doomed.

Julia might have the money. Amanda didn't know how well-off her deceased husband had left her. Yet she couldn't bring herself to ask her friend for money. Even in this difficult position, she hardly knew Julia well enough to request something so personal.

Amanda paced the floor, her mind reeling. Who else could she turn to? Who else—

Nick.

Amanda gasped aloud in the quiet hallway. Nick. Of course. Nick. Why hadn't she thought of him immediately? He'd been supportive of her refuge from the beginning. He'd offered his help. He had the money—plenty of it. She needn't worry that he'd gossip all over town about what a miserable failure she was, managing the refuge. His office was right here in the Bradbury Building. Steps away.

And he was her husband, for goodness sake.

Amanda's heart soared. Thank heaven for Nick.

She hiked up her skirt and dashed up the stairway to his office, her heels clicking on the marble risers. For a moment, her heart tumbled at the thought that perhaps he wasn't in his office right now. She forced herself to stand still, to not fidget, as the receptionist went in search of him. A moment later, he appeared.

"Amanda?" he asked, looking surprised but pleased to see her.

"Oh, Nick..." She rushed to him. It took all the strength she could muster not to throw her arms around him on the spot.

"What's wrong?" he asked, concern showing in his face.

Amanda became aware that faces in the office had turned their way. Surely, they were curious about the woman their employer had wed. No sense giving them a show.

"Could I speak with you, please?" she asked, forcing herself to calm down. "Privately?"

"Certainly." Nick gestured down the hallway.

A door bearing his name in gold letters stood open. Amanda stepped inside. The room held heavy, walnut furniture, dark-green carpet and drapes, brass accents

Nick closed the door. "Sit down."

Amanda eased onto one of the leather chairs that faced his desk and glanced at the wall clock. Fifteen minutes. The ceremony would begin in fifteen minutes.

Nick dropped into the leather chair behind his desk. "I'm surprised to see you here, Amanda. I thought—"

"I need your help." Amanda sprang to her feet, twisting her handbag in her fingers.

He sat forward quickly. "What's wrong?"

"Everything—just everything," Amanda declared. The whole sordid story poured out of her, unchecked. She couldn't tell him fast enough, couldn't unburden herself quickly enough. She didn't bother to sugarcoat any detail, or soften it. She just wanted to tell him, knowing that, somehow, he would fix this awful mess she found herself in.

Nick eased back in his chair, listening intently. By the time she finished, Amanda had twisted her handbag strings into a knot and was on the verge of crying—or screaming. She'd never been so desperate in her entire life.

"We only have a few minutes," she pleaded. "The ceremony should be starting any moment."

Expectation crackled in the air as she looked at Nick, waiting. Then, to her extreme relief, he nodded slowly.

"What would you like me to do?" he asked, and sat forward, folding his palms on his desk.

"Money. I need money," Amanda said, the words gushing out. "I have to replace the funds Clifford took from the account. Everyone is assembling at the ground-breaking ceremony at this very moment, waiting. I have to appear there with the bank draft for the architect. Can you imagine what people will think if that doesn't happen?''

''Yes, I can,'' he said thoughtfully. He eased back in his chair again. ''Of course I'll give you the money.''

Amanda thought she might swoon. Relief swamped her, weakening her knees. She clasped her hands to her chest. ''Thank you. Oh, Nick, thank you so much.''

''Is there anything else you need?'' he asked.

Amanda thought for a moment. With her major problem solved, a spurt of anger flooded her.

''I'd like you to hunt down Clifford Sullivan,'' Amanda declared, ''and get my money back.''

''Of course,'' Nick said. ''Anything more?''

''That Mr. Rayburn wasn't very nice to me. In fact, he wasn't nice at all,'' Amanda said, pointing in the general direction of the bank. ''You could fire him—or whatever it is one does with a banker.''

Nick nodded. ''Something else?''

Amanda fumed for a moment. Finally, she shook her head. ''No, I think that's all.''

''Fine, then. I'll handle everything right away.''

''Oh, Nick, I owe you a huge debt,'' Amanda said, heaving yet another sigh of relief. ''Thank you. Thank you so much. I'll figure a way to repay you, somehow. I swear I will.''

''You already know how.''

Amanda stopped abruptly. Nick gazed steadily at her. He didn't flinch, didn't blink. Just looked at her.

"You already know what I want," Nick said, his gaze lazily assessing her from head to toe.

Heat rushed through Amanda. Color rose in her cheeks. She leaned back slightly. "What—what do you mean...?"

Nick lifted one shoulder. "If you'd like me to spell it out, I will."

She blinked across the desk at him. "You want me—us—to...?"

"I want you in my bed, Amanda."

She gasped, too stunned to speak.

"You're my wife, if you'll recall," Nick said. "This shouldn't come as a complete surprise to you."

Her mouth dropped open. "I—I can't believe that you'd suggest such a thing."

Nick shrugged. "It's your decision. Do you want to show up at the ceremony today penniless? End all possibility of building your refuge? Disappoint all those women and children?"

"You wouldn't do this," Amanda declared. "You're a decent man. You wouldn't let the refuge fail just to get me in bed with you."

A little grin pulled at Nick's mouth. "Wanna *bet?*"

Amanda drew in a quick breath. The heat that had consumed her turned to ice. She wanted to slap his face for making such an indecent suggestion. He deserved it, for putting her in this position.

But what were her choices? Nothing palatable. Nothing remotely acceptable.

"You'd do this?" she asked. "You'd buy your way into bed with me?"

"Sure."

Amanda drew herself up and pushed her chin a

little higher. "You can buy my body, but not my heart," she told him.

Nick shrugged. "I'll take your body for now."

If the desk didn't separate them, Amanda would have slapped him. Instead, she stood where she was as Nick rose from his chair, fetched his hat and gestured grandly toward the door.

"Shall we go to the bank?" he invited, not bothering to hide his grin.

Amanda put her nose in the air and sailed past him, with the uncomfortable feeling that he was staring at her bottom the entire way down the hallway.

They conducted their business quickly. Nick, true to his word, fired Mr. Rayburn as the refuge project's banker. Mr. Rayburn, sputtering and stammering, followed them to the door as Nick assured him that he himself would never do business with his bank in the future.

Nick's own bank was just down the street. He arranged for the draft and they left within minutes.

Under the circumstances, the fact that he'd stood up for her, rescued both her and her refuge, brought Amanda little pleasure—not with what she faced once they got home this evening.

The ground-breaking ceremony went smoothly, despite lengthy speeches from the mayor and Mrs. Chalmers. Amanda presented Mr. Avery with the bank draft, then picked up one of the red-ribboned shovels and scooped out a patch of earth along with the other dignitaries.

She could hardly focus on the ceremony. Nick stood only steps away, eyeing her intently. While he showed no more attention to her than was decent in public, he gave off an energy Amanda couldn't ignore.

His gaze seemed more intense, more personal. He seemed to see right though her—and liked what he saw. He radiated a warmth, a heat that was unmistakable. Her skin crackled with it.

Finally, when the ceremony ended and polite conversation was concluded, Nick took her hand. He gazed into her eyes and his thumb stroked her palm, sending a shiver up her arm.

"Good day, Amanda." He leaned closer and smiled. "I'll see you...*tonight.*"

Chapter Twenty

Nick eyed the door to Amanda's bedchamber. Inside, he heard feminine voices and knew she was awake and that her maid was with her.

Annoyance rippled through him. Here he was, married all this time, and he'd seldom seen his wife in her bedchamber, preparing to retire for the evening.

Was she already snuggled into bed? he wondered. Her dark hair fanning over the white linen pillowcases? What did she wear? A loose gown that slid over her silky skin, rising to reveal—

Nick growled and pressed his lips together, trying to shake off yet another surge of desire for her. He'd hardly slept in the past weeks, aching for her. All afternoon following the ground-breaking ceremony he'd squirmed in his chair, barely able to sit at his desk, thinking about this moment.

Amanda was his. Finally.

Yet as glad as he was that this moment had finally arrived, an unwelcome thought tickled his conscience.

Truthfully, he wasn't all that proud of the ultimatum he'd handed down to Amanda this afternoon in his office. Under any other circumstances, it would have been unthinkable of him.

But Amanda was his wife—*his wife.* And all he wanted was for them to have a normal conjugal relationship. What was so wrong with that?

They'd have had it long ago if she weren't so stubborn, so determined to see things through her own narrow view of the world.

True, Amanda didn't know what Nick knew about love and marriage and such. She hadn't seen the things he'd seen. She had no idea what the curse of love could do to a marriage.

Why couldn't she just trust him?

Nick stared at the closed door in front of him. Of course, he'd never told her the circumstances that drove his decision. Perhaps if he did…

He gave himself a mental shake, tossing aside the idea. He doubted Amanda was in a mood to listen to much of anything he had to say—especially on the subject of love and marriage. And especially tonight.

The look on her face when he'd delivered his conditions for bailing her out floated in his mind. Shock. Outrage. Indignation.

Yet was there something more lurking in her eyes? Nick wondered. Had he seen a hint of wanting hidden just beneath the surface?

Or was it only wishful thinking on his part?

No matter, he decided. He had what he wanted—finally—and what he wanted was Amanda.

He opened the door to her bedchamber without knocking, and walked inside.

Seated at her vanity, Amanda gasped softly as her door opened and Nick strolled in. He wore the same suit she'd seen him in earlier today, but his jacket was off, his necktie missing and his collar open. The sleeves of his white shirt were turned back, revealing wrists and forearms brushed with dark hair.

He crossed the room, then stopped behind her. His dark, smoldering gaze met hers, reflected in the big, oval mirror in front of her.

Amanda's stomach bounced. She knew why he was here.

Nervously, she pulled at the sash of her dressing gown and saw Nick's gaze drop to her waist as her movement drew his attention to that spot. Heat rippled through Amanda, and she fought off the urge to cross her arms in front of her, dash behind the dressing screen, throw on every article of clothing she owned. Anything to escape Nick's penetrating gaze.

"Good evening," he said, his voice thick and low.

"Good evening." Amanda managed a stiff reply.

Nick turned to Dolly, who was folding down the coverlet. "That will be all," he told her.

Amanda's stomach jolted. She turned on the bench as Dolly murmured, "Yes, sir," and left the room. It annoyed Amanda that he would come into her room and order her maid away as if he owned the place, even though, in fact, he did.

Then the door closed with a soft thud, leaving Amanda alone—utterly alone—with Nick, and all she could think of was what lay ahead for her this evening.

She'd thought of nothing else since leaving the ceremony this afternoon. Her initial anger and outrage had finally melted down to fear and anxiety. Now, with Nick in her bedchamber, those feelings intensified. The moment was here.

Warmth washed over Amanda. She faced the mirror again and saw that he stood even closer now, gazing down at her. Her anxiety grew at his nearness. From the look on his face, there would be no turning back.

Silently she fiddled with the items on her vanity, straightening them, aligning them just so, anything to keep her hands busy, anything to ignore Nick a little longer.

That proved impossible.

"What's this?" He leaned over her shoulder and, from the array of bottles and jars, picked up an atomizer with a feather sprouting out the side.

"Perfume," she said, and was surprised at how soft her voice sounded.

He raised the pink bottle to his nose and sniffed, then shrugged as if the scent pleased him. "Smells good," Nick said, and set the bottle down. "Smells like you."

He just looked at her, studying her reflection in the mirror. Amanda gazed back at him, determined not to let him see how uncomfortable, how intimidated she was at the moment. But she was no match for him. The power of his masculinity overcame her. Amanda glanced away.

"Your hair is...quite lovely," Nick said softly.

Before she could look up at his reflection, Amanda felt his fingers in her hair. Slowly, gently, they dug deeper, caressing the back of her head, then dropping lower to the bare flesh of her neck.

His touch vibrated through her. Warmed her. Threatened to melt the very core of her.

Was this what he wanted? What he intended? That she would come completely undone by his presence, his touch, and fall at his feet? Did he think she'd willingly give herself to him after all they'd been through? After he'd coerced her into sharing her body with him?

Well...perhaps. Amanda's thoughts evaporated as both Nick's hands caressed her neck, and his fingers eased inside the collar of her dressing gown. Gracious...how delightful. His touch, the simple feel of his fingers, sent shivers through her. Her eyelids closed.

Then as quickly, they popped open again. Good heavens, what was she doing? Giving in to him when she knew good and well he didn't really love her? When she'd been his prize in a wager? When he'd taken her most treasured dream and used it against her?

Amanda wrestled out of his grasp and pushed to her feet, anger and resentment filling her. She'd taken his money this afternoon and agreed to his terms. She'd made her deal with the devil. Now it was time to pay up.

"Let's just get this over with," she snapped.

She marched to the bed, flung herself down on it and squeezed her eyes closed. "Go ahead. Do it."

Nick followed her to the bed and gazed down at her in the room's dim light. Amanda, his wife, the woman he'd lusted after for weeks, lay on the bed, arms stuck to her sides, feet pressed together, lips clamped shut, rigid and tense and stiff.

Not exactly the way he'd envisioned this moment.

Yet he feasted on the sight of her. Her nightclothes clung to her many curves, with nothing underneath. Her hair was down. Thick and dark, she'd caught it up with a simple ribbon and left it to curl down her back. Now it fanned out on the bed beside her. Her soft feminine scent floated up to him, wound through him, making him want her all the more.

And here she was. Available, if not completely willing.

Nick paused, looking down at his wife, trying to push aside the thoughts that suddenly filled his head.

Sure, she was obligated to him now. She would go along with their lovemaking tonight because she'd given her word. But was that how he wanted her? In bed with him because of their agreement?

The truth of the matter insinuated itself into Nick's thoughts.

How much better if she were here because she wanted to be. Because she was excited about their union. Because she truly wanted them to live as husband and wife.

Still...here she was.

Nick eased onto the edge of the bed. It shifted beneath his weight. He watched her for a moment, silently willing her to relax. She didn't.

Gently, he touched his finger to the hair at her temple and smoothed it behind her ear. He ran his fingertip down her jaw to the soft flesh of her throat.

She didn't flinch, didn't react at all, except to open one eye.

"Hurry up, will you?" Amanda said. "I have an early appointment in the morning."

A surge of desire nearly overcame Nick. God, how he wanted this woman.

"These things take time…if they're done right." Nick smiled slowly, sliding his finger along her jawline once more. "And I do intend to see that it's done right."

"Really?" She opened both eyes now and her voice softened, sounding hopeful. She relaxed slightly.

"Oh, yes," Nick assured her.

With one hand he threaded his fingers through her hair, as the other caressed her long, lovely throat. He leaned down and laid his cheek against hers, pressing them together. At last, he felt her relax a bit more. He raised his head and saw her eyes drift shut.

Slowly, Nick plucked open the top few buttons of her dressing gown. Beneath lay the white, creamy flesh where her nightgown dipped low. Desire pumped harder through his veins as he slid his hand inside.

Nick clamped his lips together to keep from moaning as his fingers brushed the swell of her breast. His own eyes closed. Soft. So soft. Warm. Inviting. Urging him to push deeper.

He gave in to the desire and slipped his hand farther beneath her gown, cupping her breast. Oh, how he wanted her. He'd wanted her for so long. Now here she lay, his for the taking.

Nick opened his eyes, anxious to see Amanda's expression as they shared this moment. But her face was turned away, tight and pinched with—

What? Fear? Revulsion? He wasn't sure. Whatever it was, he knew it wasn't right.

Nick withdrew his hand and sat up.

Amanda turned to him, confusion on her face. "What's wrong?"

He rose from the bed. "Good night."

"I thought we were going to..." she waved her arm "...you know."

"We are. But not tonight."

"Well...*when?*" she demanded.

"When I say so."

Amanda gasped and sat up, fumbling with her dressing gown to pull it closed. "You expect me to just be here, at the ready, whenever the mood strikes you?"

He shrugged. "Yes."

"Of all the nerve!" Her mouth flew open. "What makes you think I'll allow that?"

"Because of this."

Nick dropped his knee onto the bed and swept Amanda into his arms, pulling her halfway off the mattress. His mouth claimed hers. He pushed his tongue inside with a deep, hungry kiss, pouring out all the desire that had raged inside him for so long.

She didn't protest. Didn't struggle. Just hung in his embrace, accepting his very thorough kiss.

He released her, allowing her to drop back onto the bed. Desire raged in him. He wanted her. He wanted her now.

But not like this.

Nick turned and left the room.

Chapter Twenty-One

It happened *again.* And all he was doing was staring at her *door.*

"Hell..." Nick pulled at the back of his neck, grumbling as he stood in the sitting room in front of Amanda's door. His body's reaction to mere *thoughts* of her were almost too much to bear. Even his chilling morning bath had done little to alleviate his condition.

If he didn't make things right with Amanda soon and get her into bed, he wouldn't be held responsible for his actions.

Nick fumed silently, angry with himself. He'd missed his chance last night. No two ways about it.

Mentally, he kicked himself for his actions—or lack thereof. He should have made love to Amanda when he had the opportunity. Done it and gotten it over with. After all, once they made love he was certain Amanda would enjoy it. He'd see to it that she did.

Yet last night something inside him wouldn't let him go about it that way, had stopped him from bedding her when he had the chance. Because what he really wanted was for Amanda to come willingly to him. He wanted her to wish that their marriage was a real one.

Nick shifted uncomfortably, still staring at the door. At least that's what he'd wanted last night. This morning, trying to deal with this ever-present ache, he thought himself a fool for letting the moment pass.

If only he could make Amanda want it as much as he did.

Was that even possible?

Hell, no.

But still… Nick nodded slowly as an idea grew in his mind—no easy feat, given his condition.

What if there was a way? What if he could, in fact, make Amanda want him as much as he wanted her—or a close facsimile thereof? That would certainly ease his conscience—and a few other things, as well.

Nick stroked his chin, pacing about the sitting room. Perhaps if he quit chasing her so hard, she'd stop running away so fast. Could he then entice her? Lure her into his bed? Make her anxious to join him in consummating their marriage—a couple dozen times a night?

Maybe. Nick stopped his pacing. This plan would require a certain charm, the right amount of finesse on his part. Could he pull it off?

Truthfully, the whole notion went against his grain. He preferred an all-out effort. He wasn't much for holding back.

Nick sighed in the quiet room. What other choice did he have? He'd already tried everything else. And the fact that he was still sleeping alone, taking icy baths each morning and lusting after his own wife were indications of what a miserable failure he'd been so far.

Quickly, he ducked back into his own room, gave instructions to Jackson and sent the valet off to the kitchen, then returned to the sitting room.

Drawing in a fresh breath, Nick headed toward Amanda's door, anxious to put his new plan into action. What did he have to lose?

"Good morning," he announced, striding inside her bedchamber.

She stood by her closet, wearing her dressing gown. Morning sunlight beamed through the window, highlighting her hair, which hung loose around her shoulders. Nick's knees trembled. Lord, she was beautiful. He wanted her. Desperately.

What the hell kind of stupid plan had he just come up with?

Nick forced himself to stand still. It took all the strength he could muster not to sweep Amanda into bed immediately.

"Beautiful day, isn't it?" he said brightly, walking to the window and gazing out, trying to keep his body under control.

Nick turned back in time to see Amanda run her fingers down the buttons of her dressing gown, insuring they were all fastened. The simple action made him want her all the more.

"Don't let me disturb you," he said, waving his hand toward her. "Go ahead with what you were doing."

"I was dressing."

He smiled. "Then, by all means, don't let me stop you."

Amanda flushed slightly as she headed for her vanity, annoyed at the liberties he was suddenly taking with her. Bursting into her bedchamber unannounced and uninvited. Of all the nerve.

"This really isn't a good time," she said, seating herself on the vanity bench. "I have an appointment this morning and I'd really like to—"

"Nice mirror," Nick said. He walked up behind her and, as he had last night, met her gaze in the reflection. "Mine seems to be broken."

Amanda's cheeks colored at the mention of his mirror, which she'd smashed when she'd thrown the Scotch at him on their wedding night. She glanced at the bottle now sitting on the corner of her vanity. Dare she do it again?

Nick leaned forward slightly, tweaking his necktie. "Is this straight?"

Amanda glanced up at him in the mirror. Dark, smoldering eyes—first thing in the morning. A warmth shuddered through her. Did that mean he intended to demand his husbandly rights—*now?*

"Your necktie is fine." Amanda tore her gaze from his and snatched up her hairbrush. Deliberately, she ran it through her hair, staring at herself in the mirror. "Why haven't you had your mirror replaced?" she asked.

"It's on order."

His hand dropped to her shoulder. Amanda jumped.

"Where are you going this morning?" he asked, his fingers lazily skimming the skin of her neck.

Her breath quickened. Gracious, his touch was gentle. Comforting, almost.

"Julia and I have plans," Amanda said, her words coming out in a breathy little sigh.

He placed his other hand on her shoulder and slowly massaged, running his thumbs up her neck and into her hairline. Amanda refused to allow herself to acknowledge his touch. Yet it was so light, so intriguing, she couldn't help herself.

Nick leaned down. Amanda felt his breath on her cheek, then his jaw against her neck. She should storm away from him—or at least protest. If he wanted to take her to bed—first thing in the morning, of all times—she shouldn't make it easy for him.

Yet instinctively, she leaned her head sideways, giving him access to her throat. An unexpected thrill passed through her as his lips skimmed her face.

"Amanda?" he whispered against her ear. "It's time."

Time? It was *time?* Time for her to make good on their agreement?

A little tremor shook her. Yet here, now, at this moment, with his hands working a strange magic on her neck and shoulders, and his lips teasing her flesh, the idea didn't seem so terrifying.

"Very well..." she whispered.

Amanda rose from the bench and turned to Nick. Her whole body seemed alive, suddenly, as it never had before.

What would happen next? she wondered. Would he sweep her into his arms, as he'd done last night? Give her another of the kisses that had left her breathless and kept her staring at the ceiling half the night?

Instead, he gestured toward the connecting door to the sitting room. "After you."

Amanda frowned, glanced at her bed, then back at him. "But you said it was…time."

"For breakfast," Nick said. "Time for breakfast."

Heat rushed up Amanda's neck and into her cheeks. Gracious, why had she thought such a thing? Simply because he'd kissed her cheek and touched her neck, she'd assumed he wanted her in bed—now….

"We agreed to have meals together," Nick pointed out. "Remember?"

Amanda fought off her embarrassment. Yes, she remembered agreeing to have meals with Nick, even though he hadn't insisted upon it before now.

She touched the skirt of her dressing gown. "I can't go downstairs for breakfast with you. I'm not properly dressed."

His gaze dipped to her feet, then rose to her face. "You're dressed perfectly…for what I have in mind."

Her insides flamed again. What did he mean now? That they would consummate their marriage on the dining room table? Linens and candlesticks flying, china crashing to the floor?

He opened the door to the sitting room, and Amanda saw that one of the servants had set the small round table with their breakfast.

Nick seated her at the table, then took the chair across from her and picked up his fork.

"A good meal is always desirable before strenuous activity," Nick said. "Don't you think?"

Amanda clutched her napkin in her hands. Good grief, what did *that* mean? That he intended them to make love after breakfast? On a full stomach? Was that *done?*

"What's this appointment you and Julia have?" Nick asked, as he began to eat.

Flustered, Amanda had to think a moment to remember what she'd planned for the day.

"We're meeting with a teacher interested in tutoring the women who'll live at the refuge," she finally said. "Some may need to brush up on their studies to get a job."

Nick continued eating, giving no sign that he was about to toss her over his shoulder and head off to bed. Yet her gaze was drawn to his hand as he gripped his fork. A big hand. With long fingers brushed with fine, dark hair. Strong, but so gentle against her neck. What would it feel like if he touched her—

Amanda clamped her lips together to keep from gasping aloud. Good Lord, what was she thinking?

She turned her mind to polite mealtime conversation.

"Anything new on Charlotte Moore?" she asked, forcing herself to eat. "Did your attorney contact her about selling the land so your Whitney project can get under way?"

"Actually, the woman is a little tougher than I'd anticipated," Nick said, helping himself to a muffin. "Claims she doesn't want to sell."

"You don't seem upset, considering that this will ruin your entire project."

Nick sipped his coffee. "She's just angling for more money. I told my attorney I don't give a damn what it costs, just get me that land."

"So you haven't actually met this woman yourself?"

Nick shook his head. "No need. My attorney is going out there again this morning. He'll talk to her again, get this thing settled."

"But what if she really doesn't want to sell the land?"

"She'll sell." Nick grinned devilishly. "I have a way with stubborn women."

Before Amanda could respond, he tossed his napkin on the table and pushed himself up from his seat. Her senses went on alert again. What was that gleam in his eye? She'd seen it before. Last night. When he'd come into her room.

Her stomach clenched. The moment was upon her. She knew it.

"I'd better get to the office," Nick said.

"You're—leaving?" Amanda asked. He was going to work? Now? She'd sat here worrying and wondering if he intended to take her to bed after breakfast, and now he was simply walking out?

Amanda rose from her chair. "When will you be home?"

A little grin pulled at his lips and he eased closer, almost but not quite close enough to touch. Still, heat from his body wafted to hers.

"Anxious for my return?" he asked in a low voice.

Amanda flushed. Anxious? Hardly. But she did want to know when to expect him. Surely he wouldn't wait much longer to take her to bed.

"Do you have plans for the afternoon?" Nick asked.

"No," Amanda said, glad for something else to focus on.

"Good. I might slip home this afternoon for a few hours."

A few *hours?* Amanda's heart thudded harder in her chest. How long did such things *take?*

Without warning, Nick slid his hand behind her neck and leaned down, covering her mouth with a hot kiss. Then, just as quickly, he released her and left.

Stunned, Amanda grasped the chair back for support. He *might* come home this afternoon?

Her lips still burning from his kiss, Amanda knew there was only one thing Nick would come home for.

Her.

Chapter Twenty-Two

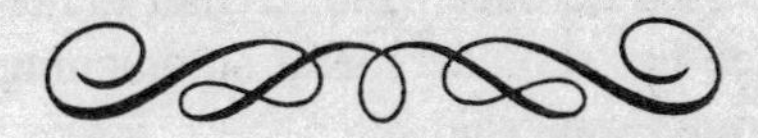

When Julia arrived at the house, Amanda was so relieved to see her that she rushed to meet her in the foyer. She needed a diversion from her own thoughts. All morning she'd fretted about her encounters with Nick last night and over breakfast. First he'd insisted on claiming his husbandly rights, then he hadn't followed through.

Was he no longer interested? she'd wondered as she dressed this morning. Yet if he weren't, why did he keep kissing her? *Really* kissing her?

Finally, Amanda had decided to ask Julia's opinion. After all, she'd been married for several years. Though a widow now, she knew about men, and Amanda didn't feel awkward asking Julia's opinion on so sensitive a subject.

Yet when she saw Julia in the foyer, Amanda's own problems flew from her head. At a glance she saw how upset her friend was, her eyes puffy as if she'd been crying.

Julia sniffed, struggling to hold back tears. "I have to speak with you."

Amanda took her into the parlor off the rose garden. She couldn't imagine what was wrong. In the time she'd known Julia they'd become good friends, but Amanda had no hint of her problem this morning.

They settled on the mauve settee. The French doors to the rose garden stood open, filling the room with sunshine and a fragrant breeze.

Julia pressed her lace handkerchief to her lips, then straightened her shoulders as if summoning strength. "I'm leaving," she said.

"Leaving?" Amanda asked. "Leaving the city?"

"Yes."

"But why?" Amanda couldn't imagine what had happened to drive Julia away.

"Because...because I have to." Tears again pooled in her eyes.

"Where are you going?"

"New York," Julia said, dabbing at her eyes with her handkerchief. "I have family there. I'm leaving right away. This afternoon, actually. I've told no one but you, and my aunt, of course. It's not something I'm anxious to advertise."

Amanda took Julia's hand and gave it a quick squeeze. "Tell me what's wrong."

"Everything!" A wave of tears overwhelmed her. She sobbed softly, clutching her handkerchief to her lips, then composed herself again. "I...I saw Ethan yesterday."

An ugly suspicion wound through Amanda as she remembered how he'd shown interest in Julia in an effort to win the wager he'd made with Nick.

"Did he say something to upset you?" Amanda demanded.

"Yes." Julia gulped, then tears misted her eyes once more. "He said that he'd enjoyed the times we'd spent together, and—and that he *missed* me."

Julia collapsed into another crying fit while Amanda just stared at her, trying to figure out what was happening. The last she'd heard, Julia had broken off her involvement with Ethan, and he'd agreed to respect her wishes.

"Julia," Amanda said, after her friend had gotten her tears under control once more, "I don't understand. I thought you weren't interested in Ethan."

"Oh, but I am," Julia wailed. "But I shouldn't be. Don't you see? Tom, my husband, has only been dead for a little over a year. I loved him so much. I've been absolutely lost without him...until Ethan came along."

"And now you feel guilty that you're interested in another man?" Amanda asked.

"Yes. Yes, I suppose that's it." Julia closed her fist around her handkerchief. "I don't know what it is that I feel, really. Am I genuinely interested in Ethan? Or just using him as a substitute for Tom?"

"Oh, dear, I see what you mean," Amanda said. "But is leaving the right thing to do?"

"Yes. I'm sure of it," Julia said, though she looked absolutely miserable at her decision. "I need time to think. I don't want to involve Ethan, possibly end up hurting him."

Amanda wondered if she should use this opportunity to tell Julia the reason behind Ethan's initial interest in her, despite her promise to Nick that she wouldn't. If Julia knew the truth, perhaps she wouldn't be so concerned about Ethan's feelings. Perhaps she would question, as Amanda did, whether Ethan, in fact, had any feelings for Julia at all.

But at the moment, with her friend in tears, it seemed cruel to tell her about the wager. Surely the truth would only make her feel worse.

Yet Julia had reported that Ethan claimed he'd missed her. Did that mean he genuinely cared for her, after all?

"Maybe you should stay and talk to Ethan," Amanda said.

Julia shook her head. "I've thought this through. I have to leave."

They were quiet for a while, except for Julia's ragged breathing. Finally, Amanda patted her hand.

"You'll stay in touch, won't you?" she asked.

"Yes, of course." Julia looked at her for a moment, then clutched her hand. "You're so lucky, Amanda, to be married and settled. I envy you."

Stunned, Amanda just sat there while Julia rose and hurried out of the parlor. She thought her settled? Even envied her?

Of course, Julia didn't know what had transpired between her and Nick. No one knew how positively *unsettled* things were between them.

A deep longing arose in Amanda's heart. She and Nick. Happily married. Settled.

If only it were true.

Rose Arbogast, the teacher who'd applied to work at the refuge, arrived for her interview precisely on time. Amanda met with her in the music room.

The tiny, white-haired woman presented her credentials and talked for some time about her extensive teaching background. At first glance, Amanda could see she'd be perfect for the job, yet she didn't offer her the position. After the fiasco with Clifford Sullivan, Amanda intended to have everyone investigated by the Pinkerton Agency before employment. Even dear, sweet old Mrs. Arbogast.

Amanda promised to let her know something definite in a week or so, then saw her out the front door.

"What did you dream last night?"

Amanda turned in the foyer to find Winnifred coming down the staircase. Since the woman's return from San Diego, Amanda had seen little of her—or Constance either, for that matter, thanks to Charles Osborne's devoted attention. Though she liked Winnifred well enough, Amanda had wanted to avoid her probing questions about her dreams. How could she tell Nick's aunt about her recurring nightmare, in which Nick was trying to lure her off a cliff to her death?

"Well?" Winnifred asked, stopping in front of Amanda. "What did you dream?"

Cornered, Amanda searched her memory to come up with a dream she'd had in the past. "Let's see," she said pensively. "Oh, of course. Actually, I had this dream just a few nights ago. I dreamed I was wandering through a large house, opening doors, discovering rooms I didn't know existed."

"I see." Winnifred's brows drew together. She drew in a breath, then let it out slowly. "Was anyone speaking a foreign language?"

"No."

"Were you a public official?"

"Well, no."

"Were there root vegetables in the house?"

"No."

"Hmm..." Winnifred pursed her lips, her frown deepening, then cried, "Aha! I know what your dream means."

Amanda waited patiently, wondering what the woman had come up with this time. Truthfully, Amanda didn't put much stock in Winnifred's analysis.

"Your dream means that you are in a situation where new opportunities are opening up to you," Winnifred explained.

Amanda paused, startled, because Winnifred's assessment actually contained a grain of sense. "Really? New opportunities?"

"Oh, yes. And you're excited about them, gleefully running from room to room to see what else awaits you." Winnifred frowned again. "Either that, or you have a fear of being struck by lightning."

The woman went on her way, leaving Amanda to contemplate her dream analysis, barely aware that the doorbell had chimed. Perhaps Winnifred was correct. New opportunities had opened up—and were still opening up—in her life. And she was enjoying them. Most of them, anyway.

"Oh, Amanda, dear?"

She turned to find Winnifred standing in the parlor doorway. "A word of caution—just be careful *which* doors you choose. Once opened, some can't be closed again," she said, and went on her way.

A chill passed over Amanda. Which doors, indeed.

"Excuse me, Mrs. Hastings," Vincent said, approaching her. ''The carriage has arrived with a message from Mr. Hastings. He'd like you to join him.''

Amanda was surprised because Nick had said that he intended to come home this afternoon. For a few *hours.*

''Join him?'' she asked. ''At his office?''

''No, ma'am,'' Vincent said, without really looking at her. ''At the Merrimont Hotel.''

Her stomach jolted. ''The Merrimont Hotel? When?''

''Immediately.''

They were going to consummate their marriage in a *hotel?* In the very city in which they lived? In the middle of the afternoon?

Was that proper?

Amanda's cheeks flamed as she sat in the carriage, the very carriage that was at this moment taking her to the Merrimont Hotel.

Winnifred's dream analysis came back to Amanda. Was this a door she shouldn't open? This one, surely, could never be closed again.

Amanda pushed that thought from her mind and allowed a thread of anger to take its place. Who did Nick think he was, ordering her around? Sending a carriage for her. Insisting that she join him. Immediately. At a hotel. A *hotel.*

Amanda shivered, despite the afternoon heat. The thought of Julia floated into her mind.

Would she still envy her life if she knew Amanda was on her way to an afternoon tryst with her husband?

A little sadness settled in Amanda's heart. Yes.

Given Julia's circumstances, she would probably envy her greatly.

When the carriage arrived at the Merrimont Hotel, the driver helped her down. Amanda stood in the street, pedestrians pushing past her. She leaned her head back, gazing up at the four-story hotel.

Was Nick upstairs in one of those rooms, waiting for her? Was this the moment when they would become husband and wife in the truest sense of the word?

Amanda gulped. Why would Nick have brought her here, of all places, if he intended otherwise?

She touched her hand to the skirt of her lavender dress. Was this appropriate? Should she have brought something with her? She'd never heard her aunt or any of her cousins or friends comment on what should be worn for such an occasion.

Gracious, why did she keep finding herself on such unfamiliar ground where Nick was concerned?

Drawing in a deep breath, Amanda entered the hotel. The lobby was large and airy, filled with maroon and blue furnishings, dark woodwork, palms and spring floral arrangements. Several men in business suits sat scattered about the lobby, reading newspapers. Were any of them here to meet their wives? she wondered.

Finally, Amanda spotted Nick pacing across the far side of the room, head down, pulling at the back of his neck. She'd seen that expression on his face before and knew by the way he carried himself that something was wrong.

"Nick?" Amanda came up behind him and touched his arm.

He spun, startled at seeing her. ''Amanda, I'm so glad you're here.''

''What's wrong?'' she asked.

He shook off his mood and forced a smile. ''Nothing. Nothing's wrong.''

''Nick, please,'' she said, refusing to give up. ''Don't put me off like that. Something's wrong. I know it. Tell me what it is.''

The smile he'd forced for her sake transformed into a more sincere one, and he relaxed a little, as if it were a relief that he didn't have to pretend with her.

''I promise I'll tell you everything afterward,'' Nick said.

''Afterward?'' Her brows rose. The reason she'd been summoned here sprang to the front of her mind again. ''After what, exactly?''

''Lunch.''

''Oh.'' Her cheeks colored slightly. ''Yes, of course. Lunch.''

He offered his arm. ''Shall we?''

Amanda walked with him into the hotel's dining room. Here the walnut tables were laid with blue linen and china. Waiters in white jackets moved silently among the guests.

Nick asked about her morning and seemed content to listen as they ate. She told him about Mrs. Arbogast and her qualifications for teaching at the refuge.

''She seems nice enough,'' Amanda said. ''But I'd like to have one of those Pinkerton detectives look into her background.''

Nick grinned. ''So you're a believer in investigations now?''

"I'd be a fool not to be," Amanda said, pausing over her plate, "considering...everything."

"Which reminds me," Nick said, slicing into his steak. "I put the Pinkertons on the trail of Clifford Sullivan."

"You did?"

During her tirade in Nick's office the afternoon of the ground-breaking ceremony, she'd meant it when she'd asked him to hunt Clifford down and get her money back. But now the idea bothered her a bit. After all, Clifford had a mother and seven younger brothers and sisters to care for—if what he'd told her was true. Given that he'd stolen her refuge money, Amanda guessed it wasn't beyond him to lie, too.

"What will they do to Clifford when they find him?" Amanda asked.

"Whatever I tell them to do."

"Oh."

"They're not the police. They're under no obligation to arrest him, cart him off to jail." Nick raised an eyebrow. "Unless that's what you want them to do. Is it?"

Amanda laid her fork aside. Regardless of what Clifford had done, the thought of having him arrested, prosecuted and sent to jail bothered her.

"At any rate, I'm sorry I've put you in this position, Nick," she said. "You really have enough to do already without dealing with Clifford Sullivan."

Nick smiled gently. "You're worth it."

By the time dessert was served, she and Nick had talked about nearly everything and everyone they knew. He seemed relieved by the distraction, glad for something to focus on other than whatever had been troubling him earlier.

Amanda found herself wishing their lunch didn't have to end. How nice, sitting here with Nick. Gazing across the table at him. Sharing their lives.

"Could you help me with something tonight?" Nick asked, as they finished the sinfully rich chocolate dessert he'd ordered for them.

An odd flutter began in Amanda's stomach. She couldn't recall Nick ever asking for her help before. "Certainly. If I can."

"I've invited Charlotte Moore to the house."

"Danton Moore's heir? The owner of the land you want?"

"Yes. That's her," Nick said.

Suddenly he looked tired, weary, worn down. Amanda's heart sank. "She's still refusing to sell, isn't she."

"Yes," Nick said. "I'm beginning to believe that she really isn't going to sell me that land, regardless of how much money I offer."

"Oh, Nick. Your Whitney project..." Amanda reached across the table and laid her hand atop his. He'd worked long and hard on this project, sunk a great deal of money into it, to say nothing of the blow to his pride if it fell apart.

"I want to meet with her personally," Nick said, "discuss the situation, see what can be done. She's an older lady, and I'm afraid she might be uncomfortable speaking with me privately. I'd like you to be there, too, Amanda. Would you do that for me?"

"Of course," she said, pleased that he'd asked her.

"Thank you."

"So," Amanda said, as the waiter cleared away the last of their dishes, "are you going back to the office now?"

"Nope. I'm doing what any successful businessman would do when faced with an expensive project teetering on the edge of collapse." Nick smiled and gave a carefree shrug. "I'm taking the afternoon off."

He rose from his chair and offered his hand. "Are you ready to go?"

"Go where?"

Nick smiled. "To play."

Chapter Twenty-Three

They were going to make love in the carriage. Weren't they?

Amanda sat back on the leather seat, watching Nick across from her as the carriage pulled away from the Merrimont Hotel. When he'd escorted her out of the dining room, she'd assumed they would take the stairs up to a room he'd surely rented earlier. Instead, he'd swept her out of the hotel and into the carriage. Just where they were heading now and what would happen next, Amanda didn't know. His cryptic comment that they were going "to play" still baffled her.

Finally, the carriage rolled to a stop on Wilshire Boulevard, the city's most fashionable shopping district. Nick helped her out, tucked her arm through his and gestured to the store in front of them.

"Playtime," he announced.

The shop window was filled with dolls, wooden trains, drums, baby carriages, and a sign overhead read Lyons Brothers Toys and Games.

"What's this all about?" Amanda asked.

"I'm buying toys for the children at your refuge,"

Nick said. "I thought it would be fun if we picked them out together."

Amanda's heart melted. "Oh, Nick, how generous of you. And what a wonderful idea."

She started forward, but stopped, seeing the Closed sign dangling in the window. "Oh, no. They're not open."

"Don't worry. I stopped by earlier and made special arrangements to have the store to ourselves." Nick rapped on the door and a smiling shopkeeper appeared, hurrying to open it.

"Good afternoon, Mr. Hastings, ma'am. Just make yourself at home and let me know if there's anything you need."

He locked the door behind them, then slipped through the curtain at the rear of the shop, leaving Nick and Amanda alone in the store.

Shelves and tables were filled with toys, games, books and puzzles, everything imaginable to please growing children.

"I hardly know where to begin," Amanda said, looking around. Her gaze fell on a display of baseball bats and wind-up trains. "You'll have to be my expert on purchasing toys for little boys."

He picked up a tin soldier and saluted her. "At your service, ma'am."

"So tell me, what do boys like?"

"Girls."

Amanda giggled. "You're going to be no help at all."

"Probably not," Nick said, trying out one of the baseball bats.

They made their way along the aisles, looking at

china dolls dressed in satin and lace, flannel dogs, monkeys, cats and donkeys, kaleidoscopes, trick boxes, toy clocks, doll houses, infantry and cavalry soldiers, a puppet theater, tin tea sets, boats, wagons and circus trains.

"These dolls are beautiful," Amanda said, holding up a blond baby with sparkling blue eyes.

"Where were all these toys when I was a kid?" Nick muttered, picking up an artillery cannon.

By the time they were halfway through the store, Amanda was overwhelmed.

"This is too much. I hardly know where to begin. I'll need toys for all age groups, for both boys and girls. I don't want to slight anyone." She gestured to the display at the rear of the store. "And we haven't even considered the books and puzzles yet."

"What the hell," Nick said, spinning a top on a glass counter. "We'll buy one of everything."

Amanda gasped. "Nick, you're not serious."

"Lyons!"

The shopkeeper bustled through the curtain. "Yes, Mr. Hastings?"

"One of everything," he said, setting the top aside and waving his hand. "I'll let you know when I want the order delivered."

"Yes, sir. Oh, yes, sir. Right away, sir." Smiling, the shopkeeper fumbled to open the door, still thanking Nick as they climbed into the carriage.

As they got under way, Nick settled back in the seat, watching Amanda across from him and listening to her as she spoke about how thrilled the children at her refuge would be having so many wonderful toys available to them.

But really, he wasn't listening all that closely. How could he when watching her was so much more fascinating?

How pretty she looked in her hat, its wide brim dipping over one eye, feathers swaying each time she moved. Her dress clung in all the right places. Her lips were full and pink, and her smile made her eyes sparkle.

Seating her at the table in the restaurant of the Merrimont, he'd watched her lovely round bottom descend onto the chair. Now Nick couldn't stop thinking about it, seated mere feet away and so accessible.

More intimate pleasures filled his head. The two of them were alone in this carriage. She was done up quite properly in her dress and undergarments, but Nick could free her of them with little more than a flick of his wrist—or a rip of his teeth.

Thoughts of last night crept into his mind—of when he'd had her in bed, when he'd kissed her. Her breathing had quickened at his touch. She'd enjoy the feel of his fingers against her neck. And when he'd cupped her breast—

Nick wiggled on the seat, trying to ward off the cravings that overtook him so easily. His heated blood told him very plainly that he should have made love to Amanda last night when he had the chance.

But the rest of him—that small portion of his brain that still functioned—knew he'd done the right thing. It might take a while, but he would lure Amanda into his arms. He'd entice her into his bed. Tempt her. Make her want him.

Of course, he hadn't counted on this new plan of

his being harder on himself than it was on Amanda. Who was he really enticing? Her or himself?

Nick gritted his teeth as Amanda drew in a deep breath and her breasts rose and fell. This new plan had better work fast. He couldn't take much more of this.

When the carriage pulled to a stop at home, Amanda wished their journey hadn't ended. She wished her afternoon with Nick could go on forever.

Such a lovely day. They'd talked—really talked. He'd been sweet and thoughtful, generous and kind. Just the way she remembered him from that snowy night in Tahoe ten years ago. Just as he'd been during the weeks he'd courted her.

This, Amanda knew deep in her heart, was the real Nick. The one she'd loved for so long.

Why couldn't things be like this always? Why couldn't every day be just like this one?

Her hand warmed in his as he helped her from the carriage. Her feet touched down and she gazed up at him. The moment caught them, held them in its grasp. Why couldn't they find a way to hold on to this day forever?

Because Nick didn't love her.

The realization hit Amanda like a wave of icy water. Here she stood, immersed in his presence, losing herself to his charms. But the truth was that he didn't love her.

He'd bargained for her hand in marriage. He'd bargained for her body in bed.

Amanda pulled away from him and hurried into the house.

Nick didn't love her.

She'd do well to remember that.

Inside the house, Amanda had intended to dash up to her room, but Vincent stopped them both.

"Begging your pardon, sir, but perhaps you and Mrs. Hastings would care to take a moment to visit with Mrs. Hastings in the parlor," he said, and moved silently away.

Amanda shared a troubled look with Nick. Vincent would never have made such a suggestion were the circumstances not dire.

Together they went to the parlor. Constance stood near the fireplace, worrying a handkerchief in her hands.

"What's wrong?" Amanda asked, going to her.

"Oh...nothing, really." Constance gulped, forcing down her emotions. "But, actually, everything."

"What happened?"

"Charles just came by," she said, trying to make her voice sound light, airy.

Amanda glanced up at Nick. "Charles Osborne was here? What did he want?"

"He...he came by to tell me that he's going to Europe." Constance drew in a ragged breath, then touched her handkerchief to the corner of her eye. "He has some family business—very important business—to attend to and...and he won't be back for quite some time. A year, perhaps. It...it came up quite suddenly."

"I know you'll miss him," Amanda said, looping her arm around Constance's shoulder.

"Yes." She glanced down at her handkerchief. "I'd grown to enjoy his company. I'd grown quite fond of Charles, actually."

Constance shook herself, straightened her shoulders. ''Well, no matter. It's done now. He's leaving and that's that. If you'll excuse me, I think I'll go lie down.''

Nick leaned down and hugged her. ''I'm sorry, Mother.''

Constance gazed up at him. ''I'll be fine, dear. No need to worry about me. I'll manage. You know that.''

Nick paled, and his expression tightened as his mother left the room. Amanda watched him, certain something had passed between them that she didn't understand.

But she intended to find out.

''What do you know about this?'' Amanda asked.

Nick glanced at her, but didn't say anything. He strode out of the parlor.

Amanda followed him down the hallway into his study. There, he did something she'd never seen him do. Nick opened the cupboard, pulled out a decanter and glass and poured himself a drink.

''You know something about this,'' Amanda said.

Her accusation caused him to glance up at her. But he didn't speak. Instead he gulped down a large swallow of liquor.

''Answer me,'' she demanded, advancing on him. ''What is it? What do you know that—'' She gasped abruptly. She knew! She knew what he'd done.

''You had the Pinkerton Agency investigate Charles Osborne, didn't you? You really did it.''

Nick glared at her for a moment. ''Yes.''

''Nick! How could you have *done* such a thing?''

He strode around her, pushed the door closed with a thud. ''She's my mother. I want her protected.''

Amanda followed him across the room. ''You have no business interfering in her personal life.''

''The hell I don't.'' Nick slammed his glass down on the bookshelves. ''You want to know what Pinkerton found out? Osborne is a fraud. He'd lost all his money, his home, everything, before he showed up here.''

''Just because he'd fallen on hard times doesn't mean he was a threat.''

''Yeah?'' Nick challenged. ''Then why did he leave?''

''Maybe he was embarrassed.''

''Or maybe he was up to no good.''

''But, Nick, your mother is devastated.''

He squeezed his eyes shut for a second, his shoulders sagging, the fight leaving him. ''I didn't think she'd cry.''

''What did you think she'd do?''

''Do you honestly believe I wanted to make my mother miserable?'' he demanded.

Amanda flung out her hands. ''I don't know what to believe!''

''Charles Osborne isn't who he claimed to be,'' Nick said. ''I went to him, told him I knew the truth, and gave him the option of leaving town quietly. And that's exactly what he did. He duped my mother. He probably just wanted her money. Did you think I was just going to stand back and let that happen?''

''And let what happen? Let him marry her when he didn't really love her?''

Anger twisted Nick's face. "This isn't about us! This is different."

"Different how?"

"I genuinely care about you, Amanda."

"You *genuinely* want me in bed!"

"Of course I do! What the devil is so wrong with that? I want us to have a marriage, a real marriage. To have children. To wake up together, to sit across the table from each other—forever. You're what I want. I've told you that a dozen times. You're my perfect wife."

"How can you say that? How can you say it to my face? How can you delude yourself? How can you claim I'm the perfect wife when you know you don't love me?"

"Because I don't *want* to love you!"

Amanda gasped, as stunned as if he'd slapped her. Nick froze, as surprised as she by the words he'd blurted out.

He stalked to the other side of the room. Amanda watched him, too numb to understand what had happened, to ask what he meant.

He didn't *want* to love her? He wanted a wife, but not one he loved? That was his idea of perfection?

For a long moment Nick stood with his back to her. He shoved one hand into his trouser pocket and pulled at the back of his neck with the other. The air, the energy seemed to vanish from the room. In its place was an empty chill.

"There's something more," Amanda said softly. "Something beyond Charles Osborne, beyond you and me. Something about your mother. What did she mean just now in the parlor, Nick, when she said she'd 'manage'? That you knew she'd be all right? It was an odd thing to say. Why did she say it to you?"

Nick bent his head and shoved his other hand into his pocket. A moment dragged by in silence. Finally he turned and drew in a deep breath.

"My father had a mistress."

Amanda just looked at him. "But—how did you know?"

"We have extensive holdings throughout the state, including in Sacramento," Nick said, his voice almost flat, devoid of emotion, as if that were the only way he could tell the story. "I'd gone there with some friends during my college days and saw Father and her together."

"You must have been devastated."

Nick just nodded, his eyes vacant, remembering. "Shocked. Angry."

"Did you and your father discuss…the situation?"

"Later, when we'd both returned home, he told me the whole story," Nick said. "He'd known Suzanne—that was her name—for years. He'd asked her to marry him when they were young, but she turned him down. He married my mother."

"Married her on the rebound? Without loving her?" Amanda asked, and couldn't help but hear how judgmental her own voice sounded.

Nick eased onto the corner of the desk. "Actually, he loved my mother very much. Took one look at her, fell hopelessly in love and married her."

Amanda frowned. "I don't understand. If he loved your mother, why did he renew his romance with Suzanne?"

"I asked the same question. My father told me that

the answer would become clear at supper that night.'' Nick rose from the desk and sighed heavily. ''And it did. My father and mother barely spoke. They had nothing in common. No mutual interests. Nothing connected them. Sitting there, I realized it had always been that way.''

''But why would your father live that way? Why not just make a clean break of things?''

''Because he did love my mother. He loved her very much. But she couldn't talk to him about his business, his friends, the world, politics—everything that was important to him. And he couldn't relate to anything that mattered to her.''

''So he stayed married to Constance, but kept Suzanne in his life.'' Amanda shook her head. ''Did Constance know?''

''Wouldn't a woman know? For chrissake, Amanda, look at me. Is there any doubt in your mind how much I want you? If I was off with some other woman, wouldn't you know it?''

''Yes, I suppose I would,'' Amanda said. ''Did your father ask you to keep his secret?''

Nick shook his head. ''No. He told me to tell Mother, if I wanted to. But I could never bring myself to do it, knowing what would result.''

''After her comment in the parlor just now, I guess we can assume that Constance knew about your father's mistress all along.''

''Yes, I suppose so.''

Amanda shook her head. ''I can't believe they were both content with that sort of marriage. I wouldn't be.''

''Nor would I,'' Nick said.

Amanda looked across the room at him, realization finally dawning on her. ''So that's why you wanted a wife who was compatible.''

''Yes.''

''You didn't want to become entangled with a woman whom you couldn't even have a conversation with over supper.''

''Love be damned,'' Nick said. ''Compatibility is what's important.''

''And that's enough for you?''

Nick drew in a breath. ''The question is, Amanda, is it enough for *you?*''

Chapter Twenty-Four

Women. They required the patience of a saint—every last one of them.

Nick sat on a chair in the parlor, trying not to fidget. He'd never liked this room. Pink. Whoever heard of pink furniture? And the food on the tray in front of him was supposed to be nourishment? The tea he'd finished was tepid because the cup was so thin, and he'd eaten just enough of those silly little sandwiches to make himself hungry. He damn well knew that he'd come completely undone if the conversation being bandied about the room didn't change pretty soon.

But this was what women liked. Nick reined in his impatience. Thank God Amanda was here.

What now felt like an eternity ago, Miss Charlotte Moore had arrived at the Hastings home to discuss the sale of her property to Nick. He would have preferred to get right down to business, but women didn't do that. Amanda had taken command of the situation, seated Miss Moore in this hideous pink parlor, put her at ease immediately, then served this miserable excuse for refreshments. Soon the two of them were conversing as if they'd known each other for years. At the moment, they were discussing the flowers in bloom in Miss Moore's yard.

All quite proper. All quite maddening.

Nick struggled to keep his patience under control, and contented himself with the thought that at least this gave him time to size up his adversary. Though seeing her now, it was difficult to think of Miss Moore as such.

He guessed her age at around sixty, judging from her white hair and lined face. Her clothes were not expensive; they couldn't hide her thin, frail frame.

Once again, Nick wished he'd gone to Miss Moore's home for this meeting. But she'd planned to come into the city to visit friends, and having her on his own turf couldn't hurt anything.

He'd known from the beginning that this meeting would require a great deal of patience, but it couldn't have come at a worse time. He wasn't in the proper frame of mind to negotiate a crucial business deal.

Instead, he found himself second-guessing his decision to confront Charles Osborne. He'd given the man the opportunity to tell his mother that trumped-up story about going to Europe on family business, and leave town quietly, and Osborne had taken him up on it. Despite the momentary hurt his mother felt, Nick knew he'd done the right thing. But still it bothered him.

Almost as much as the incident with Amanda that had followed. Now, with those things on his mind, Nick felt on edge. He'd never have managed Miss Moore's visit without Amanda.

His ears perked up as the conversation changed.

"I hope you won't think I've accepted your hospitality under false pretenses," Miss Moore said, glancing from Amanda to Nick. "But truly, Mr. Hastings, I have no desire to sell that plot of land."

Nick sat forward, ready to get down to business, anxious to focus on something he knew and understood.

"I've made you a very generous offer. Several very generous offers, actually," he said. "I'm sure we can come to terms you will find agreeable."

Miss Moore shook her head. "My needs are simple. I have no desires that I can't currently fulfill."

"Perhaps you have a charity that would benefit from a donation in your name?" Nick suggested.

Miss Moore paused for a moment, then shook her head once more. "Very generous of you. But...no, thank you."

"Miss Moore, I don't understand your refusal—"

"Perhaps," Amanda said, gently interrupting him, "you could explain to us why you don't want to sell the land, Miss Moore. I get the impression that your decision is for personal rather than business reasons."

"Yes, dear, that's true," the woman admitted.

Nick leaned forward eagerly. Finally, they were getting somewhere.

"It began many years ago," Miss Moore began, "when I was a young girl."

Nick nearly groaned aloud. He sat back in his chair.

"The farmhouse on the property was my home growing up." Miss Moore smiled at the recollection. "So many happy memories."

"You don't want to see your family home destroyed?'' Amanda asked. ''Is that the reason for your reluctance?''

''No, it's not that,'' Miss Moore said. ''It's the tree.''

Nick blinked across the room at her. ''The tree?''

''Yes. That lovely old oak tree in front of the house.'' Miss Moore's smile faded. ''That's where my dear, sweet Alfred courted me. That's where he asked for my hand in marriage.''

''I didn't realize you'd been married,'' Amanda said.

''Oh, but I haven't,'' she answered. The lines in her face deepened. ''I rejected Alfred's proposal, though I did love him dearly.''

''Then why reject him?'' Amanda asked.

Miss Moore shrugged her thin shoulders. ''Believe me, I've spent my life wondering why I turned him down, and I know now that it was fear. Alfred wanted us to move up north. Start a business of our own. But I was afraid to leave the farm, the security of my family, and venture out into the world. I was afraid that our love wouldn't sustain us, worried about what a future with Alfred would really hold.''

''So what happened?'' Amanda asked.

''Alfred left without me. I never married.'' Miss Moore drew in a thin breath. ''I keep that land with the tree. It's all I have left of him. Sometimes I go out there and just sit...and think about what might have been.''

A deep silence fell over the room. After a moment, she rose, bringing Amanda and Nick to their feet as well.

''I'm sorry, Mr. Hastings, but I can't let that land

go. Thank you for your hospitality. I'll see myself out.'' Miss Moore left the room.

''A tree?'' Nick muttered a curse. ''I'm losing the perfect location for my factory—and a fortune—because of a damn *tree?*''

Amanda watched as Nick started pacing. She was almost envious of his anger. How nice to feel that emotion instead of the sadness that had wrapped her heart and squeezed it painfully.

Miss Moore, who'd missed her chance at love, and lived an empty life of regret, with nothing better to fill her time than to ride to a deserted farm, sit beneath a tree and speculate on what might have been.

''I'm rather partial to that old tree myself,'' Amanda said.

Nick spun toward her, anger contorting his features.

She managed a smile. ''You kissed me there. Remember?''

He glared at her, his foul mood finally draining away. ''Hell...''

Amanda drew in a deep breath, trying to fortify herself against the overwhelming sadness of the day. Only steps away stood Nick, big, strong, sturdy. How she wanted to go to him, throw her arms around him, soak up some of his strength. He was troubled, too. She could see it. What was more natural than for a husband and wife to seek comfort in each other's arms?

But that wouldn't happen. Not between the two of them. The sadness, the futility of their situation overwhelmed Amanda.

''This is all too much,'' she said, tears filling her eyes. ''Julia came by this morning to tell me she was leaving town, too troubled over Ethan to stay. Your mother is devastated over Charles. And now, Miss Moore.''

Julia had lost the man in her life, as had Constance and Miss Moore. Amanda had her husband, the man she loved, but they were as far apart as any two people could be.

Amanda gulped, trying to hold back her tears. ''And you and I...''

All the hurtful words, the ultimatums, the bargains sprang up between them as they gazed at each other. Their future and what it surely held presented itself.

Could they fix this? Amanda wondered, looking at Nick. From his expression she knew his thoughts were the same. The two of them so close, yet so distant. Was there a way to bridge the gap between them?

Nick turned away and walked to the window, staring out at the closing darkness. Finally, shoulders hunched, his hands shoved in his pockets, he turned to her, looking as lost as she'd ever seen him.

''I don't want to live like this anymore,'' he said.

''Neither do I,'' Amanda said, and she'd never meant anything more in her life.

''What are we going to do about it?'' he asked.

She shook her head. ''I don't know....''

Stay or leave?

Try or give up?

Amanda strolled through the gardens at the rear of the house as evening shadows stretched across the grounds, the incidents of the day pounding in her head...and squeezing her heart.

She and Nick. What would become of them? Of their marriage? Should they throw it away, admit defeat and go their separate ways?

And if so, what kind of future did that offer?

Only this afternoon she'd advised Julia to stay in town, confront Ethan, give the two of them a chance. But Julia had pulled away from Ethan. Left town. Run away.

True, Amanda had stayed in her marriage. But she'd made no effort to work through their problems. She'd simply held tight to her own beliefs. She hadn't tried at all.

She may as well have left, as Julia had.

Amanda paused, gazing at the last remnants of sunlight disappearing below the horizon. Would she end up like Charlotte Moore? Old, lonely, clinging to memories of what might have been? Would she become so desperate for companionship that, like Constance, she'd fall for a man who was possibly after her family money?

Yet how could Amanda stay in her marriage? How could she live her life with Nick, knowing he didn't really, truly love her?

She'd grown up in a home where she was accepted but not loved. Was she wrong to expect more than that from her husband, of all people?

Despair overcame Amanda. She leaned her head back and gazed up at the house, to the windows on the second floor that belonged to the bedchambers of the master suite. Nick. How she loved him. He cared for her, in his own way. She was, as he'd said, his perfect wife.

What would become of them? Amanda didn't

know. All she knew for certain was that they couldn't go on like this.

She went back into the house, tired and weary, ready to crawl into bed, though it wasn't very late. She'd missed supper, but doubted anyone else had been at the table to eat. Nick, maybe. She didn't know where he'd gone. Constance was surely in her room. Who knew where Nick's aunt was at any given time?

To her surprise, Amanda saw Winnifred heading up the staircase. She hurried to catch up, feeling the need for closeness with another person at the moment.

"Retiring early?" Winnifred asked as they climbed the steps together.

"I'm a little tired."

"Bad dreams lately?" Winnifred asked hopefully.

"No. Nothing like that."

"Oh," she said, and sounded disappointed. "I'm going to look in on Constance. I suppose you heard that her Mr. Osborne has departed."

"Yes," Amanda said, feeling the loss in the pit of her stomach again. "Please give Constance my good wishes."

"I will. Good night, dear. Sweet dreams."

Sweet dreams, indeed. As if that would be possible tonight.

She glanced at the next doorway down the hall—Nick's room—and saw a ribbon of light beneath it. Apparently, he was as tired as she and had retired early. She wondered if he would get any rest tonight.

Amanda doubted that she'd be so lucky herself. If she got any sleep at all, she'd likely conjure up a nightmare—or be tormented by her recurring bad dream.

Amanda stopped abruptly at her bedchamber door. "Aunt Winnie? Could you interpret a dream for me?"

"What? Oh, why yes. Of course." Winnifred hurried back to her.

Amanda wasn't sure why she'd even asked for Winnifred's help, except that Nick consumed her thoughts tonight and she'd wondered about the meaning behind the dreadful dream in which he played so prominent a role. Was it possible Winnifred could give her guidance? Winnifred's last interpretation had been helpful. Could she now clear this awful dream from Amanda's mind once and for all?

Or would she only confirm the fear that lay in Amanda's heart?

"Go ahead," Winnifred said, pursing her lips and frowning.

"In the dream, I'm standing on a very high cliff. A voice—Nick's voice, actually—calls to me, wanting me to come to the edge."

Winnifred's frown deepened. "To the edge? The very edge?"

"Yes." Amanda shuddered, remembering the fear she'd experienced in the dream. "He keeps insisting that I come closer and closer. But I can't. I'm afraid. Afraid I'll fall."

"Hmm..." Winnifred lapsed into thought for a moment. "It's Nick's voice you hear? You're certain of that?"

"Oh, yes."

"And he keeps urging you to come closer to the edge?"

"Yes," Amanda said. "Does it mean he wants me to fall?"

"Fall? Well, perhaps." Winnifred looked thoughtful for another moment, then tilted her head. "Or you just might *fly*."

Amanda gasped, and her heart thudded in her chest as Winnifred headed off down the hallway and disappeared into Constance's room.

Fly? She might fly? Never once had she considered that. She'd been so sure, so positive that she'd fall.

Amanda went into her room and switched on the lamps. In the dream, Nick had urged her to come to the edge. Was he really encouraging her so that she'd fly? Oh, how she wished she could do just that. Fly. Soar. With him.

But how could that be possible?

And then Amanda knew. She had wings. Perhaps it was time she tried them out.

Dashing to her closet, she pulled off her clothes, struggling with the fasteners, but not wanting to wait for Dolly's assistance. Then she slid her nightgown over her head and yanked on her dressing gown. She grabbed the bottle of Scotch from her vanity and held it up to the light.

The day after their wedding, Nick had arrogantly predicted she'd use this bottle to offer a toast the day she invited him into her bed.

Amanda headed for Nick's bedchamber.

Chapter Twenty-Five

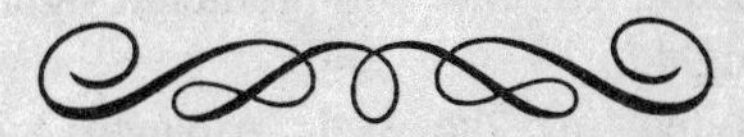

Amanda hesitated in the sitting room, staring at the thread of light beneath Nick's bedchamber door. In her hand she clutched the bottle of Scotch.

Amid all her conflicting and confusing thoughts, the one thing she knew absolutely was that she loved Nick. She'd always loved him.

She knew, too, that Nick wanted her. In his own way, he wanted her.

Yet they were hurting each other, tearing each other apart, breaking hearts and inflicting misery. They couldn't go on this way. It had to stop.

That meant leaving—or staying. And if she stayed, things would have to be different.

Amanda knew of only one step that could be taken now.

And only she could take it.

As she threw open the door to Nick's bedchamber, her stomach clenched, as if she'd actually stepped off that high cliff in her dreams. She said a silent prayer that she wouldn't fall, but fly.

Nick sat on the edge of his bed, pulling off his

socks. His shoes lay on the floor at odd angles. Jacket and necktie were already discarded, and his shirt hung open, revealing his white cotton undershirt.

His gaze came up quickly and he jumped, startled at seeing her, seemingly unsure of what was happening.

Amanda lifted the bottle of Scotch. ''I'm here to suggest a toast. The one you predicted right after our wedding night.''

Nick bolted off the bed. Amanda turned and walked back into her own bedroom. He followed, as she hoped he would.

But he still wasn't smiling as he stopped in the doorway of her bedchamber. He eyed her suspiciously and deliberately held back. ''What the devil are you talking about?'' he asked cautiously.

''You predicted we'd drink a toast the night I welcomed you into my bed. Don't tell me you've forgotten.''

''No, I haven't forgotten,'' Nick said, and carefully took a step into her room.

Amanda waved the bottle. ''Well, cheers.''

Nick blanched. ''You—want—we're going to—we can—''

He stuttered and stammered incoherently, then stopped abruptly. Anger contorted his features.

''Look here, Amanda, after all we've been through, if you think you can simply wag your finger at me and I'll hop into bed with you, well—'' Nick glanced at the bed, then back to Amanda again ''—well, you're absolutely right.''

A slow smile lit his face as he walked to her. ''And while it would be fun...''

"It would be fun?" she asked, gazing up at him.

"Oh, hell yes," Nick assured her. "But I'd like to know that things are settled between us. That this isn't just a passing fancy of yours."

Amanda clutched the bottle in front of her. "We can't go on as we are. Something has to change. We've done things my way and they keep getting worse. I thought we'd try it your way and see if they get better."

Nick nodded slowly. "I like your thinking."

"I can't promise anything," Amanda cautioned. "You understand that, don't you?"

Nick glanced at the bed. "It's a risk I'm willing to take."

"Actually, you have your aunt to thank for this leap of faith," Amanda said.

"Remind me to thank her when we go down for breakfast tomorrow," he said, moving closer. "Or the next day…or the next…or whenever we're finished up here."

Heat sizzled through Amanda. "Do you want some of this?" she asked, lifting the Scotch higher.

"No." Nick pulled the bottle from her hand and set it aside. "All I want is you."

He closed the doors, then switched off the lamps, leaving only one on the dresser burning.

"You're beautiful," he said, standing in front of her again.

Self-consciously, Amanda touched her hand to her hair and felt it still wound atop her head. She gasped. "Oh, dear, I should have taken it down. Sorry."

"I'll take care of it," Nick said softly. "I'll take care of everything."

He guided her to the vanity and seated her on the bench in front of the mirror. Gently he dug his fingers through her hair, searching out the hidden pins. He pulled one free, then another and another, allowing her hair to fall over his hands and down her back.

"Beautiful..." he whispered, combing his fingers through her silken tresses.

Amanda relaxed, the feel of his hands mesmerizing.

Nick picked up her hairbrush and drew it through her hair, the long, languid strokes sending shivers down her spine. Never had she imagined a man performing so personal a task. Never had she imagined it would be so seductive.

In the mirror, she saw Nick bend low and reach around her. His mouth nuzzled her neck and his hands found the buttons of her dressing gown. One by one he opened them, then untied the sash and pulled the garment down her shoulders and off her arms. He caught her hands and laced their fingers together as he kissed her throat, her cheek, her ear.

Warmth raced across her flesh, coiled inside her. She turned her head to meet his lips, but Nick straightened and pulled her up with him. Amanda turned in the circle of his arms and looped her arms around his neck.

They gazed at each other in the dim light. Nick touched her hair, then dragged his finger down her jaw.

"You're sure?" he whispered.

"Yes," she said.

"Nervous?"

"A little," she admitted.

"Me, too."

Amanda's eyes widened. "You are? But—why?"

He grinned. "After making such a fuss about this for so long, I want to make sure you know it was worth the wait."

Amanda lifted her shoulders. "You could do it quite badly and I wouldn't know the difference."

"I won't do it badly."

Amanda blushed. Heat from his body wafted over her, drawing her closer. He settled his hands on her hips and lowered his mouth to hers.

Heaven. Surely this was what heaven tasted like. With a low moan, Nick deepened their kiss. Desire bloomed inside Amanda and she rose on her tiptoes to meet him, pressing closer.

Her breasts brushed his hard chest. He eased her hips nearer, pushing himself against her intimately. His blatant desire startled her, but he wrapped her in his arms, driving away her fear.

With all his strength, Nick held back. He wanted to have her, to ravish her, to make her his—finally. The feel of her soft curves, her scent, her flesh hot against his was nearly too much. His heart pounded and his need for her nearly overcame him as he struggled to maintain control. Above all, he had to pleasure Amanda tonight.

She didn't make it easy for him. Amanda slid her hands down his chest, her soft fingers branding him with trails of fire through his undershirt. He wanted to yank it off, feel her flesh against his, yet didn't. Then her hand dipped lower, brushed his fly, and his knees nearly gave out.

Nick swept her into his arms and laid her on the

bed. He sat beside her, tugged down his suspenders, struggled to free his hands from the sleeves as he pulled off his shirt, then whipped off his undershirt, sending it flying.

Head on the pillow, her dark hair fanned out around her, Amanda watched him. "Such muscles..." she whispered, and laid her palm against his chest.

Nick groaned and leaned down to claim her mouth once more. Her hands searched his chest, driving him to return the favor. She gave a little breathy gasp as he pushed aside the fabric of her nightgown and cupped her breast. Unable to stop himself, Nick dipped his head to taste her. He tugged and teased her with his teeth until she moaned again.

Too confined in his trousers, Nick shucked them off, along with his drawers, and stretched out beside Amanda. He folded her in his arms and kissed her again.

His hand swept the curve of her hip, sliding lower until he caught the hem of her gown. He raised it, her flesh scorching his palm, then pulled the garment over her head and tossed it aside.

A groan rumbled in Nick's chest at the exquisite feel of her soft, hot flesh. Under his hand, Amanda pressed herself closer. He slid his palm down her belly, lower and lower until she gasped.

Warm silk at his fingertips made him throb and ache for her with an intensity he hadn't expected and could barely resist.

He lifted his mouth from hers, gritting his teeth to hold back his desire. In the soft light, he saw Amanda's head thrown back on the pillow, her eyes closed. She seemed hopelessly lost in this new sensation he'd created for her, and Nick's heart soared.

Pushing aside his own needs, he caressed her. Her breath quickened, puffed hot against his face. Her hips rose and fell with his hand.

A need Amanda never knew existed built inside her. She couldn't understand it, couldn't explain it—could only experience it. Nick's warm, hard body alongside her, his mouth tugging at her breasts, his hand—goodness, his hand. An urgency drove her faster, demanded more. Then Nick pulled his fingers away, leaving her wanting.

She opened her eyes and saw him move above her, between her thighs. Another stronger, more intense feeling overcame her as he touched himself against her. He claimed her mouth once more.

A deep, primal ache surged through Nick. He'd wanted to wait, wanted to hold back, but the feel of her was too much. Curling his fists into the pillow, he eased himself into her. Gently, he rocked against her until she accepted him.

She moved, caught in his rhythm. He pushed deeper. She grabbed his hair.

This strange urgency reclaimed Amanda, stole her breath, his movements stoking the fire inside her. Hotter and hotter it built until it raged, then suddenly burst within her. Amanda called his name as great waves broke deep inside her.

Nick groaned, holding back until her writhing eased. He couldn't wait. Not another second. He pushed himself into her over and over, until he was spent.

* * *

"I was wrong," Amanda said softly.

Nick roused from a light sleep and pushed himself up on his elbow to gaze down at Amanda, lying beside him. How beautiful she looked, her head resting on his outstretched arm, her hair tousled, the pristine sheet barely covering the swell of her breasts. They'd made love once more some time ago; Nick wasn't sure how long. He'd fallen asleep afterward and just now opened his eyes to find Amanda wide-awake and, apparently, thinking. Something he hadn't been up to in the past few hours.

"Wrong?" he asked, his brain slowly engaging.

"Yes."

"Wrong about what?" Nick asked, and heard the fear in his voice. "About us? This?"

"No, not about us. Or *this.*" Amanda smiled, then dragged her fingertip down his bare chest. "Actually, I rather like…this."

"Oh, well…good." Nick collapsed onto the pillow again and his eyelids closed.

"Don't you want to know what I was wrong about?" Amanda asked, rolling against him.

"Hmm? What?" He blinked at her.

"Don't you want to know?" she asked again.

"Uh, well, all right." Nick rubbed his eyes and gazed up at her. "Sure, I want to know."

"I was wrong not to ask for your help with building the refuge," Amanda said. "I shouldn't have been so stubborn. I should have taken your advice and listened to your suggestions."

"It's always easy to second-guess yourself. You did what you thought was right at the time." Nick grinned and playfully tugged at a lock of her hair. "But you are stubborn, I won't argue with that."

"Me? What about you and Miss Moore's piece of land you were determined to buy?"

"That was a wise, well-informed, educated, carefully thought out business decision."

"It was stubbornness."

"That land is perfect. When I find something that's perfect I go after it. As you well know."

Amanda laid her head on his shoulder and strummed her fingers across his chest. "I'm sorry that land purchase didn't work out for you. Miss Moore seemed adamant. I don't think she'll sell no matter what."

Nick grunted. "Hell, maybe you're right. Maybe it was just stubborn arrogance on my part. Maybe I was wrong to pursue it as long as I did."

A moment passed while they lay against each other in the darkness.

"Maybe I was wrong about Charles Osborne," he said softly. "Maybe I should have listened to you and stayed out of it."

"Maybe we could both do with a little less stubbornness and a little more openness," Amanda admitted.

"Can't argue with that." Nick brushed a kiss against her forehead. He pushed up onto his elbow again and looked deep into her eyes. "I wish Mother could find happiness. Being with you, Amanda, having you in my life has made me very happy. You're perfect for me in every way."

He kissed her gently on the lips, then lay down beside her again.

Amanda snuggled against him, contented. She'd never felt such closeness with another human being before, never suspected she'd experience it with a man…a husband.

Trying it Nick's way had its advantages, even if he still hadn't said that he loved her.

But was it enough?

Chapter Twenty-Six

Something was wrong.

Nick swiveled his leather chair away from his desk and stared out on the rear lawn. Clouds darkened the midday sky as the gardeners went about their work, clipping the hedges, weeding the flower beds. He sank deeper into the chair and folded his hands across his chest. Something was wrong. With him.

But what?

He rose and paced across his study, thinking, trying to pinpoint the cause of the odd feeling that he couldn't shake. He didn't know what it was. He'd never experienced anything like it.

To add to his confusion, Nick knew he should be feeling on top of the world. After all, he'd awakened this morning in bed with Amanda, following a night of lovemaking more glorious than he'd ever hoped for. Despite her nervousness, her shy reluctance, Amanda had been giving and caring, anxious to please and be pleased.

He'd heard other men comment from time to time on sexual encounters that were less than satisfactory.

Nick had never understood their complaints. The worst he'd ever experienced had been absolutely spectacular. And Amanda, despite her inexperience, had been beyond everything he'd wished for.

He'd only left her bed this morning because she'd insisted she had an important meeting scheduled that she absolutely could not miss. He'd hung around her room until her maid came in, then had dressed hurriedly and waited in the hallway until Amanda finally emerged from her bedchamber. When he laid eyes on her, all he could think about was carrying her back into her room, peeling away all those clothes she'd dressed in, and making love to her all afternoon. He'd walked her through the house to the driveway, assisted her into the carriage, then stood there watching until it disappeared around the corner. Even then he'd been tempted to run after her. Standing there alone in the driveway, he realized that his cheeks hurt because he'd been smiling all morning long.

Nick paused in his pacing and glanced at his desk. He'd tried to read reports for the last hour, but his mind kept wandering. He couldn't concentrate.

Just as well he hadn't gone to his office. He'd have never gotten any work done. Besides, he couldn't bear the idea of Amanda returning home and him not being here the moment she arrived.

He felt jumpy, anxious, on edge. Warm, despite the cool day. He hadn't eaten breakfast, either, and he always ate breakfast. But this morning his stomach was unsettled.

An odd set of ailments, Nick thought, walking back to his desk. And stranger still that they would pick this particular morning to strike. Though, really, they'd been nagging at him for some time now, and he'd been too busy, too preoccupied to concern himself.

He did now, though. But he didn't know what they all meant. He'd never heard of an illness with these sorts of problems, except when—

Nick stopped abruptly as a recollection struck him like a bolt of lightning. That day at Westlake Park, in the little rowboat with Amanda. She'd said—

"Oh God, no..." Nick collapsed into his chair and covered his face with both hands.

Thank heaven she'd had an excuse to leave the house this morning.

Amanda gathered her satchel from the carriage seat as the driver stood waiting, holding the door open. Her errand had been accomplished quickly—too quickly—and already she was home again.

She allowed the driver to assist her from the carriage, then entered the house slowly, holding tight to her satchel when Vincent offered to take it from her. Amanda had used her errand this morning to give herself a little distance from Nick, to think through what had happened. To decide...

In the early morning hours, as she lay entwined in Nick's embrace, she'd never felt more contented in her life. His boast that she'd like being his wife in the truest sense of the word had been correct. Nick had been warm and tender, gentle, coaxing her through their lovemaking, driving away her fears.

All the more reason to love him.

Yet was it enough? She'd thought of nothing else since dawn.

Was what he offered—marriage without a declaration of love—enough? Would it sustain them through the years to come, the trials and tribulations that awaited a husband and wife?

She didn't know. She didn't have enough experience in love or marriage to predict.

Perhaps, ultimately, Nick would prove to be right. Her love for him, his pleasure at having a compatible wife, would be enough.

Her spirits rose a little at the thought that, maybe, one day, Nick would learn to love her. After last night, after the intimacy they'd shared, Amanda couldn't understand how two people could create that connection and not feel the love that came with it.

Dare she hope that Nick would grow to love her?

But what if he never did?

Amanda glanced down at the satchel she carried as she went into the study. Her inner turmoil vanished when she laid eyes on Nick.

He stood gazing out the window. In profile, he looked as she had seen him so many times before—hands thrust in trouser pockets, shoulders slightly hunched forward, brow furrowed in concentration.

Oh, how she loved him.

Yet something was different about him today. Something was wrong. Amanda's heart rose into her throat and worry clenched her stomach. She set the satchel aside and unpinned her hat.

"Nick, what's wrong?"

He glanced back, his gaze stopping her a few feet away, at the corner of his desk. Something dreadful had happened. She knew it.

Nick turned back to the window. Several long,

tense moments passed while he stared outside. Each passing second made Amanda's head pound harder. Just when she thought she couldn't stand another silent second, he glanced back at her. "I'm not well."

Amanda gulped. The stricken look on his face sent her imagination flying. Was he seriously ill? Dying?

"What—what's wrong?" she asked, taking a few steps closer.

His frown deepened and he looked outside again. "I realize now that it's been coming on for some time now. I just didn't...understand before."

"Have you seen a doctor?"

"I don't think a doctor can help," he said, and shook his head slowly.

Amanda's hands began to tremble. "What, Nick? What is it? Tell me."

"I'm not positive what, exactly, it is, though I have a suspicion." Nick turned to her. "I'm certain I know the cause."

"What is it?"

"You."

"Me?" Amanda reeled back. "Me? But how could I possibly—"

"Please, just listen to my symptoms." Nick drew in a ragged breath. "My heart. It keeps beating faster than it should. I'm warm when I shouldn't be. My palms sweat. I have trouble concentrating. My thoughts wander."

Amanda shook her head, confused. "Really, Nick, how could I possibly cause those symptoms?"

"There's more," he said. "I find myself wearing a silly grin without realizing it."

"A silly grin? Nick, that's hardly a symptom of an illness. I don't understand—"

"Worst of all—" Nick laid his hand on his belly "—my stomach feels...let me see, what was that term? Oh yes, 'squishy.' My stomach feels squishy."

Amanda gasped. That day at Westlake Park. The two of them in the rowboat. The list of ailments she'd reported to him regarding her cousins. Tears welled in her eyes.

Nick drew in a big, fortifying breath. "I believe what all this amounts to is...love."

"Love?" she whispered, emotion closing her throat.

"Yes." His gaze met hers. "I believe I've fallen in love with you."

"Oh!" Amanda went to him. Tears spilled onto her cheeks as she swatted him on the chest. "You're in love with me? Gracious, Nick, I was worried sick, thinking you were dying!"

He just looked at her, his gaze hard and intense as he searched her face. "I realize now that I've loved you all along. I just didn't understand it, or didn't want to face it, or accept it. But I love you, Amanda. I love you with all my heart."

Nick folded his arms around her and hugged her to his chest. She sniffed as she burrowed closer. He kissed her cheek.

Amanda eased away and brushed the tears from her eyes. "I wondered this morning if we could make a go of our marriage, if I should stay."

"You're not going anywhere." He caught her in his arms again and pulled her close. "You're not leaving me here with this big, stupid grin on my face all the time—and nothing to do about it.''

Amanda laughed gently. ''You realize that if you're in love with me I'm no longer your perfect wife.''

''Yes, I'd thought of that.'' Nick nodded solemnly, then smiled. ''Oh, well. I suppose there are worse things than being in love with your wife.''

''You're sure? You're absolutely sure?''

A little grin tugged at his lips as he gazed down at her. ''Absolutely sure.''

Nick closed his arms around her and leaned his head down, taking her lips in a warm kiss. Amanda pressed against him and sighed contentedly.

''Say it. Please?'' she said softly.

Nick's grin widened to a big, stupid smile. ''I love you.''

She smiled, knowing her grin was as stupid-looking as his. ''Again. Please.''

''I love you. I love you—''

''Nick! Nick!''

Amanda and Nick turned to see Ethan charge into the study. His necktie crooked and his jacket open, he looked slightly rumpled and absolutely panic-stricken.

''Nick, I need your help.'' Breathless, Ethan stopped in the center of the room.

''What's wrong?'' Nick asked.

''Wrong? What's wrong? Everything's wrong!'' He flung out both arms. ''She's gone! I just went by her aunt's house and learned that she's gone! Julia's left town—for good!''

Nick shrugged. ''So what do you care? Last time

we spoke, you said to hell with her, she could do as she damn well pleased."

"Yes, but I didn't think she'd *leave.*" Desperation bulged his eyes. "What should I do?"

"Go after her," Nick declared. "If you love her, go after her. Don't let her get away."

"But I don't know where she is," Ethan exclaimed, curling his hands into fists. "That battle-ax of an aunt of hers refused to tell me."

"New York," Amanda said. "She told me she was going to New York to visit family."

"Thank you." Ethan pressed his palm to his chest. "I have to go there. Now. Today. I'll get the train and leave immediately."

"Call the Pinkerton Agency before you leave," Nick advised. "They can track her down while you're en route."

"Right. Right." Ethan hustled out of the room. "Thank you!"

Amanda raised an eyebrow. "You and your Pinkerton agents. At least they're serving a worthwhile purpose this time."

Nick dropped his hands to her waist and pulled her close. "I'll have you know that I've used the Pinkerton Agency for other worthwhile purposes."

She gave him a skeptical look. "Oh?"

"I heard from them just this morning," Nick said. "They've found your embezzler, Clifford Sullivan."

She gasped. "You're kidding."

"Nope. He moved his mother and all those sisters and brothers of his up to Sacramento. They have family there. He bought a house for them, got the children in school."

"So he was telling the truth—about his family, anyway."

"It seems so," Nick said.

"What did you tell the agents to do? Report him to the police?" Amanda pressed her lips together. "You didn't do that, did you?"

"I must be getting softhearted—all this being in love business, I suppose." Nick shook his head. "I told the agents to leave Sullivan alone."

"Oh, Nick, that's so sweet of you." Amanda rose on her toes and kissed his cheek.

"I'll go up there in a few weeks and talk to the young man, explain to him the error of his ways," Nick said.

Amanda smiled. "Well, the money was intended to help needy families. I guess it served its purpose."

"I did something else," Nick said. "I told the Pinkerton agents to track down Charles Osborne and bring him back."

"Nick!" Amanda flung her arms around his neck. "That's wonderful. Your mother will be thrilled."

"She won't be so happy when she finds out that I caused him to leave," Nick said. "But, hopefully, he will turn out to be an honest man who has fallen on hard times and things will work out for them."

Amanda smiled up at him, stroking her fingers through the hair at his temple. "You're full of surprises today."

A devilish grin parted his lips. "Does *this* surprise you?" he asked, and pushed himself against her.

She gasped, feeling how he wanted her. "No. It doesn't surprise me at all."

"Can we go upstairs?" he asked, grinning stupidly.

She couldn't help but grin, too. "Yes, we can—oh, but wait." Amanda pulled away from him.

Nick huffed impatiently and followed her across the room. "Amanda..."

"I got you something today," she said, opening the satchel she'd left by the door.

"Can't it wait?"

"No. You'll like it. I promise."

Nick grunted as if he doubted it. "Can you at least hurry up?"

Amanda presented a large envelope. "Consider this my wedding gift to you."

Nick eyed the envelope warily, then ripped it open and pulled out the stack of documents. His jaw sagged.

"Amanda..." His gaze impaled her. "This is the deed to Charlotte Moore's land. The land I need for my Whitney project. It's signed and—and—how did you manage this?"

Amanda smiled, altogether pleased with herself. "I went to see Miss Moore this morning. She's still in town, visiting friends."

"But how did you get her to sell me the land?"

"I hope you don't mind, but I agreed to a small concession on your behalf."

His brow furrowed. "What?"

"You have to leave the oak tree standing. Make it a little park with a bench or two. I thought a bronze plaque would be nice, commemorating Miss Moore's contribution to the project," Amanda said. "What do you think?"

"I think I'm in love with the smartest woman in the world." Nick took her in his embrace and kissed her soundly on the mouth. "Can we go upstairs now?"

"I suppose I should revel in your attention while I can," Amanda said. "You'll have no time for all this lovemaking once your Whitney project is under way."

Nick swept her into his arms. "Wanna bet?"

* * * * *

JUDITH STACY

gets many of her story ideas while taking long afternoon naps. She's trying to convince her family she's actually working, but after more than a dozen novels, they're still not buying it.

Judith is married to her high school sweetheart. They have two daughters and live in Southern California.

HHIBC622